I0520049

# Renaissance
## A slave's voyage of self-discovery

### Part II of a Trilogy

## Christopher Charlton

EmOhErotica
Leeds, UK

Published by EmOh Erotica,
PO Box HP346, Leeds LS6 1UL, UK

British Library Cataloguing-in-Publication data: Christopher Charlton

Renaissance; a slave's voyage of self-discovery – Part II of a trilogy,

1. Title

ISBN    978-1-873031-33-9 (Kindle)
        978-1-873031-39-1 (Paperback)

Cover design: Ben Matthews

# TO
David M and Dave R

ALSO BY CHRISTOPHER CHARLTON

Revelation –
Part I of a Slave's Voyage of Self-Discovery

Retirement –
Part III of a Slave's Voyage of Self-Discovery

The Key to Life:
How to Get More Out of Chastity for Men

# CONTENTS

## Acknowledgements

I should like to thank my many friends and brothers who, over the years, have encouraged me in my thoughts, allowed my imagination to run free and provided me with the experiences from which this story later flowed, including Robert, Albert, Sam, Bob, Skip, Paul, Pandy, Gordon, Matt, Alex, Roger, Bryan, Rob, Craig, Andrew, Bart, John, Jan, Morgan, Peter, and Mr B, as well as those whose writings have also been inspirational, including Elissa Wald, Larry Townsend, Joseph Bean, 'Fledermaus', Race Bannon, John Preston and Guy Baldwin, Tom Henderson and Jacob Morrison.

CC

# Meeting Marc

I was standing, paying the bartender, when the hand patted me on the butt.

Although there were a number of bars in the city where I lived, I rarely used them. Being sociable could be hard work. There were many times when I preferred my own company, and a measure of whiskey, the warmth of my own home, a cheap novel or brain-dead television. That evening, I'd felt like seeing the sights. There was another reason why I avoided the bars; smoke, cigarette smoke.

It wasn't so long, perhaps nine, may be ten, years since I'd stopped. I'd smoked heavily. On a tough, long, working day, I could go through two packs. I could also drink more. Now, sometimes even before I'd finished a first beer, I'd be outside, crying, the pain in my eyes so great. If there was a God, I thought sometimes, he was into health education by vengeance. That night, I was overcoming my prejudice and taking a risk.

I turned to see who was paying me the compliment of attention. I'd gone into the bar alone. Although I'd been living in the city a couple of years, I wasn't a scene-queen. There were a few faces I knew. There were fewer people I'd spoken to.

I picked up my beer as I turned. It was the young bank official. I grinned, smiled.

'Why am I not surprised to see you here?' I said.

He bent forward and kissed me. I raised my eyebrows.

'You were wicked,' he said. 'Would you have said that whoever had been sent to do the appraisal at your house?'

'I intended to,' I said.

He held on to my arm as he ordered a beer for himself. I reached for my pocket, but he noticed and pushed my hand away.

'Remember,' he said quietly, 'I know exactly how much money you haven't got.'

I smiled. Yes, I thought, I had to remember that. It was yet another reason why my face was a rare one in the bars. I could enjoy a reasonable bottle of wine at home for far less than the price of two or three beers in a bar.

He took a mouthful of beer before speaking again.

'You intrigue me,' he said, 'and I hope you don't mind me talking to you like this.'

'Not in the least,' I said. 'I'm honored. Thank you.'

We started to move away from the crush at the bar. I had more time to look at him now than I'd had when he came to my home with his colleague from the bank. I'd been right about his shape, I thought. His biceps were nicely defined; the plain white tee-shirt he was wearing emphasized his strong points well. He stood out from many of the others. The bar was known for attracting young, affluent men. The majority used the place as an opportunity to show off. The latest fashions and designer labels were almost obligatory. Apart from one or two ageing eccentrics, nothing at the bar seemed at all old.

This young man's white tee, his denim jeans, and I discovered, looking down to check, plain brown work boots, set him off from the crowd. The brand of tee-shirt didn't matter. It fitted him well. It was just enough to show off the curve of his pecs and the V-shape of his back without making his nipples too obvious. The jeans would be Levi 501s. They always were. They always had been.

I had time to think as he led me towards the deck away from the hubbub of the bar. There had been a time when it was only gay men who had worn 501s, when the button-fly style was almost impossible to find. Anyone who had friends in Europe would be pestered with requests for them. Then they'd gone mainstream. A few years later, Levi changed their marketing policy. They'd tried to restrict supplies to smaller stores. It was if some young, aggressive, heterosexual MBA 'suit' was completely and utterly unaware of the 'leather'n'Levi' culture. Sure, there had been some reaction, some backlash against the company, but there was something about the cut of style 501, the way it allowed comfort at the front and displayed butts so beautifully at the back that protected it. The effect for my young friend from the bank was no exception: the front was obviously well-filled; the butt as round as I'd thought under the business chinos he'd been wearing the few days before.

I was glowing by the time we'd made our way out on to the deck. It was quieter there. We found some space in the corner, away from the assembling Friday-evening crowds. We sat.

I looked at him, waiting for him to speak. He seemed less confident now.

I drank a little more beer. I looked at him over the top of my glasses. 'Yes?'

He smiled, a little embarrassed.

'Do I have to give you permission?'

The word hit home. I could see him wriggle, almost imperceptibly.

'You must think me very rude,' he said.

I looked at him directly.

'I think you are very flattering,' I said. I smiled. 'As you said, you know a lot more about me than many of my friends. I don't know you very well. I'm glad of the company, especially such attractive company.'

The young man blushed. I'd wanted it that way.

'I think I can learn from you,' he said quietly.

I had to lean forward to hear him.

It was my turn to be intrigued.

'Whatever gives you that impression?' I said.

'I've been to your home,' he said. 'I used your bathroom. I had to walk along your corridor. There were things I noticed.'

'Such as?' I said, raising my eyebrows. The young man was smarter than I'd credited. My arrogance hit me.

'Your books,' he said. 'I couldn't help but noticing. That one section of shelf.'

I smiled. I knew the books he was talking about. They were about sex, SM, in theory, practice, fact and fiction.

'It was why I'm not surprised to see you here,' he said. 'And why you weren't surprised to see me.'

I reached for his hand and squeezed. The gesture wasn't romantic so much as fraternal. I smiled. Again. It wasn't the first time a young man had confided in me. I hoped it wouldn't be the last. It pleased me. There was a special feeling in being adviser, confessor, and mentor. Perhaps it was something parental inside of me; nurturing made me feel good.

'I think I can guess some things about you, Marc,' I said, using the young man's name for the first time. 'Even the way you dress says a lot about you, but I'd like to know from you, what you see life becoming.'

His expression changed. He'd noticed that I'd used his name. There is something about how roles change according to situations and circumstances and how our behaviors change with them. When we'd met first, three days earlier, the interaction had been formal. He'd been the bank representative, in his business shirt and tie. Even though our meeting had been at my home, I too had presented myself reasonably formally in a shirt and tie. The context had been

10

a business one. We both knew that. We appreciated the rituals. We had played them out.

A bar was different. He was the cute young man, dressing down where many of the others, his contemporaries and professional peers, were dressing up for a night out. That said something about him to me for a start. I was playing that game too. I'd chosen blue jeans, a tight-fitting gray tee-shirt, boots and a bomber jacket. We stood out. We were different.

I wondered why we'd both chosen that bar, to set ourselves apart from the crowd that particular evening. The other bars in town may have seemed more appropriate for our appearance. That didn't really matter at that moment. We'd met, that was what was important. My silence as I appreciated this must have surprised him.

'What do you want to know?' he asked.

'About you,' I said. 'How you've got to be where you are today.'

'Fair enough,' he said, 'but I'd like to know about you too, Mr Evan Russell.'

It seemed a reasonable deal.

'First, Marc,' I said, 'you can stopping calling Mr Russell, and Evan. Just call me Russ. I hate Evan and everyone's used Russ ever since I was a kid, OK?'

He nodded.

'So, with the finding out,' I asked, 'who's going to go first?'

## Discovering Marc

That was how our friendship had started. He'd known quite a lot about me, but then he had to. He'd had to check my bank records before we'd even had the meeting to discuss my short-term predicament and my longer-term investments. He'd also had some of the details I'd told him during the meeting a few days earlier; a magazine that published some of my work had crashed, leaving me several thousand dollars out of pocket. Re-financing my property had been my only short-term option. There were some things about me which had not been explicit, but which this acute man had noticed nevertheless.

I wasn't sure whether it was this attentiveness or his good looks, but I was fascinated by him.

'I'm not sure where to start,' he said. 'You know I work for the bank, well, their investment division anyway, I have a reasonable degree. I'm twenty-seven in a couple of months' time. I live on my own. I'm from a small town. I have two sisters, they've both moved back home, now they're married and have families of their own. I've been living here eighteen months. I have an apartment across town and a roommate who says he's straight.'

'You wear keys, and they're on the right,' I said, raising my eyebrows. I was curious. I knew good slaves, even some bottoms, could be very self-assured and self-confident. He was polite but not overly humble. 'That says something about you too.'

'I once had a master,' he said. The words were uttered very quietly, almost reverentially. I could see tears starting to form in the sides of his eyes.

'What happened?'

There was a pause has he fought to hold back the tears. 'I'm sorry,' he said.

'You don't have to apologize for that,' I said, reaching for his hand and giving it a gentle squeeze, 'and you don't have to answer my question if you don't want to.'

'No,' he said. 'It's okay. I will.'

I gave him a moment longer.

'He died.'

I looked at him. So many had died in the 1980s and 1990s that I wasn't surprised.

'No,' he added, quickly, 'for once it wasn't Aids. It was a heart attack.'

'I'm sorry,' I said.

'Thanks.'

'Do you want to tell me about it?' I felt as if he did, but needed encouragement, perhaps even permission, to disclose the details.

'I should tell someone,' he said.

'You've told no one else?' I asked, incredulity stretching my tone of voice.

'No,' Marc said. 'Not the details.'

I finished my beer. I pushed his towards him.

'This may be the time,' I said, 'but I don't think it's the place.'

He drank.

I held my hand out to him.

We left the bar together. I could feel the eyes behind us, assuming enviously, and erroneously, that we had both scored early that night.

The cab back to my home took a little more than ten minutes. We didn't speak. A taxi wasn't the right place to talk either. He held my hand. I gave him my handkerchief. Every so often, he wiped the corners of his eyes.

'My mother told me real men don't cry,' he said as we walked from the cab towards my door.

'The most honest men re-discover their tears,' I said as I turned the key. 'It's more than getting in touch with our inner selves, you know that, I know that. It's about fundamental honesty, what we are, who we are and what we endure to find out.'

Marc held my arm. His grip was firm. He exuded sexuality and sensuality. I wanted to kneel and open my mouth. It wasn't the right time for that either. Marc was more than a sex object; he was a person and it was the person who needed attention right now.

I steered him inside and directed him to the sofa. I went to the dresser and poured us each a couple of fingers of whiskey.

He took a sip. I could see the harshness of the raw spirit on his lips. I reached again gently squeezed his hand.

'What you want, in your own time,' I said. 'You're in control. You can have my ears as long as I stay awake, and then some.'

'Thanks, Russ,' he said.

'He – Jerry – was a businessman, from St Louis, originally, I think. He'd been christened Jeremiah. Through the Eighties, he did well. He worked from home. He traded commodities or futures, something like that. He was one of the earliest people online that I'd ever met. He had computers at his home in Connecticut and in the UK. He was doing okay till the recession hit.'

I understood the same economic downturn had hit me too. The strain when a business ran into problems could be horrendous.

'That wasn't all,' Marc said. 'He was about coping. He sold the UK house and rented an apartment. It brought him enough cash to keep going, just. He cut back. He started flying coach for the first time in twenty years. I thought he was going to make it.'

I nodded. He reached for my hand this time.

'Then his father died. It wasn't the emotion, they hadn't been close. I don't think they'd spoken very much in years. The old man didn't approve of his lifestyle, he said. His mother was nice though. She visited, even stayed for a few days once. Homely, I'd say. I think she loved both of them very dearly.'

14

I waited.

'His father had had his own business too. It wasn't until he died that the mess became apparent. There were huge debts. He'd taken out loans with just about everyone in town, just to keep face. He felt he was an elder statesman of the town. He'd been mayor for many years and had never let go. He felt he should always be accorded the respect of the office, Jerry told me once. Jerry senior couldn't be seen to be having problems. Everyone at the Country Club knew the score, except they didn't talk about it when he was there. They were jovial, courteous, letting him buy them drinks, running up even more expenses he couldn't cover,' he said.

'Some of them were older money too. They knew the signs. Some never presented his checks, we learned later. But the new money was like vultures, as soon as Jerry senior's heart gave out, they were there, circling, wanting their debts paid, then and there, with huge rates of interest.

'Jerry junior only discovered this after his father died. His father had kept it all hidden from him too. Jerry, my Jerry, wasn't wanting an inheritance, that wasn't his way. He was determinedly American. He'd made his own way, made his own money. He paid for a lot while he was trying to sort everything out too. It was expensive.

'Martha, his Mom, she was in shock. She couldn't believe her predicament. There was no insurance either, the policies had been sold off cheaply a year or so before. The business wasn't that big, the small manufacturing works only employed a dozen people or so, but they were folks Martha had known all her life. They were like an extended family. She'd helped them with their children, provided care and support. Now, they were jobless, penniless and she was too. She felt responsible, even though she'd had nothing to do with it.

'Jerry, my Jerry, Jerry junior, had to go out to Kentucky to try to sort out the mess, more than once. This came at just the wrong time for him too. While he was there he saw the people he needed to see and arranged whatever payments he could.

'He'd also been trying to keep his own business going. That wasn't so easy. He was usually available within seconds at the end of a phone. For too long, he was out of touch. His business suffered,' said Marc.

He paused. I waited.

'He'd been a smoker too, like his father,' he continued, trying to hold back the tears.

'A day, may be two days, after his own bankers had called – they wanted to discuss what was going on – he collapsed. He was on his way to the lawyer's office. They called an ambulance. Someone tried to keep him alive, but it was no good. He was dead by the time they got him to the hospital.

'I was at the bank when I had a call from Martha. She'd found my number in Jerry's address book. I fought the tears, hired a car and went and took as many personal things from his apartment as I could.'

The tears were streaming down Marc's face now. He was holding the handkerchief to his eyes.

'I took what I felt was mine too. That was the last time I was in the building. The lawyers came the next day. Everything was crated and sold. The apartment was shut down within hours. The locks were changed. There was nothing left.'

'Wasn't there a will?' I asked.

'Only an old one,' he said. 'I wasn't in it. There was a little for Martha, that was all. She didn't really get much from either of them.'

'I'm sorry.' The words seemed dreadfully inadequate, but they were all I could think of to say.

'I wrote to her,' Marc said, 'to express my condolences. It was probably a very clumsy letter, but I needed to say what I did. I never heard from her again. I don't even know whether she ever got my letter.'

'And you have nothing?'

'Not now. I gave a lot of the leather away. I was so disgusted with myself, with him, with everything, that I threw a box of toys into the river.'

'You didn't go to the funeral?'

'I don't even know where he's buried,' said Marc. 'I think I know, but I'm not sure.'

It was well after two o'clock in the morning when the conversation ended. The whiskey bottle was noticeably lower, but neither of us was drunk.

Marc had fallen asleep while I took the glasses through to the kitchen. I carried him, child-like, along the corridor to my bed. I took off his boots and undid the top button of his jeans, that was all. I grabbed a spare comforter from the closet and slept on the sofa. It wasn't until I was lying back that I realized that I could have put Marc into the guest room. Ah, well, I thought, too late now.

The next thing I knew, I was being woken by the light streaming in through the window and the smell of fresh coffee brewing.

I was still rubbing my eyes when this Adonis-like figure sat down beside me and gently kissed my cheek.

'Thank you, Russ,' he said.

I reached for his hand.

'Better?' I asked.

'Much. That's the first time I've ever told anyone the real story of me and Jerry. I didn't know who I could tell, not until I came here and saw your books. Then I knew.'

I smiled.

17

'Thank you for trusting me,' I said. 'That means a lot to me.'

'I hope you don't mind,' he said as he stood and walked towards the kitchen, 'but I've stolen a pair of your shorts.'

It was unlike me not to have noticed. I grabbed my glasses just in time to see Marc's pert butt disappear into the kitchen. My focus was ready when he came out, carrying two steaming mugs.

'They look good on you,' I said.

He looked embarrassed, not for long, but long enough for me to notice.

'This is what I wore for Jerry,' he said. 'Shorts and boots. It was what he liked.'

# Shared thoughts

Marc moved in two weeks later.

I let him have the guest room. We cleared out a few boxes and put away the clothes and papers that I'd left laid out all over the bed. I hadn't used the room much. It was a luxury, especially as I rarely had anyone to stay. I admitted quietly to myself that it was good to have it used, and to get a little extra income from it, especially at that moment.

I grinned as I thought this could have been one of the solutions to my money problems that might have saved me going to the bank. I could have advertised, found a roommate, but I'd never thought of it. Marc hadn't come up with the idea when we were formally discussing my finances. I found myself grinning at how this had happened. One of life's little co-incidences? I didn't know. I'd been living alone for quite a while. Having close company, even though Marc was out at work all day, would be interesting, if not a challenge. Let's not close a door on an opportunity, I thought, as I made space for an extra towel in the bathroom.

Marc retained his own apartment. His roommate there had a friend who needed somewhere. Marc said he could have his room. The two straight men could keep each other company, he told me. Marc said his only concern was that they kept the place reasonably neat and tidy and didn't do any damage. He went back every week or so at first to collect his mail, and, I suspect, to check out the men and how well they were looking after the place.

Marc had a wicked sense of humor, and I found myself growing to love him. Gradually more and more emerged about his relationship with Jerry junior. But I also learned quickly that I hadn't to pry. Ask a direct question and he'd go silent on me. I realized that, over Jerry at least, I had to let him get to trust me gradually, accept what he said, be non-judgmental and unshockable. And so the details came.

It was slow. It happened little by little. I'd come home and find him wearing another pair of my shorts.

'Sorry,' he'd say, 'I rather liked them.'

Generously, tolerantly, I let him get away with it. He looked good, going round the house in tight shorts. He'd sometimes come home waving something new.

'They were Bob's,' he'd say. Bob was his old roommate. 'He'll never notice.'

It didn't take too long, however, before I came to feel that he was taking advantage. It didn't make sense if I thought about it though, but there was still an underlying suspicion that he was trying to provoke me. He'd do more than his fair share around the house. He'd pay his way, generously. He'd cook more days than I did. I may have held him, kissed him occasionally, but we'd never had sex. I'd seen him naked, and good he looked too. He'd come into my room some mornings, even before I'd got up, to 'borrow', he said, some item of clothing or another.

I knew this was getting to me. I appreciated other people's space and I wanted Marc to respect mine. He should do it automatically, without having to be told, I thought. Over a week, two weeks, my irritation increased. I could feel myself getting more short-tempered. It was a weekend when I finally had enough. I'd been feeling that my own scope was being cramped. I hadn't invited anyone home for months. OK, I didn't do that often, but I felt that I couldn't, that this freedom had been taken from by Marc's intrusion. I hadn't been out to play for weeks. I felt as if more and more of my time had been taken in parenting this young man.

We, he, had decided that we'd go out for the day, for a picnic. He'd been to the store. He'd packed food. He'd made a couple of calls; to one of my friends, then to one of his.

I'd been getting changed when he came into my room. The door had been open as usual. Without a word, he opened one of my drawers and started going through my swimwear. I watched open mouthed as he pulled out one of my favorite garments.

'Where,' I asked, sternly, as he turned to leave, 'do you think you are going with that?'

I was fuming.

I didn't like being angry, but there were occasions, rare occasions, when I could snap.

Marc's face changed that instant.

'I'm sorry, Sir,' he said, suddenly standing still.

The 'Sir' caught my attention. The conditioning was still there. I walked over to him and put my hand round his neck. I came back to the bed and sat down. I reached and pulled him down over my knee. I reached underneath him and undid his shorts. I could feel his cock hardening as I did so. I ignored it. He was wearing a jockstrap. I left that in place as I brought my hand down on his bare butt for the first time.

Ten minutes later I was exhausted. My arm was aching. Marc's butt was beautifully red. His cock was pushing out the pouch of his jockstrap.

I left him kneeling as I picked up the swimbriefs from the bed. I held them, tantalizingly, in front of his face.

'You may,' I said, 'but never without asking. Go and put them on and come back here.'

His head was bowed as he left the room. He came back a few moments later. His cock was still noticeably hard. It, he, looked good. He had chosen well. The swimbriefs showed him off nicely. I walked round him. I smiled. The cutaway back displayed a lot of the redness. I hoped it would last.

'Put on your shorts,' I said. 'You can take them off again later.'

Marc was very subdued that afternoon. He was courteous and respectful. He opened the car door for my friend Tim. He served the meal. He cleared up after it. He pretended not to be embarrassed when both Tim and his own friend Ian noticed the redness of his butt.

'We need to talk,' I said when we got home.

'Yes, Sir,' said Marc.

I let him put things away. I poured myself a little whiskey. I didn't like drinking too early in the evening, or on my own, but I needed to think. I was glad for the few moments while he was working.

He didn't sit on the sofa but on the floor in front of me. He looked downwards, avoiding my eye.

I waited before speaking.

'I want honesty, Marc, is that clear?'

'Yes, Sir,' he said, his face reddening again.

'If you wanted to be spanked, why didn't you ask me?' He slowly looked up at me, like a wounded child.

'I didn't know I could,' he said.

21

'I'm not sure I'm the right person to do it,' I said, 'but you still could have asked. You should have asked.'

He looked down again.

'I'm sorry,' he said, very quietly. 'I won't do it again.'

'You're right there,' I said. It was hard not to be flippant. 'What else do you need?'

'I'm not sure exactly, Sir,' he said.

I took a sip of whiskey.

'You know I'm no 'Sir' Marc, for a start,' I said. 'So you can stop that now, do you understand?'

'Yes, Russ, I understand.'

'I know what you need most, I need it too.'

He looked up at me, curious, not quite understanding.

'A master,' I explained.

I could see him lighten a little. We were making progress.

'But that's not going to happen overnight,' I said. 'Is it?'

Marc shook his head.

'So, there are two of us. We both need parameters to live within. We both have our particular turn-ons. We like working out. We like shorts. We like someone else to take some decisions for us. That's true, isn't it?'

He nodded.

'We have a simple choice then. We can either do nothing or monitor each other. Which do you think it should be?'

I knew which I would like, but I wasn't then sure whether it was sensible or it would work. I liked the idea. I could feel my own cock hardening within my shorts.

'Each other?' Marc suggested.

'Okay,' I said. 'But how?'

'I'm not sure,' he said. 'I could be top one day, you the next?'

'I'm not sure about that,' I said. 'I think we both have to be both, for ourselves and for each other.'

22

'I don't follow,' he said.

'I'll explain,' I said. 'We agree some rules. Some may be the same for both of us. If I've not performed at the end of the week, you can punish me. If you've not performed, I can punish you. What do you think?'

'It sounds okay to me, I think,' Marc said. He looked uneasy.

'You have to know what you want, Marc, what you need,' I said, 'if this is going to stand any chance of working. You do understand that, don't you?'

'I understand it, Russ,' he said, 'it's just that well, yes, I do know some of the things that I want and need, but now, well, it seems so strange that some of these could become real.'

'It won't be play, Marc. Play is different. If it is to be good, to work, to be effective, it has to be real, every day, a part of life. No opting out, saying you're not feeling like it one day. It has to be more than that.'

I could see that he was still uneasy. I felt uncomfortable myself. Marc was an attractive man, he was professional and confident too, mainly outside the home, but I wasn't sure I could maintain a strong commitment to obey Marc. I could have played with him, but in the circumstances, taking his orders would have jarred.

I had an idea.

'Alternatively, Marc, I could be your mentor, training and preparing you until you find a true master,' I said.

His face lit up.

'But, on one very important condition, that you do not regard me as a master, that you accept the arrangement as temporary and that we start a determined search to find you a new master.'

He looked up at me. A gleam had appeared in his eyes.

'You'll help me to do that?' he asked.

'Yes,' I said, taking hold of his hands, 'I'll help you to do that.'

'I hope I can be good enough,' he said.

I left Marc sitting on the floor as I went and poured myself some more whiskey. It was too late to have regrets now. I hoped that I hadn't taken on more than I could deliver.

I sat quietly thinking for a while before I spoke. Sitting silently on the floor, Marc seemed to be falling into his chosen role. I also wondered how much this exercise might change me.

'I think we need to plan this,' I said at last.

Marc looked up.

'I suggest we spend the next few days preparing, and then we can start formally either next weekend or at the beginning of next month, that's just over a week away. And, I think there needs to be a time limit.'

Marc looked disappointed. I think he already believed that his new role had started.

His behavior that day had certainly shown he was ready for it at that moment. It was important, I thought, to make sure that this wasn't some immediate, short term, display of horniness or petulance.

'You can set your own standards this week,' I said. 'But I want you to write them down. If you adopt them between now and the weekend, remember it's highly probable that I will note them and they'll become a permanent requirement. So, if you decided you're not going to use the furniture, like today, then that is likely to continue.'

I smiled.

Marc looked up at me and grinned.

# Possibilities

We said nothing more about the matter that evening. I retreated to the Sunday papers. There wasn't too much to read, but I didn't want Marc to be the focus of my attention any longer. When he noticed I was no longer interested and the subject appeared to have been dropped, he went silently to fix dinner.

I could hear him in the kitchen. I was a little surprised when he brought me a glass of wine. The white had already been poured, but he'd put the glass on a small salver. The noise had been the sound of him searching cupboards for the small tray. He knelt and put a napkin down beside me. He took my empty whiskey glass away. If he had understood me correctly, he was setting himself very high and demanding standards.

I nodded my thanks. I was almost afraid of the sound of my own voice. I didn't want to speak. I was pleased that Marc hadn't knelt. He could have done that. Some masters have that requirement; that slaves kneel before entering any room they occupy, or when presenting themselves or serving the Master.

Marc signalled that dinner was ready by coming and standing silently beside me. He had his head bowed and his hands behind his back. I smiled. It would take me a while to get used to such formality in my own home.

I was surprised to find only one place set at the table. We normally had our meals together. I'd let him do what he wanted this evening, I decided, but I wanted meal times to be talking times. If Marc was waiting table for me, that wouldn't really be possible.

I ate dinner in silence. An appetizer was waiting for me. Marc was supremely attentive. He stood behind me, waiting for me to finish each course, re-filling my wine glass at regular intervals.

When he had brought me salad, I stopped.

'Some paper and a pen, Marc, please,' I said.

I made notes as I ate. It was going to be a tough project, finding a master for Marc. I wondered how long I should allow. Three months might not be long enough. Six months would tire me. I knew I couldn't sustain a year. Six months it would be.

My notes were random. I thought about men I had known, men I had played with, men I had tried to serve. There were so few I felt who were able to benefit from Marc, his talents and his enthusiasm. Yes, there were certainly some who could, who would, use his body for their pleasure, and his. There were some who would enjoy and appreciate his domestic service. It wasn't going to be easy.

There was The Professor. He would thoroughly approve of what Marc had to offer, but he didn't seem to want anyone full time. He would take on a young man for a while, but never forever. There would be someone with him for a week, or a month. I wondered. It was a possibility. I would write.

There was Rudy. He earned himself a very good living, selling his professional services, discretely, ever so discretely, to the diplomatic establishment of Washington, DC. He was a good-looking young man, very good-looking. He was using the proceeds from pissing on visiting eastern European politicians to fund his progress through college. He'd taken to the gym, changed his diet and gone down to less than 10 per cent body fat. He was now bringing in a good return on his investment. Having a permanent slave would cramp his style.

Marc could learn from him, that was certain. Marc might even be able to add to the earning power. Pairs, especially pairs where both men were firm and well-defined, could command a premium. They could earn a great deal of money.

There were Dan and Simon. They had one of the best dungeons on the West Coast. They'd been together for more than twenty years. Others had come into their household, but only for a few months. Then they moved on. That was always the deal. If was if they were scared of someone becoming more permanent, getting between them, perhaps, but that was the way they protected themselves and their relationship. Dan was a good trainer. He was a highly skilled and experienced master. Simon was comfortable in his role as slave. There was much Marc could learn from them. Perhaps, if he could get a transfer at the bank for a while, he could spend some time in Washington state, extending his experience. I would have to find out.

There was Robert in San Francisco. I was uneasy. I had much respect for Robert. I'd seen him work on one of the runs. I had enjoyed his company. His health counted against him. It felt distasteful, but I knew that I couldn't send Marc to someone who might die prematurely. Robert was in his mid, late, forties, I thought. Medications were improving week by week, but although the cancer was being kept at bay, it was still there. I hoped Robert would live to see his sixtieth birthday, but I doubted that he would. Having lost Jerry, it wasn't fair to place Marc with a master whom he might have to nurse and see die within a decade. That wouldn't be right. Again, Marc would benefit from time with Robert, but as a permanent relationship, no, I thought, shaking my head, while it might work, the longer-term implications for Marc didn't bear consideration. Another letter, another visit, I thought.

It felt strange but beautiful, this role of agent. I knew that ritual and protocol could make arrangements difficult. Slaves, potential slaves, wondered about the appropriateness of asking masters, potential masters, about their lives, their requirements, living arrangements and characters. So much could be focused on the sexual that the practicalities and personalities could be sidelined. However much of a relationship was sexual, or carried on within erotic parameters, the individuals had to be able to co-exist with one another. However much a slave may be dedicated to a master, there was little point in pursuing a relationship if the master held, and moreover, expressed views which were not respected by the slave.

I sat at the dining table, thinking, long after Marc had cleared my plates. I think he'd had something to eat himself, washed the dishes and tidied the kitchen, I wasn't paying attention. He brought me some coffee. He knew me well enough to know that in the evening it had to be decaf. He brought me some more whiskey too.

Marc had put a small towel down on the floor against one wall of the sitting room when I finally picked up my notebook and whiskey and got up from the table. He was sitting there, quietly, reading, waiting for me to finish. He put down his book when I came into the room. As soon as I'd sat down, he got up and went to clear my coffee cup. I suspected that within a day the towel would be replaced with a small rug.

I left Marc sitting there when I went to bed. I couldn't even start to think of sleep. My mind was too busy. A transformation had taken place that day. It had caught me by surprise. Marc had set the pace. I grinned. I hadn't seen this coming. I'd been enjoying his companionship. The age difference between us made it all the more refreshing. Through his actions, Marc had told me he wanted, needed, more.

The next morning, I woke to find steaming coffee already on the nightstand beside my bed. I could hear activity downstairs.

Marc had prepared a tray for my breakfast. There was the cereal I usually had, plus some orange juice. He was dressed neatly, ready for work, when I got to the kitchen.

I was wandering around, wearing only sweat pants, when he came across to me and grasped my hand.

He kissed me gently on the cheek.

'Thank you,' he whispered into my ear.

By the time I'd turned round, he'd picked up his jacket and was out of the front door.

My normal work took second place that day. It wasn't that Marc was more important than some of the writing I was supposed to be doing. It was more that I knew that I wouldn't be able to write well until my mind was free of the distractions that Marc had created.

I found the computer already running in the room I used as an office. The mail had been slit open, but nothing had been taken from the envelopes. The trash cans had been emptied. I grinned. Marc was certainly setting himself a fierce pace, I thought. I hoped he could keep going.

Although I wasn't going to write, I decided I would try and keep as close to my normal schedule as I could. I'd work for an hour or so, then shower and dress. I'd either run later in the morning or go to the gym for a while.

It wasn't until that hour was over and I took a break that I noticed. Marc had always kept the room to his door closed. I felt that it was his way of defining his space, his privacy. Today, the door was open. It was held wide. It was as if he was saying he had nothing to hide, that he had no need for privacy, that every part of him should be claimed. It was a significant gesture. I felt it should be recognized in some way, but I wasn't yet sure how.

I was starting to formulate my plan.

I didn't shower. I changed from sweat pants into light

running shorts and a tanktop. The fall weather was still good, even for New Jersey. The evenings were closing in, but the days were not cold.

There had been some rain, but that part of the eastern seaboard of the United States had been spared the snow storms of the Rockies and the hurricanes of Florida and the Caribbean. I adjusted the rubber cockring that I always wore inside the inner brief and set out. I had a door key on a cord. I put it around my neck.

I thought more about Marc's requirements as I ran. He had certainly provided me with a challenge. I tried to review the thoughts I'd had. I would write some letters. I would talk to Marc, in detail. I wanted to know more about what had happened in the five years or so since Jerry had died. I wondered where the best place to do that would be. I enjoyed the run. I hadn't been going out as often as I should have done, but I didn't think too much about the run this time. I was concentrating on my quest to find Marc a new master.

I wondered about the letters. They would not be too difficult.

As soon as I got home, I went to my office. I didn't bother showering or changing. I booted the computer and started writing while my thoughts were fresh.

Dear Professor,

I'm sorry not have been in touch for a while, but when we last spoke, we both seemed to be very busy. This letter is a request for assistance or advice at least.

I'm fairly sure I told you I've found a roommate since we met on the run last year.

It's an interesting tale. We met when I went to the bank to refinance my home.

His name is Marc and he's twenty-seven. But, more pertinently now, when he was in his late teens and early twenties, he was in slavery. That master died suddenly five or six years ago.

He had a heart attack after experiencing a great deal of stress. Marc decided that the time has come when he should try to find a new master.

I hope, Professor, that this isn't inappropriate, but I remember you as having young men in training, for relatively short periods of time, rather than anyone permanently with you. If you should be looking for someone to be with you for a longer period, to care for you, your home and your most personal needs, I would commend this young man to you.

If you are not, I would ask that you consider him for a shorter period of training. The guidance you can provide would add greatly to his appeal. He works for the investment department of one of the major banks. It is possible for him to seek deployment to different cities for two-week to four-month periods. Alternatively, he could take some vacation for a shorter period of training or service.

If neither of these suggestions is possible, then any other advice or guidance you could offer would be very greatly appreciated.

I await your response with interest.

Respectfully,

Russ


I could have sent the message by e-mail, but it seemed more appropriate that it should be a proper letter. I produced it on the computer. It was neat and fairly formal. I dug around in my desk to find my fountain pen. I hadn't used it in a while, but this was a letter which I felt should be signed with the old-fashioned reverence of pen and ink, rather than rollerball or ballpoint. There was something about The Professor which kept informality at arm's length. Even writing to him had to be taken seriously. Such a bearing extended off campus, out of his elegant home, too;

when he was striding about a run site, wearing jeans and a tee-shirt, there was something about his demeanor which demanded respect.

So, it wasn't surprising that my relationship with The Professor had always been formal. I had first been introduced to him when I was in slavery. The man scared me too. He was very much a gentle-man, until he played. Then, he could be a savage. I was tempted. I had been tempted many times. I didn't dispute his abilities, only mine.

I'd deliberately kept the letter short. I'd decided that I would produce a résumé of Marc's experience and personality, but this wouldn't be ready until I had time to talk with him more. It would not be right to send it out with a first message or enquiry either.

I addressed the envelope by hand and found a stamp. I was thinking of putting the letter in the mailbox, so it could be collected. I changed my mind.

# Marc's education begins

I called Marc as soon as he opened the door.

I'd heard his pick-up pull up. I could hear him coming up the few stairs to get to the front door. Inside, he paused. His tie was askew. I suspected he'd been taking it off at the door and hadn't expected my summons.

'Come in,' I said.

He came and stood beside me.

The letter was on the desk. I picked it up.

'Go and change into running gear,' I said. 'You can then go and post this. It's my first letter seeking a position for you.'

I put the envelope down. It was his cue to go and change. He picked up the nuance. Within seconds, I could hear him taking off his work clothes. He was putting them away before putting on anything else.

I was surprised when there was a knock on my door.

I looked up. He looked beautiful. He was standing wearing a tanktop and a cockring, nothing else. In one had he had a running short with inner brief, in the other a jockstrap and separate shorts. He clearly expected me to decide what he should wear.

I enjoyed keeping him waiting while I decided.

'The jock,' I said. 'You can keep it on when you get back, but take off the shorts and tanktop.'

He nodded. He put the jockstrap on there and then. He looked good in it. He turned and vanished but was back in a moment. One pair of shorts had been put away, the other was on. I smiled. I was enjoying the transformation. On the few occasions of old when I'd needed to go into Marc's room, there had always been clothes everywhere. Sometimes, he'd had to iron a shirt in the morning, before going to work. I hoped this new-found neatness would last. I would do my best to make sure that it did.

He waited for me to hand him the envelope.

'You have twenty minutes,' I said. 'Exactly twenty minutes. There will be six strokes of the cane for every minute you are late.'

The smile left Marc's face. He looked puzzled.

'A legacy of my time in England,' I explained answering the question in his eyes, 'and very, very effective,'

The run would be hard, getting to the post office and back in that time. It wasn't a casual evening jog. I opened the clock program on the computer. I waited for the seconds to tick away before handing him the envelope. It was 6.10pm exactly.

I stood and watched him leave. He wanted to take the stairs two or three at a time. He restrained himself. I also noticed that when he'd taken off his office clothes, he'd taken off his watch. There was a clock at the post office, I knew. I did know of anywhere else where he'd be able to get a check on his progress. Coming back, he would have to run hard or increase the risk and degree of punishment.

Those twenty minutes gave me the time I wanted too.

I'd done well buying that particular home, not least because the previous owner had done nothing with the basement. As soon as I'd seen the space behind the garage, I'd known the house was for me. The third bedroom had made an ideal study and office while basement was big enough for a utility room, the two-car one-bike garage, a store room that quickly became my archive and overflow library, and a good sized playroom.

Getting it all together had taken time. I'd done quite a lot of the work myself, or had guys help me out. I'd done deals with some, letting them use the space themselves in return for painting or a piece of equipment. After a few years, I thought, it was quite nicely appointed.

I looked round the space proudly while Marc was out. I had to admit that I hadn't been using such good facilities as much as I should have been, or was much as I would have liked. Perhaps this would change, I wondered, as I pulled a punishment frame out from one wall to the center of the room.

Marc was sweating hard and short of breath when he reached the doorstep on his return. I'd been looking out for him, keeping my eye on the time. I opened the door to let him in.

'Only a minute,' I said, looking at my watch.

'Shorts, tanktop, off,' I said as soon as he was inside. 'Go down to the basement and bend over the frame.'

Despite still being out of breath, Marc moved quickly. He took the shorts and tanktop with him. He was still holding them in his hand when I followed him down the basement stairs.

I took the shorts from his hand and walked round him. I held the sweaty garment in front of his face. It took him a moment to realize that I was waiting for him to open his mouth. When he did, I pushed the shorts in. They would give him something to bite on, I thought. I could enjoy using the cane. Often, I would do it for an hour. I loved to work a body gradually, having someone standing naked, either against a frame or with their fingertips against a wall, but feet set back. I could then work their calves, thighs, inside and out, butt and back. I liked using music. With a friend, we'd called the activity 'Vivaldi-ing', because of the strict rhythm of the baroque music that was so excellent. In this fashion, a body could be played. The intensity could be built, relaxed, built up again. It was a joy and a challenge to keep someone on the edge of changing the 'oos' on their lips to 'ows'.

I'd developed the technique at several SM events I had attended. At one, a spectator had complimented me on the choreography. That was how it felt. At another, someone had been intrigued, but scared. I'd promised I wouldn't hurt him. I didn't. I had him 'oo-ing' for ages, and worked up the marks on his upper back and thighs. He had been quite high when I stopped. He'd cursed me the following morning when the bruises had matured and the intensity had had its effect. Seeing that rainbow across his shoulder blades was a moment I remembered with pride.

I'd had lots of good fun with the canes I'd brought back from England with me, and others that friends had given me too. So many all-American young men found the different implement a surprise; they're been raised in the land of the ubiquitous paddle after all. Paddles could be effective, I knew, but there was something about the nice, thin, clean welt lines that a well-placed cane could raise across a man's butt. The broader impact of a paddle may also hurt, but its legacy wasn't the same. Bruising after an intense caning could last a good few days, reminding the recipient of his endurance for several days, every time he wanted to sit down. Denying someone underwear in favor of rougher pants could also extend the effect. Marc, I thought, might be spending more of the coming days in a jockstrap than he had anticipated.

Much as I loved such creative caning, it didn't get me hard. Somehow, for some reason, caning someone hard, hard enough to leave bruises did. I could feel myself getting hard as I picked up the cane behind Marc.

'You know what you have to do,' I said, forgetting he had the shorts in his mouth.

'Yes, Sir,' he mumbled against the material.

I ran my hand over his butt. This was not a turn-on for Marc, but a punishment. I remembered the comment about such beatings 'hurting me more than it hurts you'. I felt uncomfortable. I was actually looking forward to it. Implicitly, he had agreed to it, I said to myself. I wasn't entirely convinced, but the thought helped.

I had to admit that Marc's bare butt looked good too. It was stretched. He was bent forward over the bench. The cheeks were framed by the straps of the jock. Yes, it was an appealing target.

I stepped back. I brought the cane down against my hand. I wished for a moment there was a pillow nearby I could use for a few practice strokes. There wasn't. I would have to do without.

I flicked the cane up and down a few times, using my wrist to get the end to move most quickly, producing the nice 'swish' sound that could be so daunting. I thought I could sense Marc tense. I got into position. I placed the cane carefully against his butt, trying to get myself into the best position to make sure that it would fall horizontally across his cheeks.

I patted Marc's flank a couple of times to signal that the beating was about to begin. I felt him grasp the bench more tightly. The best way was to take a deep breath and go for it, no pausing at all, I thought. I steadied myself. I hadn't done this for a while. I closed my eyes and concentrated. It took some effort.

I opened my eyes, counted slowly to five, then brought the cane down with some force. I wanted it to hurt and I intended to leave bruises. It was important that Marc wouldn't enjoy sitting down for a while.

There was a grunt from the other side of the bench. I think Marc was trying to count.

No sooner had the cane bounced back from the flesh of Marc's butt than I raised it again. I could see the welt of the first starting to rise. I tried to aim, but precision was less important to me at that moment than impact. I wasn't really too concerned if the other strokes landed on top of that first mark.

The second hit him. There was another grunt.

The third; the grunt had an agonized edge to it. The pain was finding its home, I thought, as I raised the cane again.

The fourth; and I could hear the crying around the grunt.

The fifth; Marc was weeping hard now. I could hardly hear the sound of counting. I wasn't too worried. The sensation of the beating was more important. Counting was more part of a play scene, I thought, than this.

The sixth; I tried to bring the cane down on his reddening ass no harder but no softer than the rest. I looked at the butt.

The welts were developing quickly and aggressively. Marc would have some fine bruises. I put the cane down and

37

walked round him. I pulled the shorts from his mouth and put them to one side. It was not a time for gesture or sentiment. It was punishment. Tempting as it was to be supportive, soothing even, I had to be dispassionate. I turned and walked out of the room.

I could feel my erection as I did. I looked back quickly at Marc's developing bruises. I knew that there could be something wonderfully erotic and self-fulfilling about a bruise. There could be nice feelings when a bruise was touched. The real pain came from the impact; it may be so intense that it went off the scale of every rating system ever invented, but it was momentary. As soon as that millisecond was over, the body started to repair itself. I wondered if I could still take such a beating. I knew I had done in the past. Some had bad memories, of school, of apparent justice misplaced. Others brought smiles to my face. I rubbed my own butt.

I went to the kitchen and poured myself a glass of wine. I had to maintain the distance. I went back to my desk. I didn't really do much. I played with some e-mails and sorted a few files. It was a shamefaced Marc who appeared at the door half-an-hour later to tell me that dinner was ready.

His face was still red. His eyes were red too. There was plenty of evidence that he had been crying a lot. I looked as closely as I could at the yellow, red and black bruises across his butt as he led the way downstairs. It was difficult, but I could make out four distinct lines. I was pleased, they were almost parallel. They looked good. Then, I wasn't pleased. I was taking pleasure in the esoterics, rather than the psychology.

Marc said nothing while I ate. He stood quietly behind me. I could smell his perspiration. He hadn't showered since the run or the beating. When I'd finished eating, I turned to him before he started to clear the table.

'When you've cleaned up,' I said, 'go shower. Then we need to talk.'

## Learning more

The evening was pleasant after that. I took my wine and the newspaper on to the deck while Marc ate, cleaned up and showered. I took my notepad with me too. Another reason I had chosen the house was its privacy. The deck had shutters that could be pulled down to keep the insects out, but this wasn't one of those evenings. There were two sides, one faced south-east, the other south-west. There was sun in the morning and sun at night. I could just hear the distant rumble of traffic on the freeway a mile or so away, but the evening was peaceful. I sat quietly, sipping my wine and thinking.

Marc was very quiet when he approached me next. He looked ashamed. He put himself as close to my feet as he could. I watched as he tried to make himself comfortable. He was half kneeling, taking his weight on his haunches and keeping pressure off his butt and bruises. He looked up at me. He was asking permission. I didn't know what he wanted.

'Yes?' I said.

He inched himself forward and held my hand. He put his head on my thigh. I smiled as the tears started again. He squeezed my hand. It took him a few minutes before he could speak. I let him run with the emotion. It wasn't the time to interrupt. The dynamic could change. The effect had been felt. The punishment had made its mark. This was the right time for support and understanding.

'Thank you,' he said.

I raised my eyebrows, pretending not to understand. He

looked directly into my eyes. It was a little disconcerting. I tried not to let him see it.

'I needed that,' he said, a smile reappearing on his face at last. 'You know I did. Thank you, Russ.'

It was my turn to squeeze his hand. I had to try hard not to be facetious. That was the way I often retreated into denial, or diverted potential embarrassment. I said nothing.

I let him rest for a while. The sun was setting behind trees at the edge of the property. The long evening shadows reached Marc's naked back. They made some interesting patterns. I tried to imagine how they would look, etched in more carefully crafted bruises.

'I'll tell you what I've been planning,' I said. Marc nodded.

'The letter, the one you posted, you saw who it was to?'

Marc nodded again.

'Have you met The Professor?' I couldn't remember. The world, our world, was a small one. Most of those who were serious players or lived the life grew to know one another, if not directly, then by reputation.

'No, I haven't,' Marc said, 'not yet.'

'You know about him?'

'You've told me quite a lot,' he said. 'I have friends who know him too.'

'Good. I've written to him first. I've asked him if he will train you for a while. I'm not sure how long. It depends which classes he is teaching this year and the demands of his research. It may be a weekend, it may be a month or two, perhaps three. You know he's in California now? He's teaching at Stanford. You can be assigned to San Francisco or San José, right?'

Marc nodded.

'That's not a problem,' he said.

'And the period of time?'

'I'll take vacation if it's only a few days,' Marc replied. 'I can apply for a short-term transfer for anything from one month to six.'

'He may have others in training, either short or longer-term,' I said. 'Don't expect his sole attention. It's unlikely to be a one-on- one experience, more likely training as part of a stable. You're comfortable with that?'

Marc nodded.

'The Professor has acquired quite a reputation for himself,' I went on.

'He is well known.'

'That's not what I meant,' I said. Marc looked puzzled.

'He's been a fast developer,' I explained. 'Five, six years ago, on the runs, he'd play, but he was quiet, shy almost. He was unsure of his own skills and abilities, Marc. He knew what he wanted. He knew some of the things he liked doing. We talked then, just as we talk now, long into the evening, over tumblers of whiskey.'

It was my turn to reminisce, to dream. Marc looked up at me and nodded again.

'At first, we sat together, on chairs, on a deck, not unlike this. He told me about how he felt more of a top than a master. He found maintaining the persona of a master difficult at that time. The Professor told me he loved the beautiful reactions on a man's face as he took someone towards that beautiful zenith of agony meeting ecstasy. He loved watching bodies, watching individuals as, with his help, they strove to take, enjoy and endure more.

'He didn't always need sex, he'd told me. He said he could be erect as he took someone on such journeys into the deepest, most intense corners of their psyches. He told me he could achieve an orgasm seeing someone else reach their peak. Often, The Professor told me, he wouldn't ejaculate,

41

but the psychological effect was the same. He felt satisfied, fulfilled, as if he had achieved his biological purpose.

'It felt like a gentleman's club, talking like that. The Professor is a very gentle man, I'm sure I've told you that before, many times. He has a dignity and a presence now. Our relationship has changed too, subtly. I no longer sit on furniture when he's around, Marc, I sit on the floor, like you are now. We may both enjoy our evening whiskies, The Professor and I, but the dynamic has changed. We have both moved on since those first discussions.

'When we have seen what The Professor has to say, as he's my first choice for you, Marc, I may introduce you to others. I will ask if you can spend time with them. They represent a range of people. The Professor is in his mid-fifties. There's another. He's in his sixties, but he is a great man, one of the most highly-respected masters on the West Coast. The last I can think of is younger, not perhaps the best long- term master, but he's skilled physically and psychologically in his own way. He's still quite young. He has learning still to do. I'm allowing six months,' I said. 'I'm giving you that. I have the energy for that, but no longer than that.'

I wasn't sure of Marc's reaction. I think it was a second of disappointment at first; six months could seem a long time. Then there was pleasure; that I was prepared to make such a commitment and that whatever happened, he would at least have six months of greater structure here with me and some potentially exciting visits too. I slowly saw the smile break out across his face as he realized this.

'Now,' I said, 'I need to know more, a lot more, about you.'

'I've told you quite a lot about Jerry already,' said Marc, looking up at me from his position on the deck.

I nodded. He had told me about this man before he moved in. He'd always used his first name; it had taken him longer than I

42

had expected to be comfortable in admitting that Jerry had been his Master. His behavior had indicated formal training. I didn't question why it had taken him so long to acknowledge the true nature of their relationship. If he wanted to tell me more about that, he would, in time. He was, I knew, still grieving. Healing was slow for him. I waited for a few moments, then nodded again, indicating that he should continue.

'After Jerry died and I lost my home,' he said, almost imperceptively quietly, 'I was lost. I heard nothing from his mother. I didn't go to the funeral, I told you that. I had some things, but nothing really that was his. There were items I would have liked, that we had shared, enjoyed together. I would have appreciated something that had been very personal to him. I have nothing now.

'It didn't matter too much at first,' Marc went on, 'perhaps because I was just too shocked. I went into an automatic trance. I did my work, but it wasn't inspired. It was as much as I had to do. It was difficult at work too. They knew someone had died, someone close to me, but the relationship, well, you know, Russ, it isn't, it wasn't, the sort of relationship that you can describe easily to people. You never know if they'll understand.'

I nodded, indicating that he should continue.

'It used to be bad enough coming out as gay in the bank. That's changed though. They have made progress. It may be we're lucky having huge offices in cities where there are large, open gay populations. You can't exist in San Francisco without knowing gay people are part of humankind, an important, valuable part. With such a large office there, it's not surprising they have so many gay employees. New York was the same, but ....' Marc's voice trailed off.

'You ... and Jerry ...' I prompted.

He looked up at me, a far away look in his eyes.

43

'I'm not sure how long this lasted,' he said. 'I would go home. I'd drink, regularly, daily, not a lot, but enough. I was never really drunk. I just told myself I needed some alcohol to help me sleep. I became reclusive. I didn't go out. I had to force myself to see friends. Even then, I didn't really enjoy it. I felt I was expected to be the happy-go- lucky, brazen, showing-off, quick-to-respond, ready-with-a-quip Marc, as if I had to perform for people. Someone told me later that it looked like depression.

'Yes, sure, I like doing that, but this time made me realize that I liked doing this in my own way, in my own time, when I was ready, being myself for myself. I didn't want to perform like that when I didn't want to. I kept away from people.

'I'd jerk off, every day, sometimes several times a day, just as I always did when I was left to my own resources. I'd think of scenes we'd had, me and Master Jerry, the sex we'd enjoyed, the sex I'd been denied. Sometimes, I'd even wear a cup jock into work, for old times' sake, I'd tell myself. One day, it didn't work. I found myself in a cubicle in the men's room, crying. I threw the jock and the cup in the trash. I was angry with myself, with Jerry, with the world, for not understanding.

'Eventually, one of my friends noticed. He took charge, in a quiet way, not like my relationship with Jerry. He made me take some vacation. He took me with him. He didn't have to, but he did. We hired a cabin in the mountains for a week. We were about two miles from the nearest people. We had a view across the woods and the valleys. It was the early fall. The leaves were just starting to change color, but it was still warm. It was wonderful.

'We'd go out in the morning for a little while, perhaps to the store a few miles away. We went and looked at some of the local attractions. We sat and had coffee overlooking a

44

lake, watching as the boat owners closed up, ready for the winter. We were probably some of the last folks there, the real stragglers, coming in well after the end of the season. Labor Day was long past. The few pennies we added to the year's income for those folks and their businesses were appreciated, but we were half resented, for getting in the way of the clearing up.

'My friend slept in the afternoon. He'd been ill. He was recovering. I sat in the sun. It felt good. I wore my Speedos and a cockring. I read some cheap novels. I thought of Jerry. I wished I had his ashes to scatter among the trees.

'There were deer too. I could hear other animals. There were the birds. Eagles, I'm sure they were eagles, they seemed big enough, as they soared overhead, silent, swimming on the thermals. It looked effortless, but the concentration on searching for prey was never ending. I thought of myself as an eagle, looking down, ready to swoop for my next meal.

'But, most importantly of all, I rested. I didn't have to act with Warren. I didn't have to perform. Sure, we talked some. He knew about Jerry, although they'd never met. Warren had played some too; so he knew enough to understand me. There were times when we didn't need to talk. He'd come and give me a hug, or just squeeze my hand.

'One day, I walked. Warren went to rest just after we'd had some lunch. I remember it clearly. I put sweat pants and a tee-shirt in a small backpack, and a can of soda, but I walked wearing only my Speedos. For a while, I even took those off and walked naked along the track through the woods. The air on my skin felt cleansing, liberating.

'Warren was up, waiting, when I got back. He came and kissed me, briefly, on the lips. 'I think you're getting better,' he'd said. I'd felt so too.

'The old me went back to work the next week. There was an energy and impetus that had been missing since Jerry's death. I hit targets. I smiled. I bounced. I stopped drinking alone at home. I started going out again. I saw friends. I performed.'

Then, without warning, Marc stopped. He went silent, almost moody.

I offered him my wine. He took a sip from the glass. I waited. I could see him thinking, breathing deeply.

'And?' I prompted, having given him a few minutes.

He looked up at me again. He seemed reluctant to go on. I nodded. I wanted him to continue. He had to. There was more that he had to release. He knew that too. He took a deep breath, sipped a little more wine. He looked up at me, his eyes asking me for permission to continue.

Once again I nodded.

Marc thought for a moment before picking up his account where he'd left off.

'It was fine for five, six, months, perhaps a little longer. Then I felt I needed action again. I started going back to the bars. I'd look for the men whom I thought could deliver. I'd wait, patiently, trying to be a good slave-boy, standing, head bowed, looking down, watching them in my peripheral vision, hands behind my back. I'd get as close to them as I could without actually going up to them and saying 'use me, Sir'.

'A few responded, but something was missing. No.'

He stopped again, equally suddenly, as if he was realizing something for the first time.

'A lot was missing,' he said. 'Being tied loosely to a bed frame and fucked in the early hours of the morning didn't mean anything. If I got up first and made coffee, brought it to the bedside, I'd be regarded as impertinent. These guys made me feel like a guest in their homes, not someone ready to serve, to service them. It wasn't working. It didn't work for me. I don't think it really worked for them.

'Sure, they'd be wearing leather. They'd been working out. They looked good. They had good bodies. They tasted good, but they wanted to suck my cock as much, perhaps even more, than I wanted to suck theirs. It was vanilla, with the sharpness of the pods, I admit, perhaps with a little decoration, a little sauce, but it was vanilla all the same.'

I had to admit too, to myself, that I knew exactly what Marc meant. I'd been there too. I'd bought the tee-shirt. We'd both worn them. I think we'd both worn them out.

'So?' I said. I was sure there was more of Marc's story to come.

'So?' He smiled, almost teasing me. 'I started topping.'

I think he expected me to be surprised. I wasn't. I had started to wonder if that was what had happened.

'I wasn't sure where I was going,' he said. 'I knew about our culture, our history; some of the evolution, collective and individual, how we started as slaves when we were young, earned our leathers and became masters as we grew older and supposedly more mature. Our culture, this culture, has moved on since the early 1970s. It's evolved. It's still evolving. We're always having to look at what's around us, what we're doing, how we're fitting in.

'I was confused about age too,' Marc said, suddenly returning to his story from his philosophical thoughts.

'I felt older than many of these men. I'd been playing since my early teens, remember. Some of these guys were only just discovering their cocks for the first time when they were in their forties. It wasn't so much as life beginning,' he said, 'it was more like adolescence beginning ... for them.'

I felt him relaxing. He was starting to perform for me. I liked it. I enjoyed his company when he was less serious. I

47

also knew that we had to strike a balance. We could both be frivolous, almost silly at times.

I'm an only child, so I don't know a lot about sibling relationships. I agree with the view that gay men use camp and effeminacy as a means of self protection, of being self-deprecating. Luckily for my sanity, I'd discovered very early, when I was in my early teens, that sex for me had to be something masculine. I was into 'mansex' as if I had to prove my gender reference points through my cock, my ass and my mouth. Yet, the concept of being 'sisters' was one that I felt I could increasingly understand. I had relationships with a couple of former colleagues, women, which were distinctly open. Both, at different times, had said that they spoke to me because they felt an empathy, telling me things that they told no other men, not even their husbands.

I felt that there was a similar sort of relationship between Marc and me. Although I was fifteen years, no sixteen, his senior, I had had many of the same experiences. I had had very similar emotions. I knew everyone was, is, unique, and that consequently no two people could ever experience 100 per cent the same feelings, but, if they could communicate well enough, there was a high probability of what I'd decided I could best describe as 'common empathies'. I felt this with Marc.

I felt I understood a lot of what Marc had been through in those five or six years since Jerry's death. It was tempting to make assumptions. I knew I had to hear it from him.

'Tell me about that too,' I said.

'I think you can guess,' he said.

'I may well be able to, Marc, but I need to hear what you feel about it, what you did, what you tried to do, why you think it didn't work?'

'I was technically good,' he said, smiling proudly.

Yes, I could imagine that. I could understand the pride in

his work. 'But I couldn't maintain the role. I felt myself being like the other guys had been with me. I was as bad as they were, worse probably. I wanted to look after the guest in my home, even when I'd had him whimpering on his knees. I'd be turned on at the thought of scrubbing another guy's kitchen floor with a toothbrush, while plugged, gagged and naked, or ironing his shirts but I couldn't understand why someone might want to do it for me. Then I realized, accepted that my destiny was different. In some ways, I was just like the others, like so many of them, but unlike the guys who only let themselves play the life, I knew I needed to live the life. There was that difference. For me, it had to be all or nothing, even if it meant years of frustration, being patient, hoping, praying that I would find the right master or that the right master would find me.

'That didn't mean that I have up playing altogether. I gave some guys some good times,' he said. 'I could blindfold them and tease them, tie them to the bed, shave them, drop hot wax on their balls and tits, rub their cocks with menthol, impale them on dildos, beat their backs, even sew their cocks and balls together, but I felt as if I should have been doing it for a master.

'I had some good scenes, but they were rare, one, perhaps two a year. I'd respond to an advert. We'd exchange two or three letters. I would be turned on by getting instructions. The scene would start before we met. It would continue when I got to the guy's home. I'd strip in the lobby, put on a blindfold, cuffs, whatever. We'd play, for perhaps an hour, may be longer. I could be used quite hard, but then, we'd break, relax. The guy would let his domination slip. Once we spoke as equals, peers, something was lost. I could try saying 'Sir', but the nuance wouldn't be appreciated. If that happened, there was usually no way I could rediscover the respect, the obedience. The dynamic was lost forever.

'Some guys would call me, even write me letters with instructions, but I wouldn't go back. I was busy. Something had happened at work. I had vacation planned that week. I'd make excuses. I wouldn't go back. I'd start looking for the next, hoping that he'd be better.'

'And sometimes, when you're searching, you never find,' I said, 'and when you're not, they find you?'

'Yeh,' Marc said, 'sort of. But even when I didn't think I was looking that hard, nothing found me. I could share some of these things with one or two friends, like Warren, but, I found myself holding back, not quite being entirely honest. Despite trying to convince myself, I wondered if I was losing it altogether, whether I'd ever get another chance.'

He fell silent again.

I waited. There was more to come. I took a sip of wine. I pushed the glass towards him. He took a sip too, savoring the liquid before talking again.

'I started using the net,' he said. 'I'd go online, on the chat channels, flirting, talking with people. Some were players, explorers, jerk-off merchants. Sure, I could do that too. Getting instructions on screen could make my cock hard. I'd play with myself for an hour or two before finally getting off.

'Then, one day, I discovered this guy in Europe.'

# Disappointment

'He was older. He told me he was retired. He'd been a scientist, working in nuclear physics, he said, running a department at one of the older, more prestigious universities. He sounded cultured and knowledgeable. He sent me a picture. He was hot, but it was the image of a forty-year-old, not someone in their early sixties.

'He said his boy had died. They'd been together fifteen years, he told me. I said I wanted to visit. I wanted to be this guy's slave. There was something about him which had my attention. He got to my cock and to my head. He seemed sure in his confidence, his needs, his ideas.

'Again I asked about being his slave. No, he said. A visit? Perhaps, he said, if I was coming to Europe for any other reason. I quickly thought about the bank. I wondered if I could find a pretence, any pretence to visit the European headquarters in Paris. Once there, I could take some vacation and visit this guy.

'We e-mailed. He told me that his parents were an old Prussian family, that there was family money, that now he'd retired he was looking to relocate. I believed him. He sounded okay. There was something about the e-mails. He seemed to know what he was doing. His requirements and house rules sounded realistic.

'It took a few months to arrange, but I managed to get myself that business trip to Paris. It would be hard work. I'd have meetings with two or three different managers each day and then I'd be expected to provide specific expertise when I came back. It seemed an okay deal. I could also take the week's vacation I'd requested.

'I e-mailed this guy and told him. He'd moved, he said. He'd found a town house in Amsterdam. He had another boy too. I was a little upset by that I had to admit, but I'd learned enough to cope with the concept of the master-slave family. We arranged dates. I was feeling good. He would give me a week's try-out.

'I told Warren about what I was doing. I checked out the guy with a couple of other people in Amsterdam, friends of friends who look out for each other in this small world of ours. I hoped I might be able to see them while I was there. They were, I also knew, a safety net in case things didn't work out.

'He was away for a few days before I went to Paris. There was a leather event in Hamburg he was going to. I'd hoped he'd have a good time. I called him once I got to Paris. I called him every day. He wanted to know what I was doing, how I was doing. He sounded a little quieter than when I'd called him from home, but he said he'd caught a cold in Hamburg. I didn't think much more about it.

'I enjoyed Paris. The three weeks were hard work. I had to concentrate hard, coping with the jet lag and the meetings at the beginning, but after three or four days, I was feeling better. I'd decided I'd go out to one of the bars a few nights before I was due to take the train to Amsterdam. I told him so. He said I could have sex, even shoot, but only if it was before midnight. I wasn't, he told me, to touch myself after that.

'The Keller was surprisingly busy for just after 11pm. I'd checked out the backroom. There was action even at that time. A beautiful sight greeted me. There were three guys on a pool table. All had their heads down and their asses up. Behind two of them, a big black guy had a fist in each. He was hot, probably in his thirties, defined and good-looking. I could see the muscles of his forearms tense and relax. He was wearing a white tanktop. It made his dark skin even more impressive. I enjoyed watching.

'The third guy had two fists inside him. There was a small, wiry white guy behind him. It looked as if he was calling for a third. Together, they had attracted quite a crowd of spectators. I'd seen people being fisted at runs, but never like that in a bar.

'I wasn't sure I wanted that sort of play myself that night. I went and bought a beer. I got talking to some guys. One of them had been in Hamburg the previous weekend. He was telling his friends about a retired scientist who had been having fun with electricity. I knew that there weren't, then, quite so many people in Europe playing with electricity as there were here in the States. It gradually became clear that the guy he was talking about was the guy I was going to see. The description was impressive. And, the guy at the bar said, he was 'drop-dead gorgeous'. I felt my knees weakening, but still I said nothing.

'I'd been listening to the stories for an hour, I suddenly realized. I wondered about finding some action, whatever the quality. It seemed a pity to waste the opportunity. I headed back to the darkroom again. It more than served its purpose. The sex was anonymous, but someone went for my nipples. I don't think I have ever come out of a backroom so sore. It was enough for me still to be feeling it the following morning, the sensitivity against the cloth of my office shirt. I came out of the bar a little before midnight.

'I was on a strange high as I walked back to the apartment hotel where I was staying. It took a little while, but that's what I liked about Paris. If you weren't in a hurry, so much was walkable. I couldn't help but think about the master and the comments which had been made in the bar. The man certainly seemed to have made an impression on the event in Hamburg. I was reassured but my anxieties also rose. I wondered if I would be able to provide the level of response that the man clearly required or demanded. I wondered if I'd be able to maintain that for the trial week that we'd agreed.

'Still, there was one factor that had been dominating my thoughts. I'd told Warren about it during the two or three weeks before my departure for Europe. There was something about the opportunity. It was almost as if the guy's appearance and skills didn't matter. It had slowly become more and more apparent to me that I had to follow through. I knew that if I didn't go, I would be forever wondering whether I could have done it. It was a challenge for me personally. I needed to know that I could go back and, then, that I could go back and do well.

'Yes, I was scared. I was scared of admitting that this was still such an important aspect of me. Those days made me realize just how much I had been repressing this part of my character, of my psyche. I realized I'd been in denial, trying to be a top, trying to master others. As the days went by, I found my confidence slowly growing. Something inside me, in my heart, was telling me that I could do it. 'The clash of these emotions came as I got onto the train for Amsterdam. I'd been told that there was very little that I'd need for the week – jeans, two tee-shirts, two tanktops, two jockstraps, a jacket, boots. I kept them in the small, carry-on sized, bag that I had with me.

'I'd been out to the bar again, the night before. I'd been into the backroom, but – as far as the lack of light allowed – I'd looked and not touched. I'd felt a stirring of envy for a young man being fucked on the pool table. I'd watched as a plug was pulled out of his ass and a series of condom-covered cocks had gone in. I'd felt the stirrings of an erection as I watched a smile grow across his face as yet another man pumped away aggressively into him.

'I was up promptly that morning. I probably allowed myself far too much time, but I was nervous. I shaved from my neck to ass yet again, even though I'd only done it two days earlier. My training from Jerry came back to me too. I chose my rubber cockring and a cup jock. It felt good and reassuring, helping me to get myself into an appropriate frame of mind as I made my way through the streets of Paris, walking the short distance from the apartment hotel the bank had found for me to the Gare du Nord.

'I'd left myself more than enough time. I'd printed off the Master's e-mail messages. I sat quietly in the station, waiting to board the train, knowing that my appearance – black boots, blue jeans, white tee-shirt and leather jacket – would have been quite significant to some. I could feel the cup jock making a ridge in my jeans. I held my papers in front of me as I read yet again what he had to say.

'I knew as soon as I got on to the train that I had made the right decision. I was lucky. It wasn't that full. The seats around me were empty. I could read, and re-read, my papers. I could feel my cock hardening inside my cup jock. I could concentrate on the commitment I had made, to this master, and to myself. I felt pleased that I was there. In some ways, I had made the decision easier for myself through the arrangements. If I hadn't been going to this guy, I'd have had to have found myself accommodation and activity in Europe for a week. Either that, or I would have had the expense of changing my return flight to the US. All in all, I had convinced myself, a week's slavery was the easier and the less expensive option.

'The week was strange but beautiful. His other boy met me at Amsterdam central station. I'd asked the Master how to identify him. I'd been told he was in his mid-twenties, around six feet tall, looked good, had curly hair, liked tee-shirts and would be wearing a heavy chain round his neck.

'I saw Scott before he saw me. The Master was right. He was good-looking. I held my hand out as I walked towards him. We hugged. We kissed. We held hands as we walked through the train station. He spent those few minutes telling me about the Master and what would be expected of me. I was really pleased that we were getting along so well. I knew that I didn't have much choice but to be his friend, if we were to work together and not get in each other's way, or become insanely jealous of one another.

'He was the one who told me about the Master's health. He'd caught a chest infection during the Hamburg run which had turned to pneumonia, Scott said. He wasn't in the best of health. I was cross. I hadn't come all this way to spend time with a guy who was ill. Yet, at the same time, I was honored that he was letting me into his life at a time when he obviously wasn't at his best. Perhaps that was the best trial of a prospective live-in slave of all. That was most realistic, I thought. If I could cope with that, if he could, then there was probably a greater chance that the arrangement could last.

'I hardly noticed the distance as we talked. Scott said the Master's apartment was within a few hundred yards of the Central Station. It was. I was glad Scott was there to carry a bag for me as we pushed our way through the crowds of tourists along Damrak. I knew some of the famous bars were close by as we turned into one of the narrow alleyways between the stores.

'I was surprised by the size of the Master's apartment. It was on the upper floors of a block close to Dam Square. It couldn't have been more central.

'The first room we came to was the play room. There was a line of floggers on one wall. I certainly recognized the quality of the work that had gone into them. I wondered which had been made by Jeanette Heartwood, which by Sara Jones. There was a cage. Marc told me to hang what I needed in the closet. Inside was a collection of the master's leather. It represented the workshops of some of the finest producers in Europe at that time – Rob, Expectations and Fetters.

'Next to the play room was a shower room. I was to shower, shave and douche, Scott told me. He would go and tell the Master I was there. When I was finished, he said, there was a stool in the main living area, I was to go and kneel on it and wait. Scott said he had been banished for that first night. He'd been instructed to stay over at his own apartment, further into the Amsterdam suburbs.

'Douching took me longer than I expected, but Scott waited for me. He hugged me and led me to the stool. He made sure I was kneeling correctly before he left.

'Suddenly, I was there alone, kneeling, naked, in this apartment, waiting for a man I didn't know and had never met before in a city that I hardly knew. I hoped the efforts I'd put into my workouts for the previous few weeks had been enough. I hoped my body would give the Master pleasure. I closed my eyes and waited.

'I have no idea how long I knelt there. The Master had his bedroom and an office room on a mezzanine floor. I think he had probably been watching me since I came out of the bath room, but I didn't know that then. The first I knew of his imminent arrival was when I heard his boots on the first rungs of the iron spiral staircase.

'I didn't want to be too obvious when I looked. I opened my eyes, but kept my head bowed. I didn't look up until the Master's back was towards me. His chest didn't seem quite as large as he'd claimed, but he certainly had a good V-shaped back. His arms, in his tee-shirt, were well-defined too. His butt filled his jeans well. I melted. He almost was too good to be true.

'We didn't speak for a long time. He walked round me. He touched me, felt bits of me. He let me lick him. He worked my nipples, very gently at first then with steadily increasing intensity. Over at least two hours, perhaps even more, he slowly built up the sensations.

They became more and more fierce. There was rarely pain. He took me to the edge of agony then backed off a little, took me a little further and then back, further and then back. My threshold was moving away from me. The endorphins were firing in. Then, in a flash, I was screaming from the ceiling I was so high. The tears were streaming down my chest. My erection was so hard, it felt as if my cock was trying to burst.

'The climax of that first encounter came when he locked a chain around my neck. I was so high that I let go. It was amazing.

'We sat for a while after that. He had his armchair. I sat or knelt on the floor beside him. I think I opened his jeans with my mouth and spent time licking his balls as he lent back and listened to music. There was, I had to admit, something very, very trippy about light sopranos and some opera for that sort of sexual encounter. He worked my nipples again, gently at first and then between the nails of his thumbs and forefingers. I knew he'd stimulated me that way, but I didn't realize just how much until I came to put a tee-shirt on later and the soreness kicked in.

'I let time pass. I was happy. I had my mouth full of cock or balls, attached to a hunk of a man.

'When, later, we went out to dinner, I walked obediently two steps behind him. I opened doors for him. I wore the tightest tee-shirt I had and no underwear. I could feel the outline of my cock and balls against the inner thigh of my jeans. It felt very ostentatious. I was pleased I was wearing a cockring.

'When we got to the restaurant, I waited for him to be seated, to order first. I called him 'Sir'. I was very polite and courteous.

'I must admit that I did appreciate the envious glances as we walked back to his apartment across Dam Square. There were some good- looking men around. Perhaps it was my underlying horniness, not having come for four days, combined with the afternoon's stimulation, but they did look good.

'As soon as we were inside the apartment, I went into the shower room and stripped naked. Scott had confirmed that this was probably the most important of the Master's house rules. I folded my jeans and tee-shirt and left them there, on top of my boots. I left my cockring on.

'The Master was waiting beside the door of the playroom. I was glad I hadn't eaten too much. I'd maintained the healthy eating régime at the restaurant. I'd had some salad and seafood, but nothing with much fat. I didn't like playing on a full stomach.

'He said nothing. He directed me with his eyes. I spread my arms and put my fingers on the wall to brace myself. I spread my legs. I closed my eyes. I could feel his walking round me. I gasped as he pinched my nipples. The soreness was still intense. I tried not to move away. I remembered my training from Jerry; I tried to please this new Master by spreading my arms further apart and pushing my chest forward to make his access to my nipples easier.

'He walked round behind me and reached between my legs for my balls. I spread my legs and raised myself on to my toes as far as I could, again trying to make it as easy as possible for him to grasp and work those balls. He squeezed them, gently then firmly, gently then firmly, several times. He started pulling them. I moved away from him then, trying to increase the tension, or at least communicate that the pulling could be increased.

'When he took a flogger from the wall and started stroking my back, I leant back, as far as I could without taking my fingers off the wall, and tried to lower my head as far as I could, so that he had the best possible target across my shoulders. When he started bringing the flogger up between my legs, so it landed on my hard cock and shaved balls, I spread my legs and raised my knees. I went backwards and forwards between the two positions as elegantly as I could. I tried not to rush, not to make the movement to hurried, but to let the Master know that I appreciated his efforts and was trying to assist.

'I know that I can peak almost too quickly when I am being flogged, but this man knew what he was doing. He could see my breathing starting to quicken and he would ease off for a while, either making fewer strokes or lessening the intensity of each blow. He took me to that paradise beautifully. When he decided I could climb the last section of the journey, he started to hit me harder. My head was coming back more. My mouth was opening. Then, there was that single stroke, the one that took me through heaven's gate. I shrieked. The tears burst forth. There was another, and another, and another; then nothing.

'He came to me quietly and gently. He rubbed his hand down my cheeks and I kissed his knuckles. He ran a single finger down my spine. I tingled. He took my hands from the wall and put them at my sides. He let me lean into his shoulder. I could feel my tears dampening his tee-shirt.

'He held my hand as he went to sit down. I stood, head bowed, hands behind my back as he undid his jeans and pushed them to his thighs before he sat. Only then did he pull my hand, signaling that I should kneel. I started licking at his knees. I tried to be reverential as I moved my tongue and mouth slowly towards his cock and balls. I felt his cock hardening against my cheek as I moved nearer.

'He was breathing quite hard himself. The flogging must have been quite an exertion for him. He let me lick and suck his balls for a long while. I caught drips from his cock with my tongue. I felt him leaning back. Then, without any warning, he tapped me twice on the shoulder. He said just one word: 'bed'.

'I picked up the flogger and returned it to its hook when he had gone. I went and brushed my teeth. The Master was already in bed when I reached the top of the spiral stairs.

There was a comforter and pillow laid out at the bottom of the bed. I wondered if Scott had done that before he left. I expected that he had. He'd also left me written instructions about the Master's coffee in the kitchen for the morning.

'Sleep came quickly. I'd expected to be uncomfortable as I'd climbed under the comforter, but I'd quickly found a position half on my front which was best for my back. I could feel the bruises developing. I winced once as a nipple rubbed the sheet under me.

'The next I knew was the call for 'coffee, boy" coming from the bed. It took me a few moments to wake up and to realize where I was. "Yes, Sir," I called as I jumped up and headed down the stairs. I had to go carefully. The apartment was dark and I was making my way round unfamiliar surroundings by touch alone.

'I pissed and cleaned my teeth again as the coffee machine did its work. I put a napkin between mug and saucer to catch any spills as I crept back up the stairs. The apartment felt pleasantly warm. I appreciated that.

'I knelt and put the coffee mug down on the table beside the bed. I stayed there. I thought the Master had gone back to sleep, but he reached for the coffee and took a first mouthful. When he put the cup down, his hand went to the back of my head. It pushed me under his bedding. I quickly felt his morning erection in my face. I followed my instincts and my training. I opened my mouth, then slowly, as sensuously as I could, I guided the thick, uncut dick towards my throat.

'It was a long task that morning, and even then the Master didn't come. I licked his balls, but he wouldn't let me push his legs apart and lick his butt, not then at least. It's a nice way to start the day.

'It's hard to separate the days of that week now. I remember being naked, often with Scott, in the apartment. I didn't get out much; I would have liked to have seen more of the city, but it didn't happen on that occasion. Scott and I kept the place clean and tidy. We slept at the bottom of the Master's bed. The Master's health meant that we didn't play as much as I would have liked or, I think, he would have liked too.'

Marc foresaw my question.

'We lost touch. When I got home, I e-mailed him and wrote, but I never had a reply. I heard from one of the people whom I had met there that questions had been asked about his real identity and income. I didn't know whether it was a few people being malicious or whether it was caused by the guy's illness. It's hard trying to find answers to such questions from here in the US. I didn't want to jump to the wrong conclusion.

'Scott moved on too. He went to London. He was offered a job there. It made sense for him to go. We've written a couple of times and spoken, but I think we have both left this Amsterdam episode behind us.

'I'm sorry about it. The guy was good. He was technically proficient. He knew what he was doing with a slave's psychology. Those skills were too well refined for him to have been a complete newcomer to the scene. He'd obviously been around for many years, although afterwards none of the people I knew in Amsterdam or in Europe, or many of their friends, seemed to have heard of him. He seemed to appear for a few months and then vanish again. I did some checking. The university he said he'd worked for had never heard of him. There were no academic papers in his name. It was eerie. His dishonesty disappointed me. I felt abused.'

# Perceptions of ages past

'So, Marc,' I asked, 'what do you think you learned from that time?'

He looked at me, silent for a minute or two.

'That I could do it,' he said, finally.

'As a way of life?'

'I think so,' Marc said.

I raised my eyebrows. I wasn't sure. He recognized my skepticism.

'I think it depends on the circumstances,' he went on. 'If a master is working, and it's my responsibility to look after the home, that would be okay. If I was working and the master was at home, I think there would be definite problems.'

I paused. I grinned. I could imagine Marc as a homemaker. I wondered if he had been born a few decades too late. I remembered the stories of aristocrats and their butlers. Some, comedies or detective fiction, had underlying but unspoken sexual vibrations between master and servant. Some seemed to hide homosexuality and dominance behind class, where an aristocrat had been a serving military officer in the 1914-1918 Great War and his servant had been the ordinary working-class soldier who looked after him. I wondered how much of the gay culture of the late twentieth century or the early twenty-first was being imposed on an altogether different era, but I could empathize with the soldiers. There was a security in the affluence of the aristocracy, there was a good-looking young man, fit, well-educated, accustomed to male company from time at a harsh, primitive boarding school.

I had heard stories of male sexual activity in the 1939-45 war; I wondered how much had taken place twenty five years before that. Had all the syphilis of the major epidemics of those first two decades of the twentieth century been transmitted heterosexually? No one thought to consider any alternative. Science may not have been sufficiently advanced to have been able to identify oral or anal transmission. It was hard to believe that men hadn't been screwing, sucking or jerking each other off in the trenches. It was another generation. Masturbation was still taboo. Literacy levels weren't as great, yet it wasn't long since the trials of Oscar Wilde had been reported. Sex between men had entered the public domain. The late 19th century had seen the criminalization of homosexual activity in the UK. Members of the aristocracy were superior; they were represented in the House of Lords, they read the newspapers more. They had to appreciate what could happen, even if it had been proscribed.

I could see Marc in the glamour of the 1920s, laying out his Master's evening clothes, running his bath, perhaps even shaving him. I could see him caring lovingly for all the Master's different outfits, his uniforms, his different suits, even his nightshirt and underwear. I could see him starching the collars for the Master's shirts, making sure invitations were acknowledged, answering the door, serving tea, taking his Master breakfast in bed. I could perhaps even see him acting as a secretary, or personal assistant, dealing with some of the Master's correspondence, perhaps even managing the home, dealing with the tradesmen – they were mostly male then, of course – and arranging their travel. The relationship would be far closer, far more intimate than any between the Master and his wife.

Marc would have had pride in such a Master. He would have made sure that his Master's shoes and boots were the cleanest, the most highly-polished in the regiment or at the ball. He would have made sure that the Master's appearance was impeccable at all times. I could see him, standing to one side, chest out with pride, as his Master rode out to hounds, or took his place on Horse Guards Parade in London for the Trooping of the Color. I could see him, never in the center of the picture, but always at the side, or out of shot, at all the events of the Season – the Debutantes' balls, Ascot, Henley, Cowes Week, Goodwood, heading to Scotland for the grouse shooting and the Glorious Twelfth. Yes, Marc would have been there, truly in his element. I realized I'd been reading too many books, letting the romanticism of that time influence me. Yes, the England – and Scotland – of the Roaring Twenties, even the Thirties, despite The Great Depression, had colored my imagination.

I relished the pictures. I let my imagination roam. Although so many millions of young men had perished in those conflicts, I almost wished Marc had been a man of that time, born to a different age and different opportunities.

'You're dreaming,' he said, retrieving me from my reverie.

'I was thinking of you,' I said.

He looked surprised.

'Imaging you in times gone by, as a butler, or footman, serving an aristocratic master, domestically ... and sexually ....'

Marc smiled. I could see him taking up my thoughts and running with them.

'I wish,' he said, a moment later.

My perception of Marc was slowly falling in to place. I could use that description of the butler. The exact phrase came to me in my sleep: he was an ideal 'gentleman's gentleman'.

The arrangement had to be more than that of an employer-employee. I regretted that perceptions of relationships had, at least in Western cultures, changed in the late twentieth century. There had to be a longer commitment for Marc. The aim had to be life-long. Too many work arrangements were transitory, almost temporary, contracts. No time was allowed for respect to develop. The time itself defied the establishment of any loyalty. With Marc, it would have to be different, that really had become clear.

Even personal relationships had changed. I felt as if society had been telling me that one other person – a 'partner' had to be everything to me; my sole sexual release, my best friend, my emotional support. It had taken me a long time to discover, but I felt that it wasn't surprising that relationships didn't last when so much, probably too much, was being expected from them. It was if there was a limit to the amount of energy any relationship could expect to have, as if the give-and-take was finite. No wonder some people used up all that energy very quickly.

Mistresses relieved wives of some of that burden. There may have been greater male emotional repression, but somehow relationships did survive. Perhaps by telling each other less, those involved didn't exhaust their mutual tolerance and understanding too quickly.

I was increasingly appreciating those relationships where a master had maybe two slaves, or a boy. In my thirties, I'd fallen in love. I had learned, painfully, that I couldn't expect one guy to fulfill all my needs. I couldn't expect to have all his time, all his undivided attention. I had had to learn to appreciate that part of him which I did have, which I could have. I'd applied that to my own search for a master. I tried to pass the lesson on to Marc.

It was as if we were searching for something from a time past. We didn't necessarily need to love a master from the outset, but we needed to have some respect for that person. If we found them sexually attractive, that was a real bonus. We hoped we could grow to love them. I felt an increasing empathy with the old episcopalean rite for what was beautifully called the 'solemnization' of marriage. I didn't want to be sacrilegious, but I wanted to answer 'yes' when asked if I took 'this man' to thy Master, to 'obey him, and serve him, love, honor, and keep him in sickness and in health'? Perhaps I had read too many romantic stories as a child. Perhaps the nursery rhyme endings of princesses living with Adonis-like princes who wore tights, had strapping thighs and bubble butts had had too much of an effect? Eat your heart out Cinderella.

The more I got to know him, the more I saw him choose his behaviors for himself, and adopt his chosen role, the more I felt Marc to be that 'faithful retainer', the stalwart who would 'honor and obey' so long as ye both shall live. All I had to do now was describe this in a way twenty-first century masters would understand and appreciate.

# The summons

The Professor's call came a couple of days later.

Marc had answered the phone. I could hear him from the deck.

We'd had dinner, or rather, I'd had dinner and Marc had had something to eat in the kitchen. I'd taken a draft report out to read on the deck as I enjoyed the evening sun.

I laughed as I heard him answer.

'Mr Russell's home,' he's said, 'This is Marc speaking. How may I help you?'

I just caught the 'yes, Sir' a moment later.

Some of my friends, I knew, would never let me live down such pretension. I wondered if Marc knew that. I suspected that he did. I think he was enjoying both the ritual and teasing me. I had to admit that it sounded good, if a little out of character. I thought some amendments might be necessary.

Marc brought the phone out to me, uncoiling the cable as

he moved across the deck.

'It's The Professor,' he said, 'for you. About me.'

I didn't think it was appropriate to respond directly to him, although I had to admit to myself that I appreciated his description of the call. I took the phone.

'Professor,' I said, 'Good evening.'

'Russ,' he said, 'it was great to hear from you.' He didn't leave me any time to interrupt him. 'I appreciated your letter. Sure I'll be pleased to put your boy, your young man, though his paces.

'I can take him for four weeks, over the break between semesters. It'll be at my home in San José. There's some research I still need to check using the library at Stanford. I know where to find what I want in the library there. I decided it would be easier than being here in Chicago for a few weeks. If he can work in The Bay Area, he'll be fine. It doesn't really matter whether it's The City or the South Bay. The traffic probably means Oakland's impractical. He can have use of the car if he needs it too, but I'd prefer him to use the Bart or Caltrain.'

The Professor was pushing ahead at his customary pace. He'd clearly thought things through quickly, as usual.

'You vouch for his skills and obedience, Russ?' he asked.

'Yes, Professor, I do,' I said.

I nodded for Marc to kneel beside me on the deck.

'Good,' he said. 'I trust you will brief him?'

'Yes, Professor,' I said again, 'I shall.'

'Good. We can check travel arrangements nearer the time, and dates. I'll write to you with the dates. Does he work well with others?'

'He has had some experience, Professor,' I said. 'I think he needs more. It's more a matter of practicalities than emotions.'

'I understand,' The Professor said. 'David will be here for

most of the time. His mother in Toronto has been ill. I have been sending him to see her more. I may send him for longer if your guy is good.'

'I will tell him that, Professor,' I said.

'You know my régime, Russ. He'll be here to work and to serve, to keep himself busy, fit and available. He's clear in that?'

'He is, Sir,' I said, 'and he will be.'

'Let me speak to him,' The Professor said. I passed over the phone.

I could hear The Professor speaking, but not clearly enough to hear exactly what he was asking Marc.

'I'm kneeling beside Russ, Mr Russell, Sir,' Marc said into the phone, 'I've been clearing away after dinner, Sir. I'm wearing light yellow Speedos and a cockring, Sir, plus one chain around my neck and another around my right ankle, Sir.'

The conversation became a one-way one. Marc had time for the occasional 'Yes, Sir' acknowledgement, but that was all. I could imagine some of what The Professor would be saying. I wished I could hear it more clearly. I looked down. I could see Marc's cock hardening inside his Speedos.

I was smiling, appreciating Marc's position when he handed the phone back to me.

'I think it will work, Russ,' The Professor said. 'He sounds sensible.'

I wondered how he knew, Marc had hardly said anything.

'Like I say, I'll write.'

With that, the line went dead.

I looked at Marc. There was an excitement in his body.

'Yes?' I asked.

'Yes,' he said. It was enough.

The Professor's written reply arrived on the Friday morning. The mail service was working well, I thought.

Getting the arrangements made within the week was encouraging.

Marc was already at work at the bank when the mailman called. He was a cute guy, young and fit. I suspected that he used any excuse to talk to me rather than simply leave the mail in the box. We'd spoken a couple of times. He'd driven up when I'd been working out front. I was vain enough to have noticed his appreciative glances. I'd been wearing shorts rather than brief swimwear, submitting to the social conventions and conservatism of the neighborhood, as I usually did when I was in the front yard. One day, he'd called at the door. I'd answered wearing only Speedos. After that, it seemed he'd use any excuse. I felt flattered, but I wasn't too comfortable about responding.

'There's a catalog for you, Mr Russell,' the mailman said as I opened the door. He was writing in a notebook. 'I hope you don't mind,' he said, noticing my look, 'but I thought I'd write for one for myself. I was noting the address.'

'It's not a problem, Jeb,' I said, reading his name from the tag on his uniform. The catalog came from a men's underwear and clothing supplier on the West Coast. 'I hope you find something you like.'

'I sure do, Mr. Russell,' he said as he handed me the mail. I recognized The Professor's return address on one of the envelopes. I felt Jeb was pressing for an invitation in, or some greater recognition. May be one day, I thought, but not today.

'I'm sorry Jeb,' I said, 'but today of all days, I really don't have time to stand around and talk with you. A couple of letters here really need my attention.'

'I'm real sorry, Mr Russell,' he said. I looked at him. The embarrassment and remorse seemed genuine enough.

'Another time, then?'

'That would be good, Mr Russell,' he said.

'Write for the catalog,' I said. 'And enjoy it. Order something you like.'

'I sure will,' he said as he turned and walked back to his van. I let my eyes follow him. His legs were well-formed. The calves and thighs were tanned, too, I could see and his butt filled his uniform shorts nicely. It was a pleasant sight for a Friday. He waved as the van pulled away. I nodded to acknowledge the gesture.

It was a moment before I realized that I was standing in the open doorway wearing only Speedos. Yes, I thought, I will take some greater interest in the young man, perhaps when Marc's away. I hoped my thoughts weren't too predatory. What if they were? The young man seemed to be trying to make his feelings plain enough.

# The Professor ...

I put the catalog and bills to one side. It was The Professor's letter that was most important. It was as if someone was writing orders and instructions for me, not Marc. I could feel my cock rising. I grinned as I took the letter through to the deck. Work would have to wait a while. This was more important.

I opened the letter. It had been written by David. David was the sort of guy I wanted Marc to become. The Professor kept David. The Professor was in his mid-fifties. David was in his early thirties. They'd met when David went to Stanford to study. He'd taken one of The Professor's courses in his first semester. David had become the one man in The Professor's life for whom the word 'temporary' did not apply.

I remembered staying with The Professor that Christmastime. I can't remember why now, but he'd invited me to be his guest for a few days. We'd met at a summer run a few years before that. I'd still been in slavery myself then. He'd told me to contact him if I was going to be in The Bay Area. I think we'd had a mutual attraction and wanted to play or spend a few days exploring the power dynamic between us more deeply. That was soon after he'd moved west from Chicago for the academic months and he still had to make more friends.

I remember how The Professor told me he'd been taken by the student's attentiveness. He admitted having noticed David at the first lecture. The Professor had told me that he always tried to be in a lecture theater well before the students arrived. He liked to check out projectors, any visual aids he was going to use. He also liked to sit and watch the students come in. It gave him a chance to check out the best-looking guys, he said.

He knew teachers weren't supposed to consort with their students, but he didn't think there could be any harm in looking, he'd told me, especially with discretion.

I went to a few of The Professor's lectures. I'd been curious. He'd invited me along. I knew he was being immodest. He also made himself available to the students. He'd talk to them, ask them whether his notes were clear, whether they said what he wanted them to say, whether they found his classes interesting and stimulating. He'd frequently be in the lecture theater an hour after the formal session ended, answering questions, asking questions, challenging the students, provoking them to think, to argue.

He despised lectures as information giving, he'd said. There were far more efficient ways of doing that, he'd say, given any, given half, an opportunity. He wanted to enthuse, to motivate, to excite his students.

He started his classes almost officiously. Notebooks and

audio recorders were banned from his lectures, he'd tell the students. I imagined their fear at the first. How would they remember what he had to say? The information you need is in the notes, he'd tell them. They were expected to have read about a topic before a lecture; there was more to read afterwards. He treated them as adults, capable of managing their own work schedules, planning their learning, their reading and their writing.

He remembered David from the very first lecture, The Professor told me, the young man's military haircut standing out from the longer hair of the other young men. The Professor had been sitting on the edge of his desk as the students came in. He'd been examining the new meat, as he'd call it, among the newly-enrolled young people. He'd had to concentrate hard to give that lecture, he told me. The young man with the military looks had sat at the back, paying close attention to The Professor from the moment the lecture had started. The Professor was accustomed to getting close attention from nearer the front, usually young women, he told me, who had a crush on him for a while. He'd got used to it. Coming from a young man, right at the back, had been different. It was disconcerting.

The young man had taken to sitting at the same place for each lecture. He'd stay behind afterwards. He'd ask The Professor intelligent questions. It was apparent he'd read the notes, and more. The Professor had been intrigued by the young man. His written work was far more neatly presented than that from the others. It wasn't better at first, but The Professor could see him learning. He appreciated the guy's enthusiasm and determination. He also liked his looks.

I remember The Professor describing him. The young man, he'd said, always wore clothes that were just a little too big for him. He suspected the guy had a wonderful body, and worked at it, but the tee-shirts he wore just hid his biceps, they were too baggy to cling to a well-defined chest. There was, The Professor suspected, a good- sized cock and balls hanging between the young man's legs, but the pants he wore were just too fully cut for him to be sure. The Professor had admitted being intrigued by this. He could have been shy, The Professor said, but there was a confidence that belied such behavior. It was as if, he said, the young man was deliberately teasing the world around him.

The Professor discovered the young man's identity at a smaller tutorial discussion. David Martin was the most forthcoming. He'd quickly improved from the first written work. His knowledge was greatest and his questions the most intelligent. The Professor felt that the meeting was becoming a discussion between the two of them, with the others looking on. He would either have to make time especially for David or hope that the others would benefit without the same level of contribution.

When he received David's first formal assignment, The Professor went to the school office. It was time, he thought, to find out a little more about the young man. He hadn't had a chance to ask the young man directly. Although there had been another tutorial, the young man had disappeared quickly, almost too quickly, at the end. The Professor smiled at the thought. It was almost as if the young man had been embarrassed.

David's file told The Professor a lot. He was nearly two years older than the others in the same class. He was in the military, but had won a scholarship to study at the university. He came from California and had been a good sportsman too in his teens, The Professor read, an active member of the school wrestling and diving squads. There was no mention of a relationship, not that the files always held such details, and he was living in a single room close to the university campus. David certainly seemed to have always been busy, he'd also held down jobs at school, cleaning at a local gym.

The Professor wondered about David. The young man reminded him of characters he'd read about. How close to such stereotypes would the young man turn out to be? The Professor decided he wanted to know more.

He thought about David long and hard. He knew it was inappropriate for him to be too close to a student in one of his own classes. He knew that it was not a good idea for him to make the first move. There would have to a legitimate pretence for The Professor and the student to have some time alone together.

The Professor's sexuality was common knowledge on the liberal campus. He had spoken at campaigning events and was renowned as being quietly politically active. He would make donations and was known for bringing young politicians to the university, inviting them to stay at his home and to speak to the students. He supported student initiatives too, making occasional calls to Washington and providing informal introductions.

The Professor's most intimate desires were less well-known. There were those who attended some of the runs who knew him and appreciated his skills. There was usually at least one young man at The Professor's university townhouse. Students and colleagues considered him lucky, and mature, to have butlers, housekeepers and live-in gardeners rather than a wife, even if they did seem to move on quite quickly. They did not know the strict régimes under which those individuals lived.

I been staying at The Professor's home not long after he'd first set eyes on David. I'd been working in Oakland and I had hoped to spend a weekend enjoying some play with The Professor. The idea of forty-eight hours in his dungeon had been making my cock hard for a month. Unfortunately, it hadn't worked out. One of the scientific journals had publicized a research paper produced by one of The Professor's peers. There had been uproar. Members of Congress were being interviewed on the TV news. The news agencies were demanding comments. The Professor went to the rescue.

Instead of a weekend's play, we spent two days and nights doing the rounds of the radio and TV studios. I became an informal media adviser, rather than a play partner. It was unexpected, but I enjoyed it. Nightline even dropped a planned item so Ted Koppel could interview The Professor on the Friday evening. We did the local stations on Saturday morning, CNN in the afternoon, and talked to radio stations in almost every English-speaking country in the world.

It became social too.

Associated Press sent their top science correspondent out from New York. Or, rather, it would be more accurate to say that this correspondent decided it was a good reason to come and see The Professor. We had dinner together on the Saturday evening, The Professor and the correspondent exchanging anecdotes about one of the previous year's runs. There was something beautifully incongruous about the three of us.

It reminded me of a funeral I'd attended a few months before. There had been three of us there too, experienced players and regulars at the runs. We only usually met at the runs. Conversations would take place around slings, or crosses. We'd be dressed in leather, if we were dressed at all. Then, unexpectedly, we'd met at the funeral. We'd all come from work. We were all smartly dressed in pinstripe business suits, white shirts, dark ties and shining black shoes. Without prompting, we'd looked each other up and down when we'd met. We felt our friend who'd died would have appreciated the irony.

Anyway, that evening, there we were, sitting at The Professor's elegant dining table, the correspondent and me. I can't remember who had been The Professor's butler boy at that time. We were served a delicious meal. The wine was excellent. We had enjoyed each other's company. We felt relaxed after the busy day. I think the adrenaline had been flowing for all of us. I'd ended up handling the logistics of The Professor's numerous radio and TV appearances. Litton, the correspondent, had had to write and file his piece, well in time for it to be syndicated to the later Sunday papers in the US and for others overseas. The Professor had had to be on camera, answering questions and defending the integrity of his colleague. Litton, at The Professor's insistence, had canceled his hotel room.

It was after dessert when The Professor came up with the idea.

'You know,' he said, 'after all that's happened today, I feel like doing something I rarely do, especially during term time.'

Litton and I looked at him curiously.

'Let's go to the bar,' he said, a gleam in his eye.

Litton and I looked at each other. We had nothing pressing on the Sunday morning and my flight home wasn't until late afternoon.

'Why not?' Litton said. I nodded.

The Professor called for his boy and the car. It was so nice, he said, to have a driver and someone who knew he had to stay sober. Within minutes, we'd left the dinner table and were on our way.

# ... and David

I don't think David had been on The Professor's mind that night; he may have been, but I was never to know. The Professor hadn't said anything about him. We'd talked about the day's events, the frustrations of dealing with the media and, as a complete contrast, mutual friends and the play we had enjoyed. A couple of beers at the bar seemed a good way to round off an unexpectedly busy day.

The boy had been sent to park the car. He'd been told he could come into the bar. The Professor had given him $5 for himself and told him he could drink soda. He was to stand near the door. If he wanted to piss, he had to come and find The Professor and ask for permission, but he was free to talk to others that night, The Professor said, clearly in a good mood, as long as he told them of his function. The boy did look good. His body was developing nicely and he was wearing The Professor's standard 'outdoor' uniform of tight faded Levis and a white tanktop. He wore boots and a locked chain around his neck. As soon as we were all inside the bar, the boy had handed The Professor the car keys. Then, he went to fetch our drinks. The relationship made me curious. There seemed to be little connection between The Professor and the boy. I didn't like to ask, but the dynamic was more like a business relationship than a personal one. Perhaps The Professor was looking after the young man, providing him with a home and filling his time while another master was away? Perhaps he was consolidating his training? There were many possibilities. That there was little intellectual connection or true mutual affection was very clear. The boy clearly respected The Professor, but it was equally apparent that he didn't love him.

I liked the bar. There were tables. It wasn't too noisy. It wasn't too smoky either. Although we were in a bar, it seemed natural that the evening's conversation would continue.

The Professor was clearly well-known and respected. Many nodded in recognition. Some looked surprised at seeing him there. The Professor returned their greetings as we made our way to a table. Litton and I caught each other's eye. Some had clearly seen The Professor on TV that day. Their expressions said they were in the presence of a celebrity. Litton and I enjoyed the reflected glory.

I don't know how long we'd been there, but The Professor had just caught the boy's eye. He'd been instructed to go to the bar and get us some more beers when David walked in. Litton and I both noticed the good, clean-cut, military looks, even though we didn't know who he was, other than the stereotypical male who attracted us both. If he hadn't come in alone, we'd have assumed he was one of The Professor's boys; he was wearing a plain white tanktop, Levis and boots. All that was missing, I thought, was the chain around the neck.

The Professor had been pulling dollar bills from his pocket to pay for more beers when he looked up and saw David.

'Well, well,' The Professor said, 'one of my better students. Buy him a beer too, boy.'

I still, to this day, don't know exactly why, but I couldn't help but wonder how long it would be before that young man did have a chain locked around his firm neck. I didn't even know his name, but I knew his fate had been sealed the instant he walked through that door.

Although The Professor carried on talking, I tried to watch what was happening at the bar. I was intrigued. I was pleased Litton was paying more attention to The Professor's comments. Their discussion had returned to scientific detail and the gossip of research laboratories. The professional Litton was at work too, I could hear. Could The Professor shed any light on allegations of sexual harassment at one of the government institutes in the suburbs of Washington?

I didn't hear the answer, but I did see the boy approach the young man. I still didn't know then that this was the student The Professor had been talking about. I could see him blush. I watched as he looked towards us. He was trying to acknowledge The Professor's generosity, but The Professor's attention was focused on his conversation with Litton. I tried not to stare as I watched the boy return to our table, carrying the beers, with the young man following.

I watched the behavior with interest. The boy stood to one side, still holding the beers, waiting for a break in the conversation and permission to put the bottles down. The young man followed his example, waiting, bottle in hand, to express his thanks.

I caught The Professor's eye and nodded towards the boy. Without stopping what he was saying to Litton, he nodded that the boy should put the beers down. He did. The Professor's change was put down beside him. The boy bowed, discretely, as if embarrassed to attract too much attention in the bar, and returned to his position near the doorway.

The young man waited patiently. The Professor either hadn't noticed him or was very deliberately ignoring him and making him wait. I watched and waited too. The longer the conversation with Litton continued, the more certain I became that The Professor was testing the young man. I found it hard not to smile, to recognize and appreciate what was being done.

'David,' The Professor said, eventually, standing, turning and acknowledging the young man, 'how pleasant to see you. Let me introduce you.'

The introductions were quite formal. Both Litton and I stood to shake hands with the young man.

'David Martin,' The Professor said, as we shook hands. 'Pull up a seat and join us, young man.'

The Professor's expression told us there and then that

whatever was missing from the interaction with that weekend's young servant and chauffeur was more than positive in his attitude towards David. There was a light in The Professor's eyes.

David couldn't have missed The Professor's expression. Perhaps it was that immediate enthusiasm or the unexpected encounter, but he seemed a little uncomfortable at first. We must have looked a strange quartet. Three of us were older, dressed in blue shirts and chinos, although without ties, while this young man was in jeans and tanktop. Was he out hunting? Cruising? I couldn't help but grin as I wondered if meeting The Professor, his tutor, had suddenly interrupted that evening's quest for action.

I needn't have worried. David's discomfort slowly started to fall away as he joined the discussion. He was fascinated by Litton, his knowledge of science and the politics of the scientific establishment. Litton wasn't known for his tolerance of youngsters wanting to be journalists or seeking the glamour of science, but for once, he seemed genuinely impressed and flattered by this particular student's knowledge and intelligence. It was David's overall demeanor that aroused my curiosity.

We'd come to the bar quite early, around 10pm. It didn't seem unreasonable that we should leave shortly before midnight.

The Professor had beckoned the boy and gave him the car keys.

We'd started the rituals of moving, getting ready to leave. David suddenly looked uneasy. He stepped back. It was a moment or two before The Professor noticed his anxiety.

'David,' he said. 'I am sorry. Would you like to join us for a nightcap?'

'Thank you, Professor, but ...' his voice trailed off.

'I understand. You can either stay over, or the boy can run you back. It's up to you. Even with Litton and Russ here, there's plenty of room. I think we may even run to a spare toothbrush.'

David nodded. A smile started to appear across his face. 'Thank you, Professor' he said. 'I would appreciate that.'

I was probably the quietest of the four of us as we drove home. I sat in the front of the car, beside the boy. David was perched in the middle at the back, between The Professor and Litton. The conversation was beyond me, but the three of them seemed as intensively involved as ever.

I kept watching when we got back to The Professor's home. The boy jumped out to open the car doors for us before rushing to unlock the front door. The boy was ignored as The Professor led us inside. I watched David. He sat on the floor as soon as the door was closed and removed his boots. He put them, with his jacket neatly folded, to one side of the door. Interesting, I thought, watching him so carefully that I was unaware of The Professor and Litton.

I had to admit that I had a sneaking admiration for The Professor's style. He led the way into his study. There was a whiskey decanter and glasses on a table. Without any question, he poured drinks for each of us and handed them round. I sat down to one side and kept up my vigil. The Professor sat down in what was obviously 'his chair'. Litton took another seat to one side. David crossed his legs and sat down on the mat, close to The Professor's chair. I smiled. I think Litton too had – at last – noticed.

Litton was the first to retreat to bed. I left a few minutes later. I was fascinated by the interaction between The Professor and David, but I felt my eyelids getting tired. I made my excuses, expressed my thanks and moved to leave the room. As I closed the door behind me, I just caught sight of The Professor patting the arm of the chair, signaling that David should move closer.

David was there when I went down the following morning. He smiled politely, but remained silent, reading the newspaper and drinking coffee in The Professor's comfortable study. He had found a place for himself on a mat. He was wearing the same white tanktop that he'd had on the previous evening, but had found a pair of white running shorts from somewhere. I had to admit that he looked good. Although he stood when we left, David stayed behind when The Professor led Litton and me out to brunch. We had a pleasant time. The restaurant was busy. Many of The Professor's colleagues and their families were there too. We had a steady stream of them coming up and commenting on The Professor's TV appearances the previous day.

David was still sitting on the mat, reading, when we got back to The Professor's home. Although I had a couple of hours to kill, I rode with Litton to the airport. The boy drove us.

'Well,' I said, as we sat down for a coffee after checking in, 'what do you make of that?' I hadn't wanted to ask the question in front of the boy while we were still in the car. Whatever the boy might have learned about discretion, such a conversation would still have been inappropriate; par devant les domestiques, I remembered.

Litton looked at me as if the question was redundant.

'I think,' he said, 'we are going to have to watch and wait.'

I smiled. I agreed. I felt my instincts had been accurate.

# David's story

I heard the rest of the story from The Professor at the September run. I'd been there early, setting up. They arrived by car. The Professor was waiting in line to register and get the key to his room when I saw David walking towards him. The military student looked good. I smiled. There was the uniform tanktop, the faded denim and the boots. And, yes, I noticed, there was a chain, locked around his neck. I was still hurrying around, working, so I didn't get a chance to talk to The Professor until after dinner that night. I was waiting at the bar for a drink when he came up to me and placed his hand on my elbow.

We kissed and hugged. It was wonderful to see him. I looked him straight in the eye.

'You have a tale to tell me, Professor,' I said directly, 'and I want to hear every detail.'

His expression challenged me, but my day as his media adviser had, I'd realized soon afterwards, changed our relationships. A dimension of profession respect had usurped my submissiveness. I wasn't altogether surprised when he let me steer him, politely but firmly, to a table a little way from the others. I wanted some privacy. The Professor was wise enough to understand. We sat down with our drinks. He smiled before he began.

He told me again, briefly, about David's appearance at the university and his attendance at The Professor's lectures, his contributions to the tutorials and the apparent embarrassment. The pieces of the jigsaw puzzle started falling into place.

'And when we were in the bar that night?' I asked.

'It was a pleasant surprise,' The Professor said, 'a very pleasant surprise. It was the confirmation I'd been hoping for, I must admit, but I hadn't been expecting, at least not at that moment or in that place.'

'You kept him waiting at the table deliberately, didn't you?' I asked, challenging The Professor directly, probably for the first time in my life.

'Of course,' he admitted. 'I wanted to test him. I wanted to see just how stereotypical he was.'

He smiled. I did too.

'And then when we got home, he was so beautiful,' he said.

This alone made me wonder if The Professor had fallen in love.

'The way he took off his boots and then sat beside me on the floor. I felt he'd had training from someone. It was more than the military normally offer,' The Professor added.

'And that night?'

'David slept on the floor at the foot of my bed.'

I looked at The Professor directly, challenging him to continue.

'And, no,' he said, recognizing my impudence, 'I didn't have sex with him. He undressed me, but we didn't have sex.

'Russ, I know you're dying for every detail, so I'll go back to that Saturday night,' The Professor said, taking a sip from his drink. 'When you and Litton went to bed, I really started talking to him, interviewing him. Like I say, I'd already checked out the young man's file. It had told me some, but not a lot, about him. I wanted to know find out what was missing, what was in the gaps. I'd been trying to devise the most opportune way of finding out. His arrival in the bar was like a gift. It was perfect for striking up social contact, for shedding the professor-student formalities. He's an intelligent young man, you have to admit.'

I nodded.

'So, when you'd left, I questioned him head on. I told him that he fascinated me and that I'd looked at his records. He'd been embarrassed at first.' The Professor smiled, as if relishing the memory.

'And?' I prompted.

The Professor took a sip of his drink, giving himself time to think. I sat back as he continued.

David said he knew about me. He wasn't sure whether he knew a lot, his modesty showed, but he said, well, perhaps that part of me which is public knowledge, my sexuality, my political activism. He said he'd noticed my looks. He said he'd enjoyed my lectures, they were the most mature, the most challenging, of the classes he took, he said. Some of my colleagues, David told me, seemed to treat the students as children. I addressed them as adults, he said. He appreciated that. He said I, most of all, made him think, challenged him to use his brain, his intellect. I appreciated the professional compliment. I still do. I think I value it all the more because it comes from someone who had seen something of the world. He hadn't come directly to the university from high school. He had some other reference points to compare me with. And, knowing the high standards of that particular branch of the military, I accepted his kind words.

It wasn't until we were at the bar that night that David found out more about me. He said he'd had his suspicions, that he had been wondering, curious about the extent of my interests and experience, how much was real and how much was rumor. He'd been as pleased to see me there as I had him. The key was, apparently, buying him that beer. When my boy had approached him, he said 'I've been instructed to buy you a beer'. David confessed that it was the word 'instructed'that had caught his attention. He'd already looked at the boy and noticed the chain around his neck. He was sufficiently experienced and wise to appreciate its meaning.

'And who,' David had asked the boy, 'are you?'

The response had confirmed his suspicions.

'I'm The Professor's current boy,' he had been told. The young man hadn't even given David his name.

David confessed to me that evening that his cock had been getting hard inside his jockstrap and jeans as he'd followed the boy across to our table. He'd been jealous of the boy, he even told me.

So what, Professor, I asked, was that previous experience?

Perhaps David should tell you himself, The Professor replied.

I looked up, noticing that the military student was walking towards us. The Professor waited for him to reach the table before he spoke again.

'Get yourself a drink, David,' said The Professor, 'then come back here, Russ has some questions to ask you.'

I waited patiently for David to return. He looked wonderful. The white tanktop and chain were in place. His tight butt and ample cock and balls were shown off beautifully by a tight pair of black leather shorts. The shine caught the shadows excellently in the darkness. I could see the prominent bulge at the front. I doubted whether the young man's cock and balls would be alone in their leather refuge; there was probably some metal around them or other binding. I wondered if I would be allowed to find out.

I found myself grinning as I watched David lower himself slowly to sit, half on his haunches, beside The Professor. That, I thought from experience, is a movement a man makes when he has a buttplug lodged firmly inside him. My curiosity increased.

'Russ wants to know how you come to be here,' The Professor said, once David had put down his drink. He reached for The Professor's hand and squeezed it gently.

'Mutual compatibility,' David said, quietly, looking straight into my eyes. I had to smile. I knew exactly what he meant. I wanted him to continue. I wanted to know more, much much more.

'Tell me more,' I said, wholly unimaginatively.

David looked to The Professor for permission.

The nod came.

'I was running away when I came to the university,' he said. 'I was twenty. I was older than the other freshmen. I'd been in the military two years. I was running away then too. I was scared.'

He paused. The memories appeared to be still painful. He sighed before going on.

So, David started talking

It started when I was sixteen, he said. My father had died. He was only in his forties, but his liver failed. It was quick. He was only ill a couple of weeks. He was a good-looking man. I looked up to him. If I'm honest, now, looking back, I know that I even fancied him. I knew I was gay when I was ten or eleven. I'd started playing with other boys from school, when I could. I'd invite them home, or to go out walking, or, best of all, swimming, so I'd get to look at their bodies.

I always wanted those guys whose balls had dropped, who had hair around their dicks, those who were on the way to being men, rather than boys. I'd get them somewhere alone, then bring up the topic of masturbation. I'd be curious about technique, or about what turned them on. I'd ask them to drop their pants and show me as I couldn't quite imagine what they meant. Then I'd ask if I could do it for them, or I'd grab their cocks and ask if I was doing it right. Some guys got scared and ran, but most were so horny by that time that they couldn't resist. They started to play along, slowly at first, then more greedily as they became more aroused. Sometimes I'd just get to jerk them off. Occasionally, a guy would open my jeans and start playing with me. I even got to suck a few of them. Getting my own dick played with was less important to me, far less important, than giving the other guy a good time.

One of them was older, about seventeen, I think, he started introducing me to more. He'd make me kneel and suck him. He would instruct me in the finer points, he would make me use my tongue to lick him while I had his cock in my mouth. He'd make me hold it, without moving, right at the back of my throat. He always wore Speedos under his denim. It made him look good. There was always a nice bulge in his jeans. He made me lick his cock through the swimbriefs, tonguing his balls, then up and down the length of his cock. The nylon they used then felt good too. The material held up his cock and balls nicely. He'd have the balls pulled forward and his cock up and to one side, not like the other guys who'd push their cocks down over their balls, making both more difficult to lick. This guy showed me what happened when he wound cord tightly around the base of his cock and balls. He'd wind cord around mine. He'd wind it around my balls and tug on them while I sucked him. He'd order me to keep my hands behind my back and not touch myself. I didn't argue. It just felt so good. I stopped using my hands when I went to bed. I'd put my hands behind my back and rub my cock hard against the sheets until I shot.

David paused.

It was a while before I realized just how knowledgeable this guy was, he continued a few seconds later. I wondered where he had learned all this. One day, I asked him. He'd been shocked by the question. He asked me if I really wanted to know. Sure, I'd said, I'm keen. He said if I really did want to know, then I'd have to become his cocksucking boy. I'd only be able to go with others, to get the cock even then I knew I needed so badly, if I asked him first. He said I'd have to join the wrestling and the diving squads. I was too infatuated with him not to. I'd wear Speedos more too. I found this guy's knowledge, his confidence so powerful. I didn't know it was innate dominance then. I do now. I didn't know he was appealing to my innate subservience. I do know. I did know that he had me just where he wanted me ... and I could do nothing about it. I wanted him and I wanted what he was and I wanted to please him.

One day, after dive team training, Robert – that was the guy's name – told me to wait behind. I was really excited. He'd been wrestling. I could see the outline of his jockstrap under his tanktop, framing his bubble butt. I remember my cock getting hard in my Speedos. I hoped it wasn't too obvious. He told me I wasn't to change, just wait until everyone else had left. I felt awkward. I hoped no one would ask why I wasn't getting ready to leave. I couldn't think of an excuse.

I sat quietly while all the rest of the guys showered, got dressed and left. I sat forward, trying to hide my hard cock as I looked at them all. Most were well-defined. I looked as cautiously as I could to see who was wearing jocks, who wore boxer shorts or briefs. There were some nice, big, developing cocks.

I was wondering what I'd let myself in for when Robert came back to the locker room for me. I was to walk behind him, my head bowed, my hands behind my back. I was to stop when I was told to, he said.

I followed him, obediently. I was shocked when we stopped outside Coach's office. Robert knocked. A moment later, a voice yelled "come in". Robert pushed me forward. It was difficult. I was so embarrassed, being there, following this guy's orders. Within seconds, my cock shrank inside my

Speedos. I took a few steps forward. Robert stopped me. I stood there, as he'd instructed, head bowed, hands behind my back.

I could feel Coach's eyes on me, looking me up and down, inch by inch. I felt like a piece of meat. I tried to see as much as I could. It wasn't much. I saw Coach take off his glasses and look at Robert.

'David told me he wants an opportunity to learn,' Robert had said.

My most intimate confessions were being repeated with a member of the school staff. I wanted to disappear, I was so embarrassed.

'Does he really?' Coach asked.

I think he was teasing me, enjoying my embarrassment, but I remember the exchange so clearly.

'The door, Robert, said Coach.

From the inside, Robert turned the key in the lock.

Until then, I had never paid too much attention to Coach. I'd admired him, many of us did. He'd played college and then pro-football until an injured knee had forced him out of the professional game. He'd gone to college in his late twenties and qualified as a teacher and coach. I had to admit that he was good looking. At forty-five – I knew from the records that accompanied a series of photographs just inside the locker room how old he was – he had a body that many twenty-year-olds would be proud of. He didn't have much excess body fat. Then I knew why I'd started noticing him. One day he'd shed his customary sweat pants and tee-shirt and started coaching diving wearing only Speedos and a cowboy hat. I wondered where he'd suddenly got that idea. My attention wasn't really on the hat though. There was something that definitely interested me about the bulge in the Speedos. He chose his style carefully too. I noted he had

91

a few pairs, each was a light color, green, or blue, or yellow, with a darker shade panel over the hips. They showed off the shadows, and the outlines of his cock and balls beautifully. They were too similar, too effective, to have been bought without thought. Coach had been making a statement. Then, the proverbial penny dropped, I remembered the last time I'd been with Robert. He'd been wearing the same style.

But, that day in his office, Coach was wearing an ordinary tanktop. It showed off his shoulders well. He stood up and came round the desk, ignoring Robert. He was wearing shorts too. He looked so hot. I could smell his perspiration. I could feel my own Speedos bulging again. He came and put his arm around my shoulder. He pressed his lips against mine. Despite all the sex with other guys, it was the first time I had kissed, or been kissed by another man. I could feel myself melting into him. I could feel his cock through his shorts, hard against my thigh. He pushed his tongue into my mouth. I wasn't sure quite what to do. I felt embarrassed for a moment, all too aware that Robert was there, looking on. The tongue felt like a cock, so I did what by that time came naturally, I tried to suck it. I wanted to put my hands around him and feel that hard body.

I started to move my hands.

Coach realized what I was doing and pushed them back together, behind my back.

When I grasped my wrists, he started feeling me. He ran his hands up and down my arms, feeling my muscles. He ran them up and down my sides, around my thighs, between my legs, but never, ever, coming into contact with that ever-growing bulge inside my Speedos.

I felt as if I was ready to burst when he stopped. I was trying to squirm, but felt that I shouldn't.

Coach stepped back from me. I was panting. He put his hand on my shoulders and pressed. I knelt. I wanted to stick my tongue out, to start licking him.

'Robert tells me you already have some experience,' he said.

I nodded.

'Yes, Coach ... Sir,' I said. Using the word was difficult, but it seemed right.

He walked round behind Robert and moved him until he was a few inches in front of my face. I could see the bulging outline of Robert's cock as it curved upwards inside his wrestling singlet. I could see the impression of the material of his jockstrap, stretched across his balls. Although I'd not yet wrestled properly, I knew that the sheen, the texture of the tight spandex was so hot. Robert look amazing, his thighs and V-shaped framed by contrasting colored panels. I could see Coach pull Robert's hands behind his back. He reached up and pulled the singlet's straps off his shoulders. He pulled the singlet down off Robert until it was around his thighs. There was just the material of the jockstrap between me and Robert's cock. I could see the tip trying to push up the waistband. I could see Robert's pubic hair too, pushing out at the sides of the pouch. I could feel his warmth.

I watched Coach standing behind Robert. He grasped Robert's hips and pushed him gradually forward until the balls in the pouch were touching my mouth. I could feel the erect cock against my nose. I opened my mouth to let the covered balls rest against my tongue. I could sense Coach leaning over Robert's shoulder, watching what I was doing. He held us there. I could feel Robert's breathing quickening. I let my saliva run down my tongue, dampening his jockstrap, before some drips fell onto the singlet, wedged between his thighs. It seemed a long time before Coach finally said 'lick'.

I went to it. I washed those balls. I worked up and down Robert's cock. I tried to make his jock as wet as I could with my saliva. I turned my head and chewed the material over that cock, working my lips up and down and down and up again. I pressed hard against the cleft behind his piss slit. I tickled each ball with my tongue. I kissed the cock head, then each ball individually. I went back for more. I was panting when Coach finally pulled Robert away from me.

'You've done a good job with him,' Coach said to Robert, ignoring me altogether.

I knelt, looking downwards, simultaneously almost in a trance because of what I was doing but aware of a frisson of fear adding the excitement.

Coach stepped in front of me. He undid the top button of his shorts.

'Take them off,' he said, 'using only your mouth.'

I bent forward. It took some effort to get the zipper between my teeth, but I did, I pulled it down. I pulled the sides apart, learning round him to pull the waistband over his butt.

Coach had put his hands on his hips. I looked up, into his eyes. He smiled. He wasn't going to help me at all. I discovered one of the paneled pairs of Speedos under the shorts. Coach's cock was also hard. It must have been a good eight inches long. It was also thick. I pulled the shorts slowly down his legs. When they were at his ankles, he stepped out of them. I looked up. The bulge in the Speedos looked so impressive. Without any prompting, I bent and kissed each of Coach's naked feet. It felt the right thing to do.

That afternoon, I lost my virginity.

Robert stood to one side as Coach went back behind his desk and sat down. If I wanted to learn, he said, there were two things I had focus on, my body and his cock. My cock would no longer matter, he said. I had to concentrate my desires on his. My rewards would come from the intensity and beauty of his orgasms. I wasn't quite sure then what he meant, but it sounded right. My balls too would become toys for his pleasure. He would ensure that I developed responses to their use which would give him most joy and satisfaction. I wondered what I was letting myself in for.

He had me strip out of the Speedos. He weighed me. He measured me. He measured my cock, hard. He had Robert bring in a bench.

He opened a drawer in his desk.

I watched as he lifted out a cup and seven new jockstraps, all size small and all in their packaging. He counted them. He lifted out three pairs of the paneled Speedos. I continued watching as he lifted out a wide rubber ring.

'You know what this is?' he said, looking at me directly.

I nodded.

He handed it to me.

'Put it on,' he said. 'You will only take it off with my permission from now on, is that clear?'

I nodded again.

'Yes, Sir,' I said.

It took me a while. I had to think of everything and nothing to get my cock to soften enough to go through it. It sprang back to a full erection as soon as the ring was on.

Coach then had me put on one of the jockstraps. He came round his desk to put the cup into place.

'This is the only underwear you will use from now on,' he said.

I nodded, hoping the cup wouldn't be too obvious.

'There's one for each day. You put on a clean one each morning,' Coach said. "There are three Speedos. The yellow one is for Mondays and Thursdays, the blue for Tuesdays

95

and Fridays and the green for Wednesdays and Saturdays. You won't need one on Sundays. Wash them out each night, so they are always clean to put on. Is that clear?'

I nodded, but remained silent as Coach put the Speedos into a gym bag and handed it to me.

'Is that clear?'

'Yes, Coach,' I said, 'that's clear.'

* * *

I didn't know until I got them home that night they were size twenty eight; I took a thirty even then, or that the sides were the style briefer than those Coach himself wore. At first I felt as if everyone was looking at the obscene bulge every time I changed and went through to the pool. It took me a while to come to terms with the experience, and realize that instead of feeling humiliation, I could be proud of what I was doing, and who I was doing it for.

When he'd got the cup into place, he guided me so that I was lying face down on the inclined bench. I could feel the sides of the cup pressing into my groin. I could feel my erection inside it, fighting to get out as Coach tied my hands under the bench. I'd never felt like that before. It was Robert who got the lube and pushed some into my hole. I'd wondered what it was like to get fucked. I was about to find out. I watched as Robert stood behind Coach and undid his Speedos, pushing them to the ground. He picked them up and put them over my head. The pouch, with its intense aroma, was right in front of my nose. I inhaled deeply, relishing the scent of masculinity. I could still see a little. I watched as Robert took a condom from one of the desk drawers, opened the wrapping and unrolled it on to Coach's hard cock.

I closed my eyes and raised my head as Coach lowered his

body on to mine. He was heavy, but not unbearable. I tried to open my legs, make myself more available for him. I felt as the tip of his cock made its way across my cheeks, into the divide and tickled my hole. I hoped I could take it like a man. I was scared, but more excited than I'd ever been in my life.

I was surprised by how gentle he was. He just pushed into me a little way, then came out, then in a little further and out. He'd put his cock half an inch, then an inch into me, letting my muscle relax on it, become used to it, before pulling out and then coming in a little further. I'd been afraid, but he made it a beautiful experience for me. I could feel tears welling up in the sides of my eyes. He could have been violent. He could have raped me, but he was opening me carefully, lovingly, gently.

He seemed to read my passion.

'I don't damage good property,' he whispered into my ear.

I relaxed a little. I tried to urn my face to kiss him. I managed a peck on his chin.

It took him a while before he was fully in me. There was almost white noise in my brain as his cockhead pushed through the muscle into my rectum. He rested, letting me appreciate the moment. He pushed more. A little at a time he reached my prostate. My mouth flew open when his cockhead hit it for the first time. I could feel him grinning. He tapped my chest, under my arms twice. It was a reassuring gesture.

It was only then that he started pumping. It was gentle at first. He would raise his hips, pulling his cock back to my sphincter and then pushing into me again. He'd hit my prostate most times, but not with every thrust. I realized I was starting to fly. I could feel the cup against my groin, pressed down by the combined weights of two bodies. I didn't really care about my cock, my consciousness was in my butt.

I was concentrating so much on these amazing new

sensations that I hadn't realized Robert had moved round in front of me until I felt his cock on top of my head. I think I'd forgotten he was there. I lifted my head and his cock fell down my face. I opened my mouth. I could feel him bending awkwardly so that I could take him. I could feel my brain almost wanting to explode. I tried to think what I was doing with my mouth. I tried to make sure I sucked Robert well. I had to concentrate. It wasn't easy against the distraction that my nervous system was bringing from my prostate and butt.

I could feel the tears as Coach increased the intensity of his thrusts. He was hitting the prostate quite hard now, and with every thrust. I was teetering on the edge of the abyss between agony and ecstasy. Robert seemed to pick up on Coach's increased effort too. He was pulling back then ramming his cock more forcefully into my throat.

I thought for a moment I was going to throw up. I held it back. I took deep breaths when Robert pulled back long enough. I was gagging, gasping, but I wasn't giving up.

I felt Coach reach round under the bench. His well-defined chest was pressed into my back. He squeezed my hand. Robert was holding my head, keeping it at a comfortable angle as he fucked my mouth.

I realized the climax was imminent when Coach started counting down from ten. I tried to raise my hips to meet his thrusts. I felt my throat relax and Robert enter me more deeply.

I thought Coach was counting for himself. I hadn't realized he was issuing orders to Robert too until the cum burst from the cock in my mouth.

Coach had slowed down as he said 'three ..., two..., and finally, one.'

There had been a pause.

Then, almost fiercely as he thrust into me most powerfully, did he say, simply, 'yes, cum'.

I hit somewhere I'd never been before. I could see stars in my mind's eye. I could feel Coach's quickening thrusts as he emptied his cock into the condom deep within me. I could feel Robert pumping down my throat. It was so amazing that it was a few moments before I realized that there was dampness inside my cup jock. Spontaneously, in a way that had never happened to me before, I had cum too.

It was Robert who took his cock out of me first. Picking up a towel, he wiped himself before using the same piece of cloth across my face, catching the mixture of cum and saliva that was dribbling from the side of my mouth. He lifted my head gently and wiped the tears from my cheeks. He knelt and very gently kissed me on the lips.

Coach rested for a while. His skin felt so good against mine. It was a while before I realized that there was a roughness too. He very gradually pulled out of me. My butt felt suddenly empty and sore.

He threw the condom in a trash can. It seemed almost an insult to end such a beautiful experience in such a way. I thought later that there would have been something beautiful, if sublimely tacky about keeping the condom from one's first fuck. I wished he'd emptied the condom into my mouth so I could have tasted his cum, but he didn't. After that, Coach bent down and untied my hands.

'Go and clean him up,' Coach told Robert. His tone was abrupt, impersonal almost to the point of shame. Robert helped me get to my feet.

I was unsteady. I was still flying, my brain affected by the passion and the sensations. Coach had already disappeared. I wonder where, but then I heard the sound of his shower. I looked and saw Coach's Speedos, lying on the floor where they'd fallen from my head. I bent down and picked them up. I kissed them before putting them carefully on the desk.

Robert unlocked the door. He steered me towards the locker room and the showers. It wasn't until we were under the hot water that I realized that he had been carrying more than towels.

'There's something else that's important to Coach,' he said. 'Stand still.'

I did as I was ordered as the razor appeared. I closed my eyes as the hairs I had on my chest and belly disappeared. That, I suddenly realized, was why the Coach's chest had felt rough. He shaved too. Robert knelt. The hairs on my balls and cock went too. All that was left was a neat triangle.

I felt beautifully clean and fresh when I'd dried myself off. Looking in the long locker room mirrors, I noticed how, without the hair, my pecs and abdominal muscles looked even more impressively defined. I smiled. I appreciated what Coach was doing.

I tensed my ass as Robert and I walked back along the corridor to Coach's office. Robert was carrying my cum-stained new jockstrap.

I stood there naked as Coach spoke. The focus, he reminded me, was his cock and my body. There was a strict régime, but Robert would be there with me, he said. He handed me the sheet. Each morning there was an hour in the pool, starting at seven. Each afternoon, after classes, there was another hour in the gym, using the machines or working out with weights. We'd start, he said, the following morning.

Robert waited as I got dressed and put my new kit in my bag. Coach had made me put the damp cum-filled jockstrap on again. I was never again to come without his permission, he said. I didn't want to ask him what would happen if I did. Robert answered that question for me as we walked away from the locker room.

'It'll happen on a Saturday,' he said, 'if you need

punishment. Coach will make it an extra all-day training session. You will have an hour in the pool, then an hour in the gym. They will alternate between seven in the morning and three in the afternoon.'

I nodded.

'But in between, you will have to report to his office. He will beat you. There will be six strokes each hour, on the hour. You'll know about it, take my word for it.'

Somehow I wasn't worried, David said, continuing his story. I wasn't scared either, he continued. I felt used, but valued, appreciated for my body, my attitude and my skills. That night, as I ran through every sexual, sensuous second in my mind, my cock so, so hard, the realization slowly dawned; if I hadn't found my destiny; my destiny had found me.'

# Coach and Robert

It was good, said David, continuing his reminiscences. Coach took the place of my father. Mother was pleased too. She was relieved my energies and interests were healthy. I think she'd feared I would miss my father too much. Coach was like Dad physically too. I think that was part of it.

That year was good. Robert became a firm and very close friend. We were like conspirators. We'd be there, regularly, every morning in the pool wearing identical Speedos. We enjoyed the bond that gave us. We felt special. Robert would help me. He'd be there, holding my hand, reassuring me that I could reach the next target. He knew positive reinforcement was more effective than negative.

He'd be there when we moved on to more personal workouts, in Coach's office when everyone else had left. He'd be the one who would convince me that I could complete that final set of repetitions when I was squatting with a twenty pound weight hanging from my ballsac. He was the one who would bend down and whisper in my ear as I did another twenty push-ups, kissing Coach's feet with each dip.

I hadn't realized how much I'd miss him until he was gone. All our efforts paid off. He was offered a place at UCLA. He got a modeling contract too, nothing too special, just underwear for one of the catalogs, but enough to provide him with sufficient cash to enjoy life. I'd see his picture sometimes and smile. I wondered if Hollywood would beckon for him someday.

We'd keep in touch most weeks. We'd either e-mail one another or talk on the phone. He'd even been offered money for sex, he told me one time. This guy had bought him leather, pants, a jacket, tall boots and paid him $500 to stand over him and make him lick the leather. We laughed. We both knew Robert wasn't then a natural top, but, as he said, the money and the leather were quite an incentive.

Robert sent me some leather too. Some shorts and a jockstrap. I could wear it one day for Coach as a surprise, he said, a gift. He also sent us both new swimbriefs. He'd discovered the design while doing a catalog shoot, he said. There were three each, the styles similar to the ones we'd each had before, but a little more cutaway. He found another especially brief style for me, and sent me ones which were that size too small. I cursed him, in the nicest possible way, the next time we'd spoken. Coach had made me wear them, then he'd beaten my cock with a small whip until I'd cum. The cutaway style had really emphasized the bulge of my cock and balls, making a better target, I told Robert the next time we spoke.

I took Robert's advice and wore the leather jockstrap for Valentine's Day. I'd had a good day. I felt good after my workout. I'd put it on after showering that afternoon. When everyone else had gone, I put a towel round my waist and walked back to Coach's office. I knocked on his door and waited. It was the time when he most liked to get off. There was rarely a day when I didn't suck him or when he didn't fuck me. The inclined bench had become a permanent part of the office furniture.

I hadn't quite intended it that way. I'm not sure how I'd intended it, but the towel fell away when I was standing in front of his desk. He looked up at me. He smiled. He glowered. He made me wait.

'Yes?' he said, eventually.

'It's a gift, Sir,' I stammered, 'from Robert and I, Sir.'

He waited.

'I like it,' he said, 'but I don't like the way it was presented.'

I gulped. I hadn't intended to displease him.

'I'm sorry, Sir," I said, but it was too late.

'You didn't have permission to wear anything different today, did you David?' he said.

'No, Sir,' I admitted.

'It would have been better if you had given me the garment, or told me about it, then I could have given permission, couldn't I?'

I nodded.

He pulled out the bench. I bent over it. I heard him going to his locker. I heard the swishing behind me. I looked round. I'd expected a paddle. Instead, I could see a cane. The leather jock was still in place. My cock had shriveled. I'd been paddled before, for fun, but the cane was something new. I wondered how many strokes there would be, whether I could cope with them. I found out when they were over. There were twelve. They were rapid, one after the other. I hardly had time to count them and thank him for each one. I was shocked to find when I was allowed to stand, close to tears, that my cock was harder than it had been in a long time.

I found another level that day. The caning had hurt, but there was something else. I wasn't sure then quite what it was. Coach knew something had changed too. He said he knew I didn't like disappointing him and that I wanted to please him.

'Don't you like that, David?' he asked. His rare use of my name caught my attention. My thoughts were everywhere, from thinking about trying to please, yet knowing that to add to the inner disappointment, I needed to brace myself ready for what was inevitably to come.

I thought for a minute. I had to admit that I did feel bad about letting him down, but that I also appreciated a beating. I hated the instant of impact, but after that, the sensations were taking me to a new high, a new fulfillment.

'There,' Coach said, 'I've introduced you to a new experience, something wonderful. Don't you want to repay me? You certainly don't want to disappoint me, do you David?'

I had to admit that the heat in my ass was a threshold, a step onward.

I asked Robert about the cane on the phone that evening. He told me then that Coach had served in England in the military. Coach had acquired the taste there, Robert told me, a bit like you, I hear, Russ … Mr Russell.

David smiled, catching my eye and taking a sip of his drink before returning to his narrative.

The following morning, David continued, after he had come out of the pool, Coach ordered him to the office. Coach pushed a jar of menthol jelly towards me, the stuff you use when you have a cold. He said I could jack off, but only after I'd rubbed the grease into my cock. It was a beautiful agony. He came round his desk and took some on his little finger. He pushed it into my pisshole. I jerked off, rubbing the burning ointment further into my sensitive skin with every motion. He was enjoying watching as I endured such torments for his pleasure. I wasn't going to disappoint him again, was I? I was allowed to cum only with permission. So I asked. Would Coach be so cruel that he'd let me jack off but not cum? I was relieved. I could cum, but I had to shoot into my Speedos, then I had to suck them clean. I had to lick up any drops I'd spilled on the floor. I was catching my breath when he pushed two pieces of paper and pen towards me.

'Sign that,' he said, 'and then go.'

I signed both.

He kept one.

He gestured that I should keep the other.

I read it as I walked along the corridor to the locker room. I'd just agreed – consented – that I would accept twelve strokes of the cane, each second Saturday, after working out, regardless of anything else. I could feel my cock hardening again. The first beating would be ten days later.'

## Coach's military discipline

I was so excited as the days passed, David said. I knew the caning was going to hurt. I also knew I could take it. I knew I could give Coach pleasure by taking the caning. I wasn't sure whether it was the psychology which gave him the buzz or whether it was the moment of impact. I wasn't really worried. I just knew that he'd revealed something to me about myself, which was a vital part of me.

I worked out additionally hard that Saturday. I'd been

increasing my workouts every day, adding reps or extra sets as I could. I remembered something Arnold Schwarzenneger had said about the endorphin rush from a workout being better than sex. I didn't think it was better, as such, just something wonderfully complementary.

I waited until the locker room had emptied that Saturday afternoon. As usual, I was the last out to finish. I didn't shower then. I just waited and then changed into the leather jockstrap. I walked along to Coach's office wearing the jock, nothing else. I knocked. When Coach answered, I went in. The bench was already in position. I bent forward, putting my hands on the higher end. I could feel my cock hardening.

I saw Coach walk round me to his locker. He too was wearing only a jockstrap. His cock was hard, I could see. He took a cane from the locker. He also lifted out some lube and a condom. He spread some lube onto my hole first. He put the condom on the corner of his desk.

I heard the swish of the cane as Coach familiarized himself with its balance. He took up a position just behind me to one side. I braced myself. There were no preparatory remarks, no courtesies. I closed my eyes. I opened them again and looked at the clock on the wall. I looked at the seconds, ticking away. I took a deep breath. In thirty seconds, perhaps a minute it would be over. I was already looking forward to the glow that I would feel then. I would not disappoint Coach.

I just had time to close my eyes and breathe in before the first stroke hit me. Coach wasn't playing. These beatings were a step towards a new intensity. I could feel my head moving back with the agony as the strokes hit me. I didn't have time to say 'thank you'; I just counted them. There were tears in my eyes, but my face was tensed so tightly none escaped.

I'd no sooner said: 'Twelve, Sir' than I heard him pulling off the jockstrap.

Coach fought to get the condom on. He was panting. He pushed me forward, lowering my butt ready for his entry. I could feel the heat of my cheeks. There was no beauty like that first fuck. This was pure animal necessity for Coach. I don't know how long it had been since his last orgasm, but this one wasn't far off. He entered me with a single forceful thrust. I was grateful for the little lube that was on the condom and in my hole. He held on to my shoulders with every thrust. The sex was hard and raw. I could feel the hardness of his cock. Then, as quickly as he'd penetrated me, it was over. There were three, four, perhaps five, hard thrusts, from outside my hole to as deep as he could go. Then he was holding on to me, panting, shuddering as he filled the condom.

I left the office as soon as I could after he'd pulled out of me. I didn't stop to watch him take off the condom. I could feel my ass glowing. I turned as best I could in the locker room to see the bruises developing. It seemed as if I was looking at a different person. I was glowing.

That sex had felt more like rape, but somehow it wasn't. I'd consented. I'd known it would be hard, impersonal, almost animal-like. It felt appropriate for me to be treated like that. I didn't feel bad; I felt as if I'd been able to help a good man achieve what he needed to achieve. I couldn't call such sex 'relief'. I just knew it was right for that moment and the dynamic between us. Part of me was telling me I should have felt used, humiliated, but it wasn't like that. My butt was sore, as was my hole. I felt as if my cock should have shriveled away to nothing, but it hadn't. It wasn't hard, but it was tumescent. I clenched the cheeks of my butt and grimaced. I relaxed those muscles again a moment later. I smiled. Painful and impersonal though the experience had been, it still felt right. I knew I was trying to rationalize my predicament. I knew too that I was making progress, but that I hadn't found the entire answer. I wished I could have jacked off. I felt my cock and balls inside the jock. I paused. I breathed deeply. Despite the indignity – I couldn't call it humiliation – I felt good deep inside. I squeezed my balls a little, took a deep breath and smiled.

We went along like that for a couple of months. We'd do other things during the week, but the Saturdays had their own ritual. He'd cane me, hard, impersonally and then fuck me. After the fourth or fifth occasion, I wondered if I could take it more often. There was only one way to find out.

I looked at the original letter I'd signed. Coach had produced it on his computer. Once each week, I'd use the machine to update scores and records. That week I found the letter. I altered it. I took out the word 'second' between 'each' and 'Saturday'. I ran off two copies. I took one. I put the other in my own personal file.

Coach didn't expect me that week. He was working on some papers when I knocked on his door. I was wearing the leather jock. Bruises from the previous Saturday were still clearly visible across my cheeks.

'I didn't think you were due again until next week,' he said.

'It's this week, Sir,' I said. 'You can check the file if you want to.'

I put the bench into position.

I stood.

I watched as he stood up and went to the filing cabinet.

I saw him smile as he found the letter and read it. He looked at the signature. He could see it was genuine. He looked at me, smiling knowingly.

'If you hadn't signed it,' he said, 'I'd think it was a forgery.

'Come here,' he ordered, quietly but firmly.

I obeyed. He made me kneel and kiss his feet. I took his sweat pants off with my mouth. I licked the growing cock and tightening balls through his Speedos.

'Are you sure you're ready for this?' he asked as he opened the locker for the cane, condom and lube. It was the question that I'd been dreading in some ways. It told me he'd taught me as much as he could.

'Sir,' I said, 'I think I as ready as I will ever be. I have no option. It's in the signed document. You can see that for yourself. Whether I can do it Sir, only the next few minutes will show.'

Coach stood, wondering I think, whether he should try to protect me from myself. He decided against that. I know now that he was right.

'Prepare yourself,' he said.

I reached for the lube. I squirted some into my hole. I bent and kissed Coach's feet, then each ball and the head of his cock in his Speedos. I straightened up and kissed his firm abdominals, then each nipple. I kissed his chin. I knelt again and pulled the Speedos forward over his erection with my mouth. I kissed the cockhead. I could taste the first drops of semen as they started to leak. I reached for the condom. I slowly rolled it down his cock. I looked up into his eyes, defying him to hurt me.

When the condom was in place, I turned and bent over the bench. I could hear him breathing deeply. I hear the practice swish of the cane. I braced myself.

The first nine strokes came hard and fast. They did hurt. The bruises from the previous week were still extremely sensitive. I held my head back and closed my eyes.

'Ten, Sir,' I said. There was a pause.

He waited, then brought the eleventh down.

'Eleven Sir, thank you, Sir,' I said.

I had to squeeze the words out through my teeth. That impact was truly full of pain. Just one more, I thought.

Again he waited. I waited too, braced ready for the blow.

I almost yelled when it hit me.

I hardly had time to say 'twelve, Sir' before he'd entered me. His cock was again like a hard pole. He didn't take long to come. The thrusts were few and hard and he had shot. He collapsed on to my back. I felt his lips kiss my shoulders. I knew our time together was coming to an end. I had got as much from him as he could deliver.

I changed the letter twice more after that. In May, I added another six strokes, in June another six. That was what scared me. I knew I could take more and I knew I needed more.

# Semper Fidelis

Now David had built up the momentum of his life history, there was no stopping him. It might have been getting late, but The Professor and I let him go on. I guessed The Professor had probably heard it all before, but he was still smiling, enjoying David's autobiographical account of his young life.

I finished school on the Friday, he said. On the Monday, I enrolled in the Marines. It would be the distraction I needed, I thought. It would allow me to focus on my body. Yet, quickly, they discovered I was reasonably smart too, that I had a university place, even thought I'd enlisted. Coach endorsed my application. He grinned, said I'd have fun.

It was hot. My cock was hard as the hair was shorn from my head. There were some other great-looking guys. The exercise schedule demanded all my attention and energy.

Sure I jerked off, just as all the other guys did. I got some strange looks at first, because I always wore a jock, never boxers or briefs, but I soon noticed that some of the other guys started to do the same. It was after we got our first break, the first leave off base. The next time we stripped, I noticed at least half a dozen. It was nice. It was great to see some of the butts.

There were still bruises on my butt, the first week I was there. I tried to put those desires out of my mind. I could be a good Marine. I could work my body as much as I wanted. That was OK. I wouldn't have to worry about such strange, kinky, needs any longer, I thought.

Some hope too. It was fine for the first months, but during my second year, the feelings started to re-emerge. It wasn't just the pain, I could test my endurance most days. It was wanting to focus on someone else, to give a single person pleasure, wanting not to let someone down. That feeling, that desire has been rekindled, reborn. It had started trying to take me over.

I wanted to enlist again, to do those first few months over again. But then, unexpectedly I had the chance of taking up my university place. I would return to the Marines every so often as a reservist; the education would let me go on to officer training.

I'd been doing fine, going along that route, I thought, until that night in the bar. I'd met The Professor, of course. I'd started enjoying his classes and tutorials. I enjoyed the challenge he presented. I found myself being attracted by him, so much that I couldn't face being alone with him. That's why I always left his office so quickly.

And then, that evening, in the bar, as soon as the boy had spoken, I knew. I wanted to serve The Professor. I wanted him to be the man. He was intelligent, I thought. He will understand. He will help me. Perhaps he may rescue me from myself.

111

The training from Coach fell back into place. I'd learned about sitting on furniture, wearing clothes or shoes in a master's home. I felt I should sit on the floor when we got home that night.

When you and Litton went to bed, The Professor and I talked. I told him much of what I told you. His boy was due to be moving on before too long. He wanted someone to take over. We talked for most of that night. The Professor was unsure about me being one of his students. Although I was taking his classes that semester, he was not going to be assessing any of the work for my degree after that.

He offered me a deal. He would arrange my discharge from the Marines if I agreed to a contract lasting three years, the last two of my first degree and then an initial year's post-graduate study. Knowing that military life was important to me, The Professor said I'd also stay in the Reserves. Having found me, I think he didn't want me suddenly deployed to one of the world's trouble spots. I knew too, in an instant, that there was no choice; this was my destiny and I had to follow it.

We worked out the details that afternoon, after you and Litton had left. We talked more. I was surprised by how easily it came out. The Professor provided me with a focus too. He took over from Coach. He hoped I would not have to move on so soon. The Professor said he would introduce me to others. He was also my therapist.

He started that very afternoon. He reassured me that there was nothing wrong in wanting to give so much of myself to another. The greatest danger was finding someone who could not appreciate the gift. He was to repeat that often.

# The Letter

While I knew so much about The Professor and David, Marc did not. I would have to remind Marc to ask David to tell him the story. Remembering that night at the run and David's apprenticeship was the confirmation that I needed. Yes, spending time with The Professor and David could be exactly the experience that Marc needed, wanted, so badly.

Nevertheless, David's letter intrigued me.

Dear Russ,

The Professor has asked me to reply to you. i am sure you will appreciate that most of the requirements here are His, but He has also permitted me to add some comments of my own.

As The Professor told you on the phone, He will be pleased to accept marc's submission and services. marc will act as my 'number two' while he is here. i am sure you will agree that this is appropriate.

The basic rules are fairly straightforward. marc will use my downstairs closet. (i will meet him first when he comes to California and familiarize him with some of these points.) he will be naked in the house at all times, apart from a cockring, unless instructed otherwise. he will kneel before entering any room where The Professor is present. he will keep himself clean and ready for use at any time.

marc will work with me to provide domestic service for The Professor. It will be springtime when he comes, so he can expect there to be work in the yard that needs doing too.

i get the impression from your letter – which The Professor has shown me – and from part of your telephone conversation which he passed on that i have a reasonable amount in common with young marc. his needs do not appear dissimilar to my own. i am looking forward to meeting him and, i hope, becoming friends. Do please reassure him that while my standards are high and i will be demanding in ensuring that the quality of service we provide for The Professor is of the highest quality, i will be supportive. i understand his quest and will be close to him when he needs it. he will have long and hard days.

marc can also expect to have his body worked. he will have an exercise program alongside mine. The Professor appreciates that he will be working and that this has to be taken into account. Therefore, marc will probably rise at 6am and run with me for thirty minutes or so before we return to arrange breakfast for The Professor. If there is a gym near his work, he will be expected to workout each lunchtime. The alternative is another run, if that is practical. If he is home for 6pm, then depending on what he has been able to do, he will spend some more time in the basement gym here at The Professor's home.

As this is a development period, it is likely that The Professor will have him bound or caged for a while each evening. he may be put into a chastity device or a straitjacket. he may be plugged, for anything from an hour to overnight or even longer. There may not be any sexual contact with The Professor. marc should expect that he will be flogged at least once each week. he will also be paddled at least once each week he is with us.

marc should also know that it is highly unlikely that he will be permitted an orgasm while he is here. he may also be made available to any of The Professor's guests. If he is, the 'standard' understanding regarding personal safety will be in place.

marc should bring with him his business clothes, shirts and ties. he will need five cup jockstraps, swimbriefs (these should be as brief as possible, but have a full back) and either square-cut gym shorts or square cut swimwear. he will also need running shorts and tanktops. (If he is to workout at a gym during his lunch breaks, he may wish to bring additional workout attire.) he will require business shoes, black and white socks, training shoes and boots.

Ideally, it is probably best if marc comes here on the Friday or Saturday before the Monday when he starts work here in

The Bay Area. When he travels, he will wear jeans, boots, a cup jock, boot socks, and a white tanktop under a plain mid-blue polo shirt. i shall meet him from his flight.

We will no doubt talk before then. i wish you well in the preparation. The Professor is looking forward to Marc's service and training. i must add that i am too.

Respectfully,

david

I smiled as I read it. The letter had The Professor's influence all over it.

I noted that David was using Old Guard protocols of using lower case letters for himself and Marc, regardless of the grammar in his letter.

The history of the leather community, such as it is, both in the United States and elsewhere in the world was something Marc should learn more about. Some of the books he needed to read were already on my shelves. He'd noticed them the first time he'd visited my home, as an investment adviser from the bank, rather than a boy in training. I was certain others would be in The Professor's personal library.

Marc had stripped as usual when he came in. He stood inside the front door and took off his chinos, tie, and office shirt. He had put his shoes behind the door. I saw him as he came up the stairs, carrying the clothes. He was wearing a pair of boxer briefs. He looked good.

'Put those clothes away then come here,' I said as he went passed. 'I have something to show you.'

He was at the door to my office a moment later. The boxer briefs had been replaced by light-colored Speedos. He was standing, head bowed, hands behind his back, waiting.

I beckoned for him to come in. I pointed to the table where I had left David's letter. It was obvious that David had intended that Marc should read it and know exactly what was in it. There was something important about getting used to being referred to in the third person. I watched carefully as Marc read it. I could see his cock growing inside the Speedos. I liked that. David's comments had clearly had the right effect. It was a good sign.

There was a broad smile across Marc's face when he turned towards me. I grinned too.

'It will be hard, Marc,' I said. 'You can take my word for that, but it will be good too.'

He nodded.

'Be ready, but don't be daunted. David will be there to help you. He means that. He remembers when he was learning and needed help to find himself. You can be sure of that, okay?'

Marc nodded again. His erection was still apparent.

'You will be tired and you will need a lot of energy,' I said. 'I take it the temporary transfer is not a problem?'

'No, Russ. You know how lucky I am. The investment role gives me a rare freedom. It will be a busy month working there. If I go in to the San Francisco office like that, I will have to review most of the local staff and audit a selection of their portfolios. I'll have to bring in others from around the state for training and briefing too. I already have an application lodged. All I have to do now is confirm the location and the dates.'

'Do you know the area there?'

'I've been there for a week, three or four years ago,' he said.

'And a gym?'

'I'm not sure. I'll have to find out.'

'Tell me the office address. Now that we have the initial formalities out of the way, I'll e-mail David and ask him to check out what there is in that area,' I said.

# Preparing for The Professor

During that conversation, I agreed with Marc that we'd establish a plan that weekend. I'd already been thinking about his preparation since my first letter to The Professor. I knew he'd need to be ready for something more intense from the outset, mentally and physically. I thought about the most practical, most effective ways of moving forward for Marc. I'd already asked him to note what he'd been doing during the week and to start keeping a journal.

That Friday evening had been quiet. David's letter had clearly given Marc food for thought. He was pensive, moving around the apartment more stealthily almost, as if he was trying to avoid my attention. I thought he was ignoring me, but then the nature of his actions fell into place.

I must admit I was pleased. I thought everything would have taken longer. The Professor, my first choice as a mentor for Marc, had said yes. That alone had probably saved several months' work. Arrangements were coming together. Commitments were being made. I was also pleased that I'd written to The Professor so quickly, striking while the proverbial iron was hot. It gave Marc no time to change his mind. He'd told me enough about himself to know that not disappointing another person was important to him. I felt the speed of The Professor's response and David's letter might have been enough to make sure that any escape route had been well and truly closed off. I hoped so.

Marc had prepared dinner as usual. He'd started the weekend laundry. He'd spent an hour, perhaps more, sitting on his mat, paper and pencil in hand. He'd been making notes for our discussion, he told me later.

I'd retreated to the deck after I'd eaten. I'd needed time to think too. Marc had already gone to bed when I came inside. I'd dismissed him after he'd finished clearing up. I knew we both needed time to ourselves. David's letter and the imminent confirmation by the bank of the dates of Marc's time in California meant that the dynamic between us was changing. I knew it. He knew it.

I felt he should have more time to himself, to meditate, to consider his predicament, to ready himself mentally for his experience with The Professor.

Coming into the living area, I looked around. At the end of that week, the room was tidier than it had been for a long time. Newspapers were neatly folded in a pile. Books had been put away. Shelves had been dusted. DVDs had been put in boxes and neatly stacked. I knew I'd miss Marc when he was gone. I felt too something come back to life inside myself. Perhaps, I thought, I should be more disciplined with myself.

Marc's light was already off when I passed his room. I blew him a kiss. Grow, young man, I thought. Find yourself again. Be reborn.

It was nearly nine when I woke. Marc was already up and about. I could hear him moving around. I'd no sooner got back into bed having had a piss than he was there at the door, a coffee and the newspaper in his hand. He was wearing only light blue Speedos. He looked very good. It was an exceedingly pleasant way to wake up, I had to admit.

* * *

Marc drew back the drapes. It was a beautiful February morning. The sun hadn't been up long. The house felt cozy.

I didn't rush. I drank my coffee slowly and read some of the paper. I could hear Marc more now. He was cleaning. He'd not started anything noisy until he knew I was awake. Only once he'd heard me stir had he turned on the washing machine.

I looked out at the sunshine again. It felt like a morning for going out. That, I knew suddenly, was the answer. I had felt uncomfortable about relaxing the rules that Marc had been setting himself during the week, but I also knew there had to be a different formality as we worked through his program to prepare for the coming months. Brunch out would solve that problem.

'Marc,' I called as I got out of bed.

He was there within seconds, waiting at the door.

'Shower, get some clothes on. Jeans and a sweatshirt will do. We're going out.'

'Underwear?' he asked.

'A cup jock and your cockring,' I said.

After coming out of the shower, I chose a tight polo shirt, a pair of 2(x)ist briefs, grey 501s. I felt good. My own workouts were starting to bring the results I wanted.

Marc was waiting by the front door when I came down the stairs. I tapped the front of his jeans, to check the cup was there and remind him of its presence. He smiled. He was carrying a note book and a pen. So was I. He had the keys to his pick-up in the other hand. He was ready.

'Let's go,' I said. 'Ariadne's.'

The restaurant was busy. I'd expected it to be on a bright Saturday. The owners, managers, were canny too. They had a row of tables on a deck. They were all for two, so couples could be together. The noisier, larger family groups were kept inside. In winter, the deck was enclosed with glass panels. In summer, it was either open or there were grilles for the evening. There was an amazing mechanism which lowered the panels from under the roof space.

The glass was in place that morning. We could look out across to a park. The parking lot was 10 feet or so below the deck and didn't interrupt the view. In the park, there was the customary motley weekend morning collection of joggers and a teens' football team practising their plays.

Philip, the maitre d' showed Marc and me to the end table. Marc let me sit first. When I was comfortable, I nodded for him to sit too.

Although the restaurant was gay-owned and managed, the quality of food and service attracted a broad clientele. They were principally the younger, middle-class, reasonably affluent professionals from the city. There were some ladies-who-lunched. There were some 'laddies-who-lunched' too, but they weren't likely to be seen at any time before midday on a Saturday. They'd be trying to remember the name of the trade they'd picked up the night before. The ladies clearly cost others dearly too, either in allowances or alimony. The gold was genuine and high carat. The hair-styling alone probably ran into thousands of dollars each week. This restaurant was slightly down-scale for them, but even the few who came at weekends would have Hermes scarves over their Calvin Klein sweatpants.

The other women were burdened with children. They were already, even in their late twenties or early thirties, losing the battle against weight gain and spreading hips. Some of their menfolk were too. There seemed to be two distinct categories of men; those who had given up, who would be wearing size forty pants when they were aged forty and size fifty at fifty. There were the others who were fighting valiantly. Despite the indulgence of too much beer on a Friday night, enjoying the freedom from a manic manager before returning home to the constraints of the conjugal bed, they were coping, just, to keep their physiques under control. I'd met enough of them to know that an hour's workout at lunchtime was a lesser evil than spending time in the corporate dining room, enduring the petty gossip of their co- workers. At a gym, silence was the order of the day, every day. If there was any sound, it was individual, the privacy of their MP3 player of choice. Even cell phones could be ignored, if only for a few minutes. I was letting my mind wander. I should have been concentrating.

All were represented in the restaurant that morning. Philip, the maitre d' that day, had recognized us. Without prompting, he'd guided us through to the tables for two on the deck and put us right at the end.

Although we didn't go into town much, we both knew the waiter too that day. John was someone we both loved dearly. Through the week, he worked afternoons and evenings at the local public radio station, running their news operation single-handedly most of the time, for a pittance. At the weekends, he waited table. He'd decided long ago that while he loved the work, he didn't have the ambition to stab contemporaries, either in the front or back, that was needed to progress towards the biggest media markets and mega-buck salaries. He knew where he was happy and he was staying there. He was intelligent, modest, and unpretentious.

I'd got to know him a few years before. He'd sometimes come into one of the bars on a Friday, late, after he'd finished working. When I'd been doing more journalism, we'd encountered each other at press conferences. Later, we'd got talking in the bar. He enjoyed radio, he said, because you didn't have to look good. John hadn't been one of nature's beauties at that time, but during his late thirties, he'd changed. He got rid of the beard that he'd had, he said, since his late teens. He started eating differently and going to the gym, two or three mornings a week. He lost more than forty pounds. The John in thirty-eight-inch pants went to thirty-twos within about six months. He looked a lot better for it.

'You two look as if you need to talk,' he said, seeing the notebooks on the table in front of us.

'We do,' I said.

'I know we're busy,' John said, 'but don't worry about rushing. Let me know if you want more coffee though, otherwise, just take your time.'

We did. We didn't say much, but Marc and I caught the pleasure in each other's eyes. I had to smile. Both of us I were well behaved that day. We resisted the temptation of the calories. Rather than filling our faces with pancakes, huge amounts of butter and gallons of sugar- rich syrup, we'd chosen bran cereal, fruit and dried toast. I tried not to think about the amount of high-fructose corn syrup that would have been added to the cereal, but concentrated on the fruit. That, I remembered, was the best reason for choosing Ariadne's; the generous plates of orange, apple, banana, melon and cantaloupe, grapes and strawberries, plums too. Perhaps there was a God, I thought, as I savored another forkful; it was possible to indulge and not bulge. The fruit was so delicious, just right for that morning.

I let John refill our mugs with coffee before I opened my note book. I think Marc had been more than eager to start the conversation. I hadn't let him. Patience was particularly virtuous in slaves, or would- be slaves, I remembered.

'This is what I have planned provisionally,' I said, looking at the book. Marc had abdicated much of his decision-making to me already. It was more a matter of telling him what would be happening rather than discussing it.

'In the spring, as soon as you get the dates from the bank, you will go to The Professor's home in San José. You will live there for the four weeks you're working at the bank and you'll take a fifth week as vacation, so you have some twenty-four-hour time there that isn't the weekend.

'I will still try to arrange for you to go to DC for a week sometime after that. I hope Rudy will allow you to see some of his clients with him. It is important you learn that you may not always be a slave to men you fancy.'

I could see Marc's face fall. I don't think he'd considered that option. If he had, it looked from his expression as if he'd tried to put it out of his mind as quickly as possible.

'Let me explain, Marc,' I said. 'Once we consent, we consent. There are dynamics to consent. They cover all the who, what, where, when, why and how questions.'

Marc was puzzled.

'You can think about the details of that later,' I said. 'Right now, I have something to tell you from my own experience.

'I knew a guy about ten, fifteen, years ago. He was in his late fifties even then. He was a skilled top. He was called Bernard. He lived in Atlanta. He worked as a customer liaison executive, I can't remember who for, but he would travel round the country to sort out business problems, but play wherever he went. He was always running ads in the magazines.

'He was a hot guy, Bernard was, he kept himself in reasonable shape, but he wasn't at all good-looking, not at least in my eyes. I can't say that I really fancied him. I'd have liked to have had him play with me, let him use his hands on me, but the thought of his cock in my mouth turned me off. He told me that, for him, the "real" masochist was the person who found fulfilment in the sensation or the situation; the person who was creating it didn't matter. They could be male or female, gross or an Adonis or Venus. For him, it wasn't the person that provoked the erection, but the predicament.

'I don't think you're like that Marc. I think the person has some importance. I think, for you, it has to be a guy. I could be wrong. There may be some situations where it could be a woman. I don't want to know, at least, not now. If you are going to serve someone, to give them everything, then it has to be someone you respect, right? And,' I went on, without giving him time to answer, 'you respect people who can look after their own bodies.'

Marc nodded.

'A week, perhaps ten days, from a Friday until the Sunday a week later, with Rudy, should be enough. I'll check when I write. Then, if you can get some vacation later in the year or arrange the time some other way, you can go to back out west. Depending on how long you get, I will see whether Robert or Dan and Simon will help. Then, as a climax, we'll go to one of the September runs together. I hope I may have found someone for you by then. Whatever happens, the formality we are establishing here, this week, will definitely end when we come home then. Is that clear?'

Again, Marc nodded.

'And your thoughts?' I said.

He took a piece of paper that had been folded up inside the notebook and pushed it towards me.

Clothing: to wear only Speedos or a jockstrap in the house; to strip as soon as I come in; to wear a cockring at all times

Russ to choose underwear for me during the week and other clothing outside working hours

To eat only in the kitchen

To make dinner and wait table

To keep the house and yard clean and tidy. (Wearing shorts in the yard?)

To shave my chest, stomach,legs, armpits, cock, balls and ass each week

To work out at least four times a week

Never to touch myself or cum without permission Never to

use furniture in the house without permission Only to sit on the mat in the front room

Never to close my bedroom door

To make myself and all possessions available for inspection at all times

Never to touch any of Russ's property without permission

To speak only when spoken to

To wait for permission before entering any room that Russ is in

To develop my experience of being plugged? To develop my experience of bondage?

To manage the kitchen and household and provide the right diet


It seemed a very full list Marc was giving me. He was looking at me as if he wanted permission to speak. I noticed the question marks beside the most overtly sexual activities; it was as if he was reluctant to be so intimate with me.

'Yes?' I said.

'I feel I should tell you this, Russ,' he said. 'I knew a guy, for a year or so, before I moved here. He was a hunk. We'd work out together, and sometimes play. We'd arrange to go out for a drink every so often too. When we did, or when we went running, he'd look amazing. He'd come round wearing tight jeans, a tight tanktop and a leather jacket, or beautifully tight running shorts.

'He'd stand in my room, it was almost as if he wanted me to do something for him, but only once or twice did he ever ask, or order me. I still haven't worked him out. I'm not sure if he wanted me to go down on my knees, kiss his feet and beg for permission to touch him, whether he was embarrassed or lacked confidence, but usually he said nothing. I should have done it anyway, looking back, but I didn't. I still remember one night, he was sitting on the floor, in tight, white Levis, his bulge so inviting. I wanted to dive onto it, but he said nothing.

'I wanted that man to take decisions for me. I wanted him to call and say we're going to the bar, be ready, and wear this or don't wear that. I bought him underwear when I was away some times. He'd try it on for me, then and there, when I gave it to him, but he didn't always wear it when he did come round. There were some items I gave him I never saw him wear. I wished he'd call and say we were going for a run and that I should wear a jock or shorts. We didn't always have sex. Sometimes he played with me without even getting his cock out. There were other times when I felt I wanted to say "thank you" my way, by kneeling and kissing his feet, his fly and his butt.

'I don't want to have to ask you for those things, Russ. I don't want to have to provoke you into punishing me, like I did last week. You do understand, don't you?'

I nodded.

'Yes, Marc,' I said. 'I understand. I also accept that for the next six months you are giving me your consent to do these things, to take these decisions and you will give the same consent to The Professor and David, Rudy and the others. You say you want such decisions to be taken for you. You say you need such parameters to be set. You are making that commitment from today until the end Wednesday of the September run. You know that?'

'Yes, Russ,' he said. 'I know that. I know what it means.'

'I appreciate your list, Marc. It will start from today. We will review it in two weeks and, if necessary, add to it or amend it. If you increase the restrictions around the house, the same will apply then as it did this week; they will be added to this list automatically. We will come here, two weeks from today. If there is anything you wish to add otherwise, it will be done then. Bring it on a piece of paper as you have today.'

Marc nodded.

'Is there anything else?'

'What do you think, Russ?'

'Your list looks fairly comprehensive. I think it includes everything you've been doing. I can't remember anything else. Is there anything you want to add?'

'I'm not sure,' he said, his voice trailing away.

Was there something else? I wondered. Probably. I knew that even a few months ago Marc would take quite a lot of encouragement before he revealed some of his most personal desires. There probably would be more over the coming weeks, I realized. It was at that moment that I suddenly realized that would become apparent when he started doing them or they appeared on a Saturday morning piece of paper. That saved the problems of having to say them.

I suddenly appreciated more about Marc, and about myself. I could have the same difficulties too, even with people whom I knew understood, who had similar experiences and needs. Even on a run, there were times when I found it difficult to make the words come out of my mouth. If I'd been beside someone and they'd turned to me and said 'kneel', I would have done, I'd even have felt good doing it. If that same man had turned to me and said 'tell me exactly what you want to do now', I don't think I could have said the words 'I want to kneel at your feet, Sir'.

'I think I understand, Marc,' I said. 'You can tell me, here, you know that, or you can start doing something, or if you prefer or want more time to think about it, you can put on your list for our next discussion. You have permission to do that.'

I used the word 'permission' deliberately. I thought it might be another trigger.

127

'It's about David's letter,' Marc said.

'Yes?'

'I know that you and I, well,' the words were not coming easily to him, 'I know we're not playing and that other than Monday, we haven't been into the playroom ....'

'Yes?' I said. I wanted to hear his desires from his own mouth. I knew it was hard for him, but I also knew he needed to say something. I would help if I could, but I wasn't even going to try to put words in his mouth.

'You remember what he said about my "development period"?'

I pulled David's letter from my papers. I'd brought it with me. I re-read it again quickly. I found the passage Marc had mentioned.

'So?'

'I think I can do most of the rest, perhaps everything, Russ,' Marc said, 'but ....' His voice trailed away again.

'Yes?' I wasn't going to put words into his mouth, I told myself, again.

'Would you help me?' he said at last, 'please?'

'You know I will Marc. Isn't that what all this is about?' He nodded.

'I feel good, helping you learn. It fulfils something parental in me,' I said. Marc smiled. I felt better now he was relaxing a little. 'So, what would you like me to help you with?'

'Those aspects of David's letter,' he said. He still hadn't brought himself to say, clearly and deliberately, the specific words. I could see him wanting to bring his hands across to the letter, to point at the words rather than say them.

'Which ones specifically?' I asked.

I started to fold the letter and put it away, removing from him the temptation to reach for it.

I could see him take a deep breath. He was almost

128

whispering as he said: 'About bondage .... About being plugged ....'

'Yes,' I said, as nonchalantly as I could. 'What about them?'

'I think I need more experience of them,' Marc admitted quietly. 'And, Russ, before I go to see The Professor too. I haven't been plugged for a while. And ....'

Tears were starting to appear in the corners of his eyes. I reached to hold his hand. I nodded for him to continue.

'And,' he said, 'I haven't been in a cage since before Jerry died.'

I understood more in that moment. I took a deep breath.

'Thank you,' I said. 'I understand.'

I waited. I drank some more coffee. I thought Marc had been grieving less for Jerry recently. I should have known that there would be times, especially during this process, when memories would come flooding back. Inside, I kicked myself.

He squeezed my hand and looked at me again before he said anything else. 'Thank you' appeared silently on his lips.

'So,' I said. 'I think the best next step will be if you tell me what you think you need. You've said you're anxious about getting to The Professor not having had experience of being plugged for a while and not having been caged since Jerry was alive. Is there anything else?'

Again, it was a moment before he spoke.

'Yes,' he said, at last, breathing more easily this time. 'I'm worried about "the whole bondage thing", Russ. I'm out of practice. I don't want to disappoint The Professor by arriving on his doorstep out of practice.'

'That's up to you,' I said.

Marc looked at me quizzically.

'Think about what I've already said, Marc. You still have some choice. You can ask me directly, not right now,' I said

129

quickly, holding up my hand before he could interrupt, 'to do something. Alternatively, you can start doing it for yourself, between now and when we speak next, or you can put it on the next list.'

I paused.

Marc waited.

'I also understand that those may be slower choices. It's only a few weeks until you go to The Professor. You may not wish to lose a fortnight's practice time. So, which is it to be?'

It was his turn to pause. I could see him thinking. Once he had asked, there was no return.

'I'd like to ask directly,' he said.

'Good,' I said. 'What would you like to ask?'

He took a deep breath. I appreciated that it wasn't easy for him. I could see the challenges and desires, the reluctance, cowardice even, perhaps, fighting each other in his mind.

'Would you please help me get into practice with bondage and being plugged, Russ, please?' The words came out in a torrent. He was red and catching his breath when he finished.

I looked at him, making him wait for my answer.

'Yes,' I said, eventually. 'Of course I will.'

I smiled, enjoying the moment. Marc sighed with relief.

'I wouldn't send you off to The Professor unprepared. I thought you knew that.'

'I wanted to be sure, really sure,' Marc said.

'He uses his property hard, Marc, but The Professor takes care of everyone. He will appreciate your preparation too. He'll enjoy knowing what you're putting yourself through to be close to his standard when you get there.'

I let silence fall for a minute or two. It was almost as if he felt the subject had been dealt with, the matter over. Marc relaxed. I looked at him carefully, quizzically, raising my eyebrows, looking over my glasses. He smiled, but didn't respond. I wasn't going to let his nonchalance spoil my moment. I grinned. I wasn't going to let him escape decision-making quite so easily.

I'd learned a few years earlier that many men – I can't speak for women, I've never talked intimately with a submissive woman – see kink, SM, leathersex, call it what you will, as therapy because they feel, as slaves, boys or 'submissives', that they can abdicate decision- making to the top, to the master.

The psychology has been well documented, in fiction and by some practitioner therapists. There are the rich and powerful guys who need time to switch off, to escape from their responsibilities. There is something beautifully healing, restorative, about having someone else make the decisions. They don't have to be important decisions. It may be that they are small choices, alternatives that are almost incidental, negligible in day-to-day living. When someone else takes them, their significance grows.

In more than twenty years, I'd learned slowly but steadily that SM represents a myriad of ironies. The nomenclature is wrong, it is misleading and, in the no-time-to-think information culture that ended the twentieth century and began the twenty-first, it presented a wrong impression to society, the media and many people. That's a different argument, I thought, one to get angry about after a glass of wine too many.

It was the irony of decision-making that was important at that moment. Marc had to decide for himself what would allow him to give The Professor the greatest potential pleasure and service. He was the only one who could know what he felt was necessary so that he wouldn't disappoint.

'You don't want to let The Professor down then?' I said, looking challengingly into his eyes.

'No,' Marc replied, dropping his eyes from mine submissively. 'I don't.'

'Don't you think David would help you?'

'I'm sure he will,' Marc replied, looking up again, 'but that might be too late. I don't want to let him down from the start. You know what I mean, Russ, don't you?'

'I do, Marc,' I said. 'That's why we're having this conversation.'

He sighed again, relieved.

'So,' I said, 'where do you think you should start from?'

Marc looked at me surprised. He hadn't expected the question. 'I don't know, Russ. I was hoping you would help.'

It was my turn to nod. I waited for him to continue.

'Perhaps it's best to start somewhere near the beginning? To walk before you try to run?' I suggested, trying to encourage him more.

'Yes,' he said, quickly, 'exactly. It's easier to accelerate than slow down sometimes, especially when someone else is in charge.'

If I hadn't known better, I would have said his expression was flirting with me.

'An hour at a time?' I asked.

'Each?' he said, 'both?'

'Could be,' I said. 'What do you think?'

'It would be a start,' Marc said. 'Increasing to?'

'I don't know,' he said. 'What is The Professor likely to require? I think that should my target, for the time-being at least?'

'I don't know,' I said. 'I know he has an excellent dungeon. It was said to be one of the best equipped private spaces in the mid-west at one time. He could keep you in a cell or a cage for a weekend. Who knows?'

'Build up to twenty-four hours then,' Marc said, 'that seems a sensible minimum to aim for.'

'I'll have to think about this,' I said, 'to plan it for you.'

'I'd appreciate that,' he said.

# Marc progresses

I let Marc drive us home from brunch. I sat quietly, thinking about building up his endurance of bondage. I could use the cage, I thought. I had my pride and joy, a leather straitjacket. I tried to do some mental arithmetic. Working on six weeks before Marc was due to see The Professor, I'd have to have him in bondage four times a week if we were to build up from one hour to twenty-four. The only practical way might be to have him sleeping regularly in the cage.

I didn't think I'd take him as far as quite such long periods wearing a butt plug. Eight hours would be enough, I thought. That would take him through and afternoon and into an evening, or perhaps overnight. The Professor liked holes that would open, but that were not too loose, I thought.

I went into Marc's room as soon as we got home. I took the drawers from his room that contained his underwear, sportswear and Speedos. I put them on the floor in my own room. I was carrying the last when he came up the stairs, carrying his jeans, tee-shirt and boots. He looked surprised, as if he was about to say something. I saw him close his mouth just in time. He's remembered what he put on the paper, I thought.

I saw him waiting at my door as I was about to see what he had. I wanted us both to go out for a run, but it would take me a little time to look through the four full drawers.

'Come with me,' I said as I started to walk down the stairs.

The basement playroom was certainly getting more use now Marc was in the house. The direction his life was taking meant that it was likely to get even more use in the coming weeks. I felt good about that. It was too good a facility to waste.

When I was a bottom, a slave, I always tried to play, to perform, at a master's home. I remembered what a man called Morgan had written in a newsletter called *Checkmate* in the 1990s. I would show Marc the article.

'If you are playing away from your home area, you can be more relaxed about your personal identification,' Morgan had written, 'you're less likely to run into acquaintances who you wish to keep unaware of your fantasy proclivities ....

'As a submissive, I prefer to make the journey – and I prefer to receive if I am dominating. This way the submissive is not in conflict with social norms,' he had said. I agreed with him entirely.

I was, I hoped, changing Marc's social norms in our own home. Some, clearly, he had already changed himself. This was the next stage in his process of evolution.

'Stay there,' I said to Marc when we reached the steps to the basement. I went down. I turned on the electric heater. He'd need some extra warmth, even for an hour, I thought. I pulled the dog cage from the end wall towards the middle of the room. I opened the door at the end.

'Come down,' I called. I tried not to use his name when issuing orders or instructions. I wasn't sure quite why. It just felt better.

I think I'd again caught him by surprise. I don't think he'd expected some of his requests from the morning to have been taken up quite so quickly.

I didn't give him time to stop when he reached the bottom of the stairs.

'In you go,' I said, holding the door open.

He knelt down and crawled in. The cage was about four feet long and two and a half feet high. It was possible to sit, but with your head bent forward and your chest compressed. It was possible to lie on your back, but with

134

your legs brought up against your stomach. The most comfortable way I knew to survive in that cage for any length of time, was on my side, in a fetal position. You could always stay on all fours, I thought, seeing Marc's position as he went in.

I pushed the door closed and reached to one of the shelves for a padlock. I didn't need a large one. I wondered whether I should tether his hands to one end and his feet to the other. No, I thought, I could do that another time. I just wanted him out of the way for a while, while I went through his underwear and before we went out for a run. It would be better for him to run after some time in that cage, rather than before it, I thought.

'Make yourself as comfortable as you can,' I said. I turned off the light and left.

I made sure the door at the top of the stairs was wedged open. A little light would make its way down, but not a lot. Marc wouldn't be left in complete darkness, not yet. It also allowed me to hear him if he did have problems. There was another thing, I thought as I went back up to the bedroom, I'd have to get a baby monitor. I didn't like leaving someone locked in bondage like that without sufficient safety devices. The smoke alarms would have to be checked too, I thought.

I looked at the clock on the wall. It was twenty minutes past the hour. Marc had a good collection of underwear, jockstraps and Speedos. Just as he had stolen or borrowed some items of mine, I decided I could enjoy his too.

I found the three briefest pairs of Speedos. He could wear those around the house in rotation, I thought. There was a pair of gym shorts, with a pouch front, size small, I noticed, in a shiny blue. He could wear those if he needed to do any chores in the yard. I'd decide on what he was to wear for work, during the week, later.

135

I found some running shorts I liked too. There were two pairs, one white, one black. They were made of an extremely flimsy material. It felt almost like parachute silk, but was an artificial fiber of sort sort. They were white. There was a discrete inner brief. I bet the brief, or at least its outline, could be seen through the outer layer of the white ones. I'd never seen Marc wearing them. I knew why. I smiled. I'd seen him wearing the black ones, but never thought them anything particularly special.

I undid my boots and took off my jeans. I pulled off the 2(x)ist pouch briefs I was wearing and pulled on the black shorts. They felt good. They were very comfortable. They held my cock up against me and pushed my balls forward. I liked that.

I took off my polo shirt too. I found a black tanktop. I put it on and looked in the mirror. I was pleased with what I saw. I found a white tanktop too. That would do for Marc. I smiled. He'd look good in almost see-through white shorts as we ran through our suburban neighborhood.

I went back to his room. I found his running shoes and some white socks. He could change in the basement, I thought, and we could go straight out.

I kept an eye on the clock. I wanted Marc's first session in the cage to last an hour, no more, no less. Time was passing. I went downstairs. I waited patiently on the deck. I'd made sure I'd stayed within earshot of the basement. For the last five minutes or so of the hour, I crept to the top of the staircase. I didn't turn on the lights and I tried to be as quiet as I could. It was just possible to see a figure in the cage. I was relieved that Marc had found the fetal position I had been hoping for. I could see the broadness of his upper back and the Speedos stretched across his butt. I could see his thighs pushed up. He was a pleasant sight. I stood quietly for a few moments, appreciating the view.

He tried to sit up as he heard me come down the stairs when the hour was over. I smiled as he hit his head. He struggled to get himself on to his hands and knees. I unlocked the cage and he crawled out backwards. I looked him up and down. There was a smile on his face and his cock was more prominent in the briefs. I was pleased about that.

'That's the first hour,' I said. I handed him the shorts, singlet and shoes. He looked puzzled.

'We're going for a run,' I said. Marc was rubbing his arms, trying to relieve some of the stiffness that had set in during his time in the cage. I nodded for him to change. I was right. Marc's time inside the metal frame had had an effect on his cock. It was certainly gorged, I noticed as he dropped the briefs and put on the shorts. It wasn't until he was tying the drawstring that he realized which I had chosen. He looked at me again. I smiled.

When we left the house a few moments later, Marc was still shaking his arms. I would have to watch that, I thought, if he was going to spend longer in that cage. Alternatively, I would have to find other ways of restricting him.

'Well?' I said as we ran.

Marc looked at me.

'Yes,' I said. 'Tell me. How do you feel?'

'I'm not sure,' Marc said. 'I'd been scared I might have been bored, you know how much I like to be able to write things down when I think of them, but it wasn't like that.

'When you turned the light off, it became very peaceful, very peaceful indeed,' he said.

'I suddenly realized that there was nothing I could do, nothing at all, except relax. When that happened, I felt quite free. It was very strange. It felt far more like therapy than anything else, Russ,' he said.

'I'd have liked to have been able to stretch, to try some

relaxation exercises, to go with it, but once I'd found that position, it wasn't too uncomfortable. I did start to think about other things, about projects, about jobs that needed doing, but when I realized that I couldn't do anything about them or even make a note or two, my brain changed course. It was almost as if it had shut down.

'Sure,' he said, 'I did have some erotic thoughts. That was beautiful too. It was hard not touching myself. I could very easily have jacked-off. I thought about being there and being found by a master, no offense, Russ, and being ready to be used by him. I hoped he'd find the look of me, there, in a cage, erotic.'

'You were,' I said, quietly. 'You looked good.'

'I tried to put my hands through the wire of the cage, but the mesh was too small. I would have put them through bars, I think, and held them on the outside, to help me resist temptation. I could only just touch fingers from each hand together in your cage, Russ. It did work though. I could feel my cock getting hard, but by hands went nowhere near it.'

I smiled. Marc was learning. I tried to remember how much I'd paid for that dog cage. I wondered if it was possible to get another and link two together, so that it would be possible for Marc to lie down inside. I didn't like the idea of leaving someone with their limbs bent for more than an hour or two. The potential dangers of stress on the joints and muscles, especially at the start, seemed too great.

We only ran for about half an hour, but it was enough. I would try, whenever I could, to ensure that Marc got some exercise after being in bondage. That seemed sensible too Getting muscles working after periods of restriction and enforced rest was important.

I sent Marc to shower as soon as we were back. I went too. The idea of getting him to soap me down did cross my mind. It had been tempting. I smiled as I sent him to the shower in his own room. Hard as it might have been to say no, that pleasure could await The Professor or one of the others Marc was set to serve.

He was waiting at my door when I came out of the shower. It looked as if he'd run a razor over his chest and stomach again. He looked good. It was nice having him around, I thought, for probably the hundredth time.

'Have you done all the chores?' I asked, as I dressed.

'Yes,' he said.

'What were you planning to do?' I chose my words carefully, hoping that I'd let him realize that whatever he had planned might be about to change.

'I have some reading to do,' Marc said. 'I was going to that until it was time to get dinner.'

I left him standing there as I went into his room. I knew now where he kept his small, but extremely practical, collection of toys. There were a few cockrings, some tit clamps, two ball stretchers, some rope and four butt plugs; two cones and two 'door knobs', one small and one larger of each. There was also a reasonably-sized dildo. I picked up the smaller cone plug.

Marc could see it in my hand when I came out of his room.

'The time starts from the moment when you're back here with it in,' I said, handing him the plug. 'Oh, yes, and change into a jockstrap, I'd like to see it in place.'

It didn't take him as long to get the plug in as I thought it might have done. He had said he was out of practice. His sphincter must be very well conditioned, I thought, or it wasn't as out of practice as he'd said.

'Turn and bend over,' I said, when I saw him standing again, head bowed, hands behind his back in my doorway. He did.

I was glad he couldn't see me. I smiled as I saw the black round safety flange outside the hole. I felt a twinge of jealousy for a moment. I wondered if I should plug myself for a while to keep him company. That desire quickly passed. I'd do it another time, I promised myself, when I'd remembered in advance and had left myself time to douche, rather than that afternoon.

I remembered reading a review of a video: A guy renowned as a bottom had taken to topping. In one tape, the reviewer had said, 'there were times when I thought he was wishing someone was doing to him what he was doing to the other guy'. At that moment, I appreciated that feeling exactly.

It was tempting too to lie back on my bed and jerk off over this real-life sculpture in front of me. That was strange. I'd never considered how turned on I would be by Marc's régime. I'd had my own dreams of someone finding me sufficiently attractive to be the focus of masturbation, but I wasn't sure how others felt.

'Marc,' I said, 'stand up and turn round.' I gave him a second.

'I have a question for you,' I said. 'How would you feel if you knew someone was jerking off thinking of you?'

He didn't need to say anything in response. I could see his mouth drop a little. I don't think it was quite the question he'd been expecting. I could however see an erection developing, very firmly and very quickly, inside his jockstrap. That told me all I needed to know. I smiled. I even grinned and laughed a little. I held my finger to my lips and looked down. I felt that in his struggle to find the words he wanted, Marc hadn't realized just how hard and fast his cock had responded for him. It was a magical moment.

As soon as he realized just how prominent the bulge in his jockstrap had become, Marc's face went as red as I was sure the trapped cockhead had become. He bowed his face, partially, I suspected, so that I wouldn't see quite how red he had gone.

'Come here,' I said, sitting on the edge of my bed. 'Come and kneel down here.'

When he was in front of me, I put my hand under his chin and lifted his head. He looked directly into my eyes.

'I understand,' I said. 'There's no need to be embarrassed with me, Marc, you know that. You won't have any choice about embarrassment with The Professor or David. Remember that.'

He nodded. He looked as if he wanted to say something.

'Yes?' I said.

'You know what they say about whores, Russ? That it's a matter of financial necessity? You have to sell your body to survive?'

I nodded. The economics of commercial sex had impinged on my work as a writer.

'That's not the only reason,' Marc said. His head was bowed again now. I wasn't sure whether he was feeling pride or shame. I wanted him to go on, but I didn't want to prompt him too much. I wondered if he'd had the same feelings that I experienced.

'What is, Marc?'

'I'm not sure in a word,' he said. 'It's a need for approval. Those who are forced, financially, economically, to sell themselves and their bodies say it undermines their self-esteem, right? For me, it's great for my self-esteem. If what I am doing, or how I look, can give another guy an erection, an orgasm even, that is so much of a compliment.'

He paused for a while. I said nothing. He would continue when he was ready.

'Russ,' he said, looking up into my eyes. 'I have something to tell you.'

What he'd already said had aroused my suspicions. I nodded for him to say more.

'I used to be on the game.'

I paused too.

'Marc,' I said, 'I must admit that I am not in the least surprised.'

He looked shocked for a moment. I smiled again.

'It doesn't mean I think anything less of you. I still love you as a friend, a brother, you know what. I think I value you more for telling me, for knowing you could trust me and tell me something so intimate.'

I reached for his hands. I had to pull them round from behind his back. I held them for a moment.

'Look,' I said, 'just because some of society regards commercial sex as in some way "bad", it doesn't mean we have to accept that view, at least not without challenging it.

'Sure, I agree that it's wrong that people are forced, have no choice but to sell their bodies and sex, if they are to survive, especially when it is forced. That is bad. But there are those who want to provide such services.

'Okay, I know the idea will sound strange, crazy, to many, but you and I, Marc, we know that feeling.'

I could see his eyes widening. He hadn't expected a confession from me too that afternoon.

'I understand what you did. In a way, I'd love to be able to do that too. There's something very reassuring when someone is prepared to put money in your hand to do something with your body.'

I felt him squeeze my hands. He hadn't done that for a while.

'I want to look good,' Marc said, 'to be good, to provide great sex with a great body, not to disappoint. Being paid, especially by those guys who came back time and again, some quite regularly, confirmed that I was doing that, doing something right. In some ways, the money, the amount didn't matter, it was that feeling of being appreciated.'

I nodded. He looked up at me, almost challenging me.

'Jerk off over me as much as you want to, Russ,' he said. 'I'm flattered, you know that.'

It was my turn to be shocked. I was still sitting, open mouthed on the bed, when he got up and left.

Marc was sitting on the mat when I went downstairs. He looked up at me and smiled again. I wasn't quite sure what to think as I walked past this well-defined young man, sitting on a mat, wearing only a jockstrap and buttplug, to the deck.

The words went through my mind again as I sat down: 'doing to him what he was doing to someone else.' I could feel my own cock hardening. I took a deep breath and smiled.

I let Marc take the plug out when the hour was over. Getting him to eight hours with a plug would be easier than getting him to longer periods of bondage.

We did it though. I did the planning. Marc experienced the bondage. I managed to find an extension to the cage. Within three weeks, he was sleeping in it several nights a week. I'd throw him a comforter and lock the cellar door. I'd had him check the smoke alarms by then, of course. The only major disadvantages were having to get up early to let him out and then waiting for my coffee. I grinned. Marc's training and service was spoiling me. Still, I thought, I'd enjoy it when it lasted.

One of the great bonuses of working from home as a writer was being able to spend that extra hour in bed while others were fighting through their daily commutes. Avoiding that daily hour with your nose in a stranger's armpit on the subway more than compensated for a lower income, I thought.

My own fitness had improved during Marc's overnight bondage training. After a first mug off coffee, while he'd been showering and getting breakfast, I'd used the twenty minutes to get in a morning run. It felt good, psychologically and physically. I usually came home feeling smug, having done some exercise while the neighbors were struggling to round up their children and get them to the school or ready for the bus on time.

The weather that year was kind too. I'd started the month wearing sweat pants. For the last few days before Marc set off to The Professor, I'd ended it running in the skimpy shorts. Yes, I told myself, I do feel better for this. I wondered if I'd be able to maintain the régime while Marc was away in California. Somehow I doubted it.

I'd only started running in my mid-thirties. A good friend had encouraged me. I'd said, one New Year's Eve, that I wanted to try and get to go to the gym regularly. I hadn't expected his enthusiasm, but he'd agreed to join me a couple of times a week. The deal was that as he was a runner and usually went out at the weekend, I'd go with him. The effort had been worth it. I'd altered my eating too. I'd cut out fat and stopped eating cheese and a lot of meat. I boosted my fiber intake too. Within six months, I'd lost nearly forty pounds. By the time I was forty, I had discovered vanity.

I rarely ran on my own at that time. I did it sometimes, when I was feeling very determined or very sanctimonious, but it was hard. When I was out with my training partner, I could keep going for twenty or twenty-five minutes non-stop. Okay, he would run for two hours, but he was several inches taller than I was and had much longer legs. He was built to run. I was constructed more with a gym in mind.

Even so, on my own, I found maintaining a pace for fifteen minutes very difficult indeed. I'd have to work hard to keep in shape while Marc was with The Professor.

Everyone involved had finally sorted out the arrangements. Marc would take the Friday off work and fly out to San Francisco that afternoon. David would meet him at SFO, drive him south and have him ready for The Professor's return from the university later that day. He'd travel in The Professor's uniform; jeans, a white tanktop, polo shirt and boots. He'd also have a denim jacket with him and he'd be wearing a cup jock and cockring.

I'd let him cum on the Monday. He'd been in the cage that evening and plugged. Marc was right handed, so I'd locked his right wrist to the end of the cage. He had, I'd told him, three minutes to jerk himself off, but he wasn't to come before two and a half minutes or he'd be caned. If he hadn't come by the third minute, he'd also be caned, but while he jerked himself off. He could take off his Speedos, but he had to take them right off, using only the one hand, within the time I'd allowed. Seeing that struggle was nice too. I enjoyed watching the movement in his musculature. I smiled.

I think he'd done it deliberately. I thought he'd been ready to come in that thirty-second window. I couldn't quite see his face well enough to judge whether he was holding back. It certainly looked as if the speed of his hand had slowed considerably.

'Oh dear,' I said, when the time had run out.

I unlocked the cage and Marc's hand from the end. I beckoned for him to push the cage to one side and pull out the frame used for beatings. I bent him over it. I picked a cane from the rack on the wall. I could see his hand going back to his cock.

'No,' I said, 'I've changed my mind.'

145

He looked at me as if I had been wholly unreasonable and unfair.

'The top's prerogative,' I said, smiling at him again. 'Twelve strokes, you then have a minute. When you feel yourself cumming, start counting down from ten. I'll beat you as you cum. If you're not there within that minute, you'll get another twelve and then another minute.

Do you understand?'

Marc nodded.

'And the ten seconds after you cum are for me, okay?'

He looked at me suspiciously. I waited. He wanted to cum. He wasn't going to say no. I had to wait a few seconds more, but eventually, the nod came.

It was a routine I'd seen The Professor use at one of the runs. I'd also seen it in videos. I hadn't told Marc about it. I hoped he'd experience it again, sometime over the coming three weeks.

'When you cum, catch it in the Speedos,' I added. 'But put them in your mouth first. You may find a gag helpful.'

I could see that Marc's cock was still hard. I wondered if the erection would still be as strong after the first set of strokes.

I let the cane swish down, feeling its balance. My technique had improved too over the last few weeks. I'd caned Marc enough for my judgment and accuracy to have become noticeably more accurate. He now knew he'd have a nice set of bruises across his butt. I wanted these to last long enough to catch The Professor's attention. I knew that David would notice the remnants of bruises others had might have considered long gone. He'd want to know from Marc what had happened. I wondered if The Professor would too.

I hadn't realized until that moment that it was the first time I'd caned Marc while he was plugged. I took a step

146

closer to him and felt how far the flange of the rubber projected past the line of his cheeks. It was a little, but not far. Each time the cane hit him, the plug would be pushed further in too, perhaps even against his prostate. I pressed it now. It didn't have to go more than a few millimeters before it hit that target. I'd try and place the first stokes hits across the plug, and then some above and below it, I thought. I was glad I'd chosen a fairly heavy cane.

I got myself into a comfortable position, the angle to Marc just as I wanted. I set my feet apart. I took a deep breath and brought the cane down for the first time.

I heard Marc grunt into the Speedos in his mouth. It sounded more like him trying to count and say thank you than complain. Of course, it may have been a reaction to the plug hitting his prostate. I wondered.

I brought the next five down in quick succession. Marc grunted as soon as he could after each had hit him. The bruises were starting to develop well, even in that time, I thought.

I moved an inch or two, before continuing. The new position allowed me to land three strokes above the first six and three below. Again, each was greeted with a groan from Marc. I think he felt them differently. There wasn't the distraction of the plug hitting the prostate or absorbing some of the impact.

'A minute,' I said, 'starting now,' as soon as the last stroke of the twelve had found its mark. I noted the time on the clock. Marc's cock had softened a little, I noticed as I moved round him. He was jerking hard with his right hand, the cock responding and hardening. He'd taken the Speedos from his mouth with his left and was holding them close to the cock. I looked at his face. I could see from his eyes that he didn't really want another twelve, not at that moment.

147

I looked at the clock; twenty seconds had passed. His erection was fiercer now. He had closed his eyes. He was pumping as hard as he could. It looked as if he was using every ounce of his will power to pull the cum through from his prostate to his urethra.

Thirty seconds. He was bending forward and his muscles were tightening. Perhaps I wasn't going to get the opportunity for another twelve after all. Forty seconds, I could see his cock reddening more. Forty five.

'Ten,' he said, quietly. I moved quickly and brought the cane down across his butt, trying to hit the end of the plug.

There was a gasp.

'Nine.' I moved and landed the cane on the developing bruises above the plug end. There was another gasp.

'Eight.' I hit below the plug.

'Seven.' I went for the plug again.

'Six.' I wasn't going to set a pattern; I hit below it.

'Five'. I chose the plug end.

Marc was gasping more now. His breathing was quicker. He'd gone over the minute, but I hadn't the heart to stop him. I was enjoying it too much now. I could see the muscles in his V-shaped back and the beautiful curves of the cheeks of his butt. I felt my own cock hardening.

'Four,' he said. I went for the flesh above the plug. I increased the force of the blow. I noticed the reaction. Marc's pace on his cock slowed for a second as he grimaced and caught his breath.

'Three,' he said a moment later, his right arm again working hard and regularly. I hit the plug end. His head came back. I could see him panting. It was a wonderful sight.

'Two.' I went above the plug. I knew what I was doing now.

'One.' I raised my arm further than I'd done before. I was aiming for the end of the plug. I hit it.

'Now,' I said. I just had time to raise my arm again as Marc's convulsions started. I put all the effort I could into bringing the cane down, aiming for the fleshiest part of his cheeks, below the flange of the buttplug. The cane hit him at exactly the right moment. His head flew back. He started to scream. I could see the tears streaming from his eyes, but his lips wavering backwards and forwards between a huge 'ow' and an endorphin-high 'ah'.

Despite his best efforts, he failed to catch the first cum as he ejaculated. He was catching more in the Speedos as I dropped the cane and turned him to face me.

'My ten seconds,' I said. There was a beautiful horror in his eyes.

I grabbed the Speedos and pushed them back into his mouth. He started sucking his own cum off them immediately.

I looked at the clock as I took his balls between my thumbs and forefingers.

'Ten,' I said as I started squeezing. Marc was still high as I increased the pressure.

'Nine,' I counted slowly, building the intensity. I could see from his eyes that the pain was already reaching the sides of his stomach.

'Eight'. I smiled and pressed a little more.

'Seven.' I was watching. He wanted to open his mouth, but he was afraid of dropping the briefs. I grinned.

'Six.' He gasped. He nearly lost them, but he brought his lips together just in time.

'Five.' He started sucking harder trying.

'Four.' Marc was bending forward now. I could see from his eyes that the feeling was concentrated in the sides of his stomach.

'Three.' He held the Speedos in his teeth and dragged air passed them to breathe through his mouth. His chest was heaving now.

'Two.' I could feel my own erection inside my jeans now, almost bursting to escape.

'One.' I took a deep breath and squeezed Marc's balls as hard as I could.

The second was over. I let go. Marc's mouth flew open. I caught the Speedos. He was panting and gasping. The tears were rolling down his cheeks. He was bent forward with the pain.

'Behave like that for The Professor, Marc,' I whispered into his ear, 'And we should both be very proud.'

I held him close to me while he fought to bring his breathing under control. I pulled off my own tanktop. It was wonderful to feel his warm, hard flesh next to mine. I could feel his cock, still hard against the denim on my thigh.

Then, very slowly, I felt him kneeling. I let him do it. He put his head on the ground between my legs. It was an awesome gesture. He moved elegantly and gently kissed each of my feet. He noticed where some cum had been spilled on the floor. He moved the few inches needed to reach it. He opened his mouth and licked it up.

He knelt up. He put his hands behind his back. He leaned gently forward and kissed the outline of each of my balls under my jeans, and then my cock.

'Thank you,' he said, bowing his head again.

I bent forward and lifted his head. His eyes were closed. I kissed him very gently on the lips.

'Get cleaned up in your own time,' I whispered.

My cock was still fully erect when I got into the shower. I hardly had to touch myself before I erupted. The spurts from my cock shot up the tiles of the shower cubicle. I put a hand against the wall to steady myself. I was panting hard too.

I felt strangely guilty. It was as if I was far too turned on by what I'd been doing to Marc.

I had to confess to myself that I did enjoy this action. I'd been finding it exciting to put him into bondage in an evening. I'd had him tied up against a post. I'd had him in a straitjacket. I'd had him in the cage. I'd tried mixing different combinations and sensations. I'd put him in the cage while wearing a straitjacket.

I'd tied him to the pole with a padlock around his balls. That had been simple and very effective. He had had his hands free then. I'd found a padlock with a large clasp in a local store. It was just big enough for Marc's ballsac and a ring attached to the upright pole.

I'd smiled the first time I'd tried it. Marc had been so beautifully frustrated by it. He'd been able to move about as far as his sac could stretch. That was all. There was nothing he could do but stay there.

I kept checking on him every few minutes when I did that.

As soon as I went down the stairs to the basement, he'd put his hands behind his back and his cock would get hard. It was a beautiful sight. I trusted him not to touch himself when I wasn't there. It must have been a great temptation. I'd thought about installing a video camera, so I could watch him from the office. If the arrangement was to have been longer-lasting, I probably would have done.

These thoughts all ran through my mind as I enjoyed the hot water running down my body. I knew too that I'd miss him.

I hate goodbyes. I like partings to be sweet, yes, but swift too. I knew my relationship with Marc would never be the same. Despite the agreement that my mentoring would end in a few months' time, and my promise to take him to the September run, I could see that he was committing himself far more deeply to his vocation than I ever could.

Few words were spoken between us during those final days. Marc did what he had to do around the house. He exercised. He was plugged and caged too. We no longer needed to exchange words. We both knew that. He'd call me Sir when he had to. I tried to avoid using his name.

I'd waited patiently when that Friday finally came. Marc had taken care of breakfast. He packed what he had to pack. He'd been for a run, then showered, douched and dressed ready for the flight.

I got up when I heard him put his bags down beside the front door. I could see him checking the printed-out flight confirmation and boarding pass as I approached.

He looked up. There were tears in the corner of his eyes. I hoped he wouldn't cry. I would have lost it if he had.

Instead, he reached for the keys to the pick-up.

We'd agreed that I'd come to the airport with him and then bring the vehicle back to the house. I'd also said I'd pick him up when he came home.

I was surprised when he handed me the keys.

'You drive, please,' he said, very quietly. 'I'm too nervous.'

I nodded as I took the keys.

I waited a moment, breathing deeply.

I found myself not wanting him to go, but I knew he had to. I knew too that his life was about to change, for ever.

Marc looked surprised when I reached for both his hands. I held them.

I turned him to face me. I looked him directly in the eyes.

'Be confident,' I said. 'I know you can do it. You'll endure some of it, enjoy even more, I hope.'

I could feel him relax. His grip on my hands loosened a little. He smiled.

'I know you can do it, Marc. The Professor does. David does. Sure, they'll test you, challenge you. It may seem that they're asking you to achieve the impossible, that their expectations are unrealistic, but they'll support, encourage, nurture you too. It's in their best interests to do that.'

Marc was starting to grin. He squeezed my hands.

'Yes, Russ,' he said, so quietly I could hardly hear him, 'I appreciate that. It's the beautiful paradox of power relationships. The powerful must dominate, but they must also care. Remembering the second while submitting to the first isn't easy. I've learned that from you. I hope I will learn it more in the next month.'

He squeezed my hands again as he leaned forward and kissed me on the lips.

'Thank you, Russ,' he said. 'I appreciate this more than I can express, more than you'll ever know.'

I agreed with the first, not the second. I could, I thought, fully grasp the immensity of his actions, his commitment and his gratitude.

He kissed me again.

'I love you, you know that.'

I did, but I didn't know how to define that love. That didn't matter, certainly not at that moment.

'I love you too, Marc,' I said, leaning forward to take my turn to kiss him. I squeezed his hands too.

'You have the copy of the original letter, from David?' I asked.

He pointed to a pocket on the outside of his bag.

'Good,' I said, trying to be as encouraging as I could. 'Read it and think about it on the plane. Meditate quietly. Be ready to place yourself into The Professor's hands. Be courteous. Behave as if he was with you. Make him proud of you, Marc. Be proud of yourself.'

We kissed again, but more quickly.

Marc opened the door. He locked it behind me then

moved quickly to the pick-up, putting his bag in the back and opening the driver's door for me.

We said nothing during the drive to the airport. Marc reached for my hand at one point. He hesitated. I saw the gesture, so I reached for his. We found a new, even deeper, intimacy silently holding hands during that drive.

I was about to speak as I pulled up outside the departures area at the airport. Marc had let go of my hand by then. He put a finger to his lips, beseeching me to preserve the moment in silence, rather than spoiling it with words.

I respected his wishes as he got out and retrieved his bags from the back.

I wound the window down as he approached me. He reached for my hand, held it, squeezed it, then bent down and kissed me gently on the lips. I thought I could just read the words 'thank you' on his as I fought to keep the tears from my eyes.

I must have blinked.

When I looked again, he was gone. All I could see was the revolving airport door.

The horn of a car behind me, wanting the space to pull in, brought me back to my senses. I quickly looked round, put the pick-up into gear and pulled out, making my way carefully into the flow of traffic. I can't remember driving out of the airport. I do recall sitting in the pick-up in a parking lot crying my eyes out. I don't know how long I was there. I don't know to this day whether my tears were of sadness, for Marc's departure, or of happiness, jealousy even, for what he was going in to. I do know that the house that evening, that weekend, felt very empty indeed.

I'd been feeling low on the Sunday morning, drinking coffee, when the e-mail arrived from David.

All it said was 'he's ok'. I sat back, relieved, but still as curious as hell. I might even have been jealous.

# Academic life; Marc tells his story

Eighteen months passed before I saw Marc again. He had e-mailed me and written, a proper, hand-written, old-fashioned letter to thank me, and again with a card at Christmas, but it wasn't until the run at the end of the following summer that we actually got to see one another and I had a chance to understand why he had never come back.

We sat, quietly beside the pool one afternoon, appreciating the Michigan sun as he told me his story. He remembered everything well, as if he'd been waiting for this moment, knowing that I'd want a full, very detailed account of what had happened.

He'd cried on the plane too, Marc revealed, when we'd left each other that day at the airport, until he realized that he really should be looking forward, preparing himself, rather than looking back. However good an experience had been, he said, the past was always the past.

When me met again, after so long, he told me his story, in his own words.

As soon as I could, Marc told me, I'd reached up to the overhead locker and pulled the copy of David's letter from my bag. I kept reading and re-reading it. I thought I could almost recite it by heart.

I'd been lucky on the flight. The senior flight attendant had seen me board and quickly up-graded me. I think he just liked to look, but he was attentive. It also meant I was among the first off the plane when we got to SFO.

I hadn't got out of the baggage reclaim long when David pulled up in the truck. I'd lifted my bigger case into the back when he came round to me. He didn't say anything, but put my carry-on bag in to the cab, behind the seats. I stood, watching, realizing that I should put my hands behind my back.

David looked me up and down and then put a hand on my shoulder, pushing me firmly downwards. Even though there were people around, looking for their rides or cabs, I obeyed. I knelt. I didn't see what David was doing, but I very soon felt his hands around my neck. A collar was being locked on to me. As soon as it was in place, David put his hands under my arms and lifted me to my feet.

'In,' he said, as he turned to walk round the truck.

I'd hardly got the door closed before he was pulling away. I tried to look at him more. I could see the military high'n'tight haircut, and his muscled arms on the steering wheel, but not a lot else.

We hadn't got more than a few hundred yards from the terminal building before David spoke again.

'Boots off,' he said. I did as I was told. It was hard, leaning forward, strapped in by the seat belt, undoing the laces and pulling off the boots, but I'd done it by the time we'd reached the freeway.

He indicated that I should put the boots behind the seat.

'And the socks,' he said.

They came off. I folded them and tucked them into the top of one of the boots. I wondered how much more of a strip I'd be doing as we pulled across the southbound, Friday afternoon traffic.

'The polo shirt.'

Again, the seat belts got in the way, but I managed. I folded the shirt and put it on the ledge in front of me. I was glad for the tanktop.

'And the jeans.'

I was glad that the truck was higher than most of the cars then. Only truck drivers would be able to look down and see my naked legs. If I pulled the tanktop down over the jock, they'd never know that I wasn't wearing shorts, I thought, as

I raised my hips to undo the button fly. It took some effort, but I got the jeans off. In the cramped space of the cab, and without wanting to disturb David's driving, I folded them as best I could.

I was confused then. Part of me was wanting get excited by the submissiveness, the obedience, even the aspect of display and humiliation, but nervousness was stopping that. David had stayed silent. I'd been hoping he would have been more friendly, welcoming, supportive, but no. He was silent and distant. I wanted warmth, not this cold disdain.

I was trying to deal with all these competing thoughts when he finally spoke again.

'Open the glove compartment,' he said. 'Put on everything that's there.'

I found the little handle and pulled it. The compartment flew open.

'Look at what's there,' said David as I stared, open-mouthed, at what looked like a mass of black leather and chain, 'and think about it. You'll need to get some things in place first.'

I started to lift the items out and put them on the seat beside me. There wasn't as much as I'd immediately thought. I thought the restraints with a short chain locked between them were for my wrists, until I saw the rounded Hyatt handcuffs. I could see a gag, a blindfold, some nipple clamps and a butt plug. Beside that were two sachets of lube.

I put the ankle restraints on first, then opened one of the sachets of lube. There was a box of tissues next to the cup rests between the seats, so I lifted my butt again and put a few between me and the seat. I then used the second sachet to lube up the plug. My mind was still flying. My cock had started to get hard inside the cup jock, but I still felt embarrassed about trying to get a cone-shaped piece of rubber into my ass while being driven at seventy miles an hour down the freeway.

I managed to get myself into a position where my sitting weight was gently forcing the plug in. I rocked backwards and forwards a little as the widest bit reached my sphincter. I put the nipple clamps on next, or rather, I took a deep breath and put the clamps on. They were hard beasts. I was sure I saw David grin, just for an instant, beside me, but he was hiding his feelings well.

The gag went in next. It was a rubber ball, not too big, that sat behind my teeth, buckled from the back. I put the blindfold ready to pull down. Last of all, I snapped one, then the second, hand cuff into place. Inside the cup jock, my cock had finally become fully erect. I hoped that David's driving was good as I lifted both hands up to pull the blindfold down and shut off my view of the freeway. I didn't know whether to be excited or scared by the thought of a fire officer pulling this nearly naked man in bondage from a freeway auto wreck.

I'd been sitting quietly for a few minutes before David spoke.

'That's better, Marc,' he said.

I could feel him moving, but didn't know what he was doing until I felt his lips on my shoulder.

'Welcome to California,' he said. 'Welcome to your new life.'

His gesture and warmth came as a relief.

'Thank you, Sir,' I said, wishing I could reach out and hold his hand or caress him in some way. He must have been sensing my need, because within seconds his hand was holding my thigh.

'That's a good start, Marc. Total obedience, whatever the circumstances, does you proud. But then, I wouldn't really have expected anything less.'

I wished I could do more than gurgle behind the gag.

'Anyway, Marc, I'm not your Sir; The Professor is. He's your Master too for the next month. You should call me Mister David. Mister, not Master. Is that clear?'

I gurgled again and nodded.

'Good. Now, bring your knees a little closer together. Put a hand down on each knee.'

I did as I was told.

'That's the way you'll always sit in a car now, whenever you're not driving, or whenever you're not told to be doing something else. You're to face ahead of you too.'

I obeyed. Sitting more upright pushed the plug further into my hole. I must have flinched, because David noticed something.

'Happy boy?' he asked.

I nodded again.

David talked more as he drove. He told me – as you know – that there was a formality to life in The Professor's home, that there were always protocols to be observed, and rules to be obeyed. But, he'd said, The Professor is keen that we do not take ourselves too seriously. We must never lose our sense of humor nor must we lose our sense of the ridiculous. I'd nodded again when David had told me that. I think I'd gurgled more too. Trying to swallow was hard with the gag in place, and just having something, anything, in my mouth was making me salivate more. I wondered how long the two holes would be filled with the pieces of rubber.

It took me a while to notice that we'd slowed down, that there were more stops and turns. I guessed that the truck had left the freeway and that we were now making our way along surface streets towards The Professor's home. I started to get nervous again. David noticed. He slapped me on the thigh.

'Relax,' he said, an order that was easier said than obeyed.

When the sounds of the truck's tyres changed again, to gravel under the wheels rather than the paving of the streets, I guessed we must have reached the house.

When we stopped, David spoke again. 'Don't move,' he said, 'until I tell you.'

I thought of something you'd told me in the past, Russ, said Marc, that The Professor's house was secluded, so I didn't worry too much about being nearly naked sitting there in the truck.

I could feel my heart beating as David opened his door and got out. I heard him open the back and lift out my case. I listened as his boots crunched across the gravel and as he climbed some steps. I was aware of the smell of newly-mown grass too. I could feel the air on my shoulders and my legs. It was warm, but there was a light breeze. Deprived of sight and movement, all I could do was revel in the senses that I had left.

I was breathing deeply, trying to identify some of the scents when I heard boots coming back across the gravel.

'Out.'

David's order was clear.

The door beside me opened.

I let go of my knees and turned, letting my feet hang over the edge. I felt strong hands under my arms, supporting me. I let myself follow as I was half-lifted on to the ground.

The gravel was sharp against my feet. I felt my head being pushed upwards, then a click and a tug against my neck. David had leashed me.

'When we reach the porch, Marc, you crawl, on all fours, wag that butt for me, show me the tail in your hole.'

I followed, silently and obediently as he led me across the driveway.

The stones were sharp on my feet. I tried to tread carefully, hoping I wasn't going too slowly. I couldn't have moved too fast, even if I'd wanted to, the chain between my ankles wouldn't have let me.

I was starting to wonder how far we had to go when the sound of David's pace suddenly changed. He was on wooden steps, I could tell. I crept forward until I felt the first edge against my calf. I lifted my foot cautiously. I should, I suddenly thought, have counted the steps when David had used them before. It was too late now.

I nearly fell when I lifted my leg for a final step that wasn't there. I could hear David snigger as he turned and caught me.

'Now's the time to kneel and crawl,' he said as he helped me lower myself.

Progress after that was slow. The inch of chain between the handcuffs meant that it was more of a shuffle than crawling. I remember passing over the wood of the deck, a ridge of the door frame, tiles, carpet, and then finally more tiles.

I stopped when I felt David's boots and legs right in front of me.

'Kneel,' he said.

I sat back on my haunches. I could feel saliva dribbling out of the sides of my mouth.

I heard him moving around for a bit after that. I think he must have been putting my bags away and the clothes and boots I'd taken off when we were in the truck.

I heard him pull up a chair, something to sit on, next. I was aware that David was in front of me. He seemed different. It took me a few moments to realize that he no longer had his jeans on.

I had to blink when he lifted the blindfold from my eyes. The room was bright, and it took me a few seconds to adjust.

When normality returned, I was greeted with the most

beautiful vision. David, Mister David, was wearing a black tanktop and tight spandex square-cut shorts, the red-and-black stripes meeting in a V between his legs. His bulge looked amazing. If I'd been more relaxed, I might have shot my load at that moment.

I must have shown my admiration some how, because David bent forward and kissed me, first on the forehead and then, opening his mouth because of the gag, on my lips.

'Good boy, he said, beaming at me.

He smiled too as he reached under me to check that the plug was still in place. I let my head fall back as I tried to scream when he lifted the clamps that were still attached to my nipples. I'd become accustomed to that sensation until that moment. I spluttered as saliva ran back into my throat behind the gag, making David smile all the more.

I could see him thinking.

'Now,' he said, as much to himself, I think, as to me, 'what are we going to do with you?'

I must have been more tired than I realized, because I can't remember such detail after that. I do recall being unlocked, being showered, being shown the room which David and I would be sharing.

It was a large room, sparsely furnished. There were two wooden- framed single beds, each with ring bolts through the corner posts, plenty of closet space and French windows opening onto the back yard. There were nightstands beside each bed and thick rugs on the wooden floor.

Off this main space were other rooms. One was a bathroom, with a toilet and shower; the other office space, with two desks and computers and a music system. I didn't notice at first, but there were no doors. There was no seat to the toilet either, but the shower did have two great extra douche attachments. One was fixed to the wall, about eighteen inches up. It swiveled, so you could either squat down on it or lie down, letting the water run deep into you. The other rooms were walk-in closets.

David unlocked my hands to show me my closet space. He'd already unpacked my bags, probably checking that I'd obeyed the instructions, and laid out my clothes on the shelves. My boots, trainers and business shoes were in a tidy line under the lowermost shelf.

'We keep everything like this, always,' David told me. 'When The Professor feels he wants an excuse for punishment, he'll make a spot check. If the waistband of a jockstrap isn't exactly parallel to the wall, you'll probably know about it.'

I must have looked shocked. David grinned as he told me more.

'I know that seems extraordinary anal, but it's part of the training,' he said. 'We mustn't, ever, become complacent. He'll suddenly demand that we change the layout of this room, the closets, the kitchen, so familiarity never has a chance to breed any contempt. We mustn't take anything, least of all The Professor, for granted.'

I didn't get to meet The Professor until later that evening.

David released me from the ankle restraints, the collar, took out the gag and the plug, and even took off the nipple clamps before taking me into the bathroom.

I was thoroughly cleaned out and shaved from my eyebrows downwards. Well, all the hair was removed. David used some clippers first, trimming everything down to almost nothing. I'd been shaving my cock, balls and hole regularly, every since The Professor had permitted the visit, but nothing else. David used some cream on me. That felt and smelled strange, but it did its job. After a few minutes just standing there, the hair started to almost dissolve. It would, David told me, leave me far smoother for longer. If I did start to feel any stubble, if he or The Professor started to feel any stubble, I'd probably be ordered to shave again, immediately. The cock, ball and hole shaving would continue, David said, every morning, with one addition: the arm pits.

We'd toured the house after that. David showed me the sitting room, dining room, the deck, The Professor's study, his TV and music room, the kitchen and his personal small bathroom on this floor. Upstairs, he'd shown me The Professor's room, the closets and the bathroom, the two guest rooms too, each with their own bathrooms. Between The Professor's room and the main guest room were spaces that, I suspected, had once been closets too. Now, they were miniature dungeons. Each had a door from the bedrooms, but there was also a door between them, meaning that the two spaces could be combined or reached from either, or both, bedrooms at the same time.

Each contained a cage and an office-like moveable set of stacking plastic trays containing a range of toys, as well as condoms, several types of lube, paper and cloth towels. Everything, I suspected, had been thought about. I was still staring at the selection of floggers and paddles on the walls when David spoke.

'Sometimes The Professor likes company at night,' he said.

I looked at him. I could see experience in his eyes. He reached for my hand as I smiled.

'You'll probably find that out for yourself very soon,' he added.

I had no doubt of that. I suspected that The Professor would have been plotting for a while now, working out some formal training, but also leaving time and space for the spontaneous.

David prepared me well for The Professor that first evening. He plugged me again and gave me a protein drink.

'I hope you have no problems with feeling hungry or thirsty, Marc,' he said, 'because you know you'll only drink and eat what you're given or allowed. That is clear, isn't it?'

I'd nodded.

'Even when you're at work, or going to and from work, you may drink as much water as you like, but nothing else that hasn't been explicitly permitted.'

I was left kneeling in 'our' room when The Professor arrived home.

David went to take him a drink, then serve him dinner.

My mind was all over the place during that hour or so. I was naked apart from the plug. I could easily have touched myself, but I didn't.

I could hear David in the kitchen and the occasional words exchanged between them, so I assumed that they would have heard me, if I'd been tempted to get up and move around. I tried to see as much as I could out of the French doors. I could see impressive shrubs and a neatly-trimmed lawn. I thought back to a story by John Preston that I'd read. Trainee slaves had been put to work on a master's estate by cutting the laws with nail scissors. I couldn't help wondering whether The Professor did the same. I'd cut lawns, but always with mowers, never scissors. I wondered what the experience would be like.

David smiled at me when he came back into the room. I looked up, but as nothing was said, I stayed where I was. I heard him in the bathroom, and I could occasionally seem him in a full-length mirror. I saw him take off his brown work boots and the beautiful, striped shorts.

I felt my mouth drop in awe as I could a glance of David's huge cock and balls. That, I said to myself, smiling, was why the shorts had bulged so much. I hoped I'd be allowed to pay homage to that magnificent piece of man-meat some time. I could lick it and worship for hours, I thought, just as I could lick and worship David's beautifully muscled body.

For a few seconds, The Professor was banished from my thoughts. I continue to watch as David showered and ran a razor over parts of his body before squatting on the douche. I watched as he opened a cupboard, took out what looked like a metal plug and some lube. I saw his eyes close as he bent forward to push the heavy piece of aluminum into place. I thought I saw a flicker of a smile cross his lips as his sphincter closed around it, holding it rightfully in place.

I waited patiently while he dried himself. He smiled at me but still said nothing as he came out of the bathroom and walked to the other closet. I couldn't really see what he was carrying, other than a pair of highly-polished knee-high black boots, when he came out.

I think David was showing off, teasing me deliberately when he sat down on the bed. He picked up a leather strap and, right in front of me, spread his legs to snap it into place. It pushed each of his sizeable balls out to the side. I could see his cock starting to swell. I thought he'd picked up a jockstrap when he turned round, but the bright white underwear with the wide, jock-like waistband had a thong back.

I wished I could have helped, but enjoyed the view as the he pulled the thong into place, holding the plug even more securely in his hole. Although he had his back to me, I could see him adjusting his cock and balls inside the pouch. When he turned, the image was amazing. His cock was held vertically against his shaven pubic area, the balls framed to each side. I had to exercise every iota of self-control in my body and mind not to edge forward, my tongue hanging out. David was laughing quietly to himself. He could see my eyes standing out from their sockets, taking in his beauty.

I wouldn't have worried too much about the cock underneath, I found myself thinking, if I was allowed to work that pouch, worship the profile within it. My eyebrows rose further when David picked up a pair of tights from the bed. I'd never been into anything feminine in my life. I knew why, but that's another story, for another time and place. I needn't have worried. As David pulled his toes into the feet of the nylon and then ran the hose up his cleanly-shaved legs, I could see the effect. The musculature of his legs was being emphasized even more. He pulled the material tight around the pouch and his butt. For many of my formative years, the image of male ballet dancers had been one of my hottest fantasies. David had brought it to life.

I was so in thrall of this image that I hadn't realized just how hard my cock had become. David laughed again as he saw it. Strange as it may seem to some, I wasn't worried about it. It was David's cock and balls, his muscular thighs and deep armpits which were my focus. I wasn't sure whether I even wanted sex. I just wanted to hold him, put my arms around his hips and press my face against his bulge, to melt into his supreme manhood. I kept my hands behind my back, holding each wrist firmly to help with my self-control, as David finished dressing.

I didn't think the beauty could increase, but a grey Spandex tanktop produced a contrast to the white tights and a light black leather jacket further added to the effect. When he bent and put on the boots, the icon really had become a deity in his own right. I was speechless. I was almost breathless too.

I must have been sweating by this time, because David went into the bathroom and brought back a small hand towel to wipe my head and arms.

He squatted in front of me.

I looked down between his legs.

I wondered if I'd be able to see the base of the plug, but no, it was held firmly in place by his sphincter and the thong.

'I'm supposed to be silent,' he whispered into my ear, 'but I think you like what you see.'

I was about to say 'yes' when he pressed his finger against my lips.

I nodded instead.

'It's time,' he whispered again as he stood.

I'd take a risk, I thought.

I bent further and kissed David's boots, then as delicately as I could I touched my lips to the cock outlined in the pouch and the nylon tights. I wanted to express my desire, but leave no traces of a mark. I looked up.

David was beaming. I could see the words 'cheeky' and then 'thank you' form silently on his lips.

I glowed.

'Follow me, crawling,' he whispered.

I was putting my hands onto the floor when David bent down again.

'I would have asked you if you were ready,' he said, 'but there's no point as you don't have any choice in the matter. You have to be ready all the time, now, wherever, whenever, but that's part of the joy, the turn-on, isn't it, Marc, having no choice?'

David kissed me briefly on the head.

'Right,' he said. 'Let's go.'

I followed, feeling like a dog at heel, as David led me along the corridor towards The Professor's study.

David stopped at the doorway, and bent to kneel on one knee. I could see the base of the buttplug now, the round flange under the nylon of the tights, but held in place by the thong. His firm butt looked so inviting. I opened my mouth and started to move my tongue towards him. I was frustrated again. David stood up again before my tongue could touch him.

David moved into The Professor's room. I tried to keep my left shoulder as near to his right boot as I could.

When David stopped, I did too.

We were on a mat, thick and deep, between The Professor's desk and a fireplace. I kept my head down, but I could still see the dark wood fire surround.

David moved to turn round.

I followed his boot again, feeling more and more like a dog at an obedience show.

It took a moment, but I realized that I was also immediately in front of a deep, leather winged armchair, the sort that characterize gentlemen's clubs. Despite the intensity of the moment, I found myself remembering the famous story *The Wind in the Willows* and a line about seating for those of a 'sociable disposition'. I also thought of the famous Mapplethorpe photograph of a master, a slave and armchair like this.

I wasn't quite sure what to expect as my Friday night welcome from The Professor. I suspected that the formality and mystery would continue.

You were right about the change, Russ, said Marc. By that time it felt as if I was a world and a lifetime away from my time with you.

I tried to relax, but it wasn't easy. I was aware of David standing beside me. I felt I could smell the leather of the boots and perspiration under his tights. For a moment, I envied The Professor having such living art to appreciate, to see and to touch.

I don't know how long we were there; I kept my eyes down on the mat, but I could hear papers being moved around on the desk, the occasional sound of a pen against paper and fingers on a computer keyboard.

I must have closed my eyes, trying to ignore as much anything as I could, to enter a dream-like state where only my immediate focus would matter. I found peace of some sort, because I could feel the smile on my face when a hand touched each of my shoulders.

It was The Professor.

He was standing in front of the leather armchair.

I looked up, right into his eyes.

I straightened my back as The Professor sat down.

He reached for my hands. I could feel his power, his presence. I was nervous. It must have shown.

He suddenly leant forward and kissed me directly on the lips.

I couldn't hide my surprise.

'Welcome Marc,' said The Professor, quietly, intimately, 'I'm pleased that you're here.'

I nodded.

The Professor noticed my dilemma.

'Yes, Marc, you may speak,' he said.

I tried to respond, but my mouth was dry from the silence. I had to lick my lips and move my tongue before the words would come out.

'Sir, thank you, Sir,' I said, 'thank you for making me so welcome, Sir.'

I can only guess how I looked at that moment, but something must have been right for The Professor.

His smile grew and I could see the light in his eyes. He rubbed my head, affectionately and paternally. I kissed his hand. It seemed the right thing to do.

'Stand Marc,' he said. 'Turn round and bend forward.'

I wobbled as I got to my feet.

The Professor checked the plug in my ass. He pushed it a few times. I closed my eyes and took deep breaths as the pressure on my prostate increased.

'Good,' said The Professor. 'David will make sure that plug stays in place until you get up in the morning. You'll be plugged as soon as you get here each evening, is that clear, Marc?'

I nodded.

'Yes, Sir,' I said.

'If David is busy, then you will douche and do it yourself, understood?'

Again, I nodded. Again, I said, 'yes, Sir.'

'Turn round.'

I did, only to be greeted with the sight of David handing The Professor a pair of nipple clamps linked together with a chain.

Instinctively, I bent forward, sticking my chest out to give The Professor greatest and easiest access to my tits. He pushed me back upright. He looked at David and then, with David following his gaze, at my chest.

David knew what to do. He moved towards me, filling the gap between me and The Professor. I turned slightly making the movement easier for him. I leaned back offering him my nipples. David bent and took the right first in his mouth. He gently tongued then sucked on the flesh, working to make it more fully erect. I felt my cock hardening again, responding to David's stimulation. I opened my eyes. Looking down his back, I could see him holding his hands together. I felt my mouth opening too as the pressure on my nipple increased. David was biting now, his teeth starting to dig into me.

'Five.'

The Professor had started counting.

As he reached 'four' the pressure from David's teeth increased.

I knew what was coming. I tried to breathe more deeply, more slowly, but concentrating against such intense stimulation was difficult.

'Three'.

I bit my lips.

'Two'.

I grimaced.

My eyes were tightly shut now, my teeth clenched and my lips flared. I inhaled deeply.

'And, and, and ....'

The Professor drew the words out as David bit even harder.

'One,' he said finally.

David let go with his mouth, but almost before I'd realized that he'd let go, the first clamp was in place.

'Ah!'

My eyes flew open. The air from my throat made the sound, but with nothing from my vocal chords. It was really no more than a sudden breath, but The Professor and David both noticed.

David raised his hand, as if to hit me, but The Professor grabbed it and stopped him.

'He knows,' said The Professor. 'He doesn't need to be told; unless he does it again, of course.'

The Professor looked at me, his head slightly to one side, checking that I'd understood.

'Yes, Sir,' I said. 'I understand.'

The Professor smiled.

David was expressionless.

The Professor waited a moment, then checked the first nipple before nodding, giving David permission that he should work on the other.

The process was the same.

When The Professor thought David's tongue was achieving the desired effect, he started to count down. This time, there were even more 'ands'.

I could feel my erection starting to subside when The Professor finally said 'one'.

There were tears in my eyes too, when The Professor lifted the chain and gently pulled me closer. He kissed me again.

'Good boy,' he said, as he pulled the chain indicating that I should kneel. I bent forward a little, trying to kiss his fly. I noticed his clothing then for the first time. He was wearing smart black shoes, pinstripe suit trousers and a white shirt, open at the neck and with the sleeves rolled up to his elbows. He looked good. And authoritative.

I was kneeling up when the chain went round my neck. The links were about three-quarters of an inch long. They were black too. I felt a padlock as it snapped into place about two inches down from my neck.

'No one at work should know about that unless you want them to, Marc,' said The Professor, 'especially as you'll be wearing a tie every day.'

I kissed his hand again then, before he again lifted up my chin.

I saw as he took the leather collar from David. The piece of studded leather was a little more than an inch and a half wide; it looked new. The Professor held it for me to kiss before he placed it around my neck and buckled it at the back.

'That will go on a soon as you get back here every evening,' said The Professor. 'You will come round to the French doors in your room. You will strip, put everything away that needs to go away, hang your suit or work pants, put your shoes to one side ready for cleaning, your shirt in the laundry basket and go and piss. Then, you will go and kneel on the mat. If I am here, then David will tell me of your arrival. I may come and collar you. He might. If I'm not here, then it will be his job. You will show your appreciation appropriately, won't you, Marc?'

I nodded. I wasn't quite sure what The Professor meant by appropriately, but David would be sure to put me right if I needed guidance.

'When you're ready to go to work in a morning, and I'm in, you will come to the door of my office. You will never kneel in your work clothes unless specifically instructed; is that clear? You will stand at the door to my study or beside my breakfast table. You will bow to offer me your neck so this collar can be removed. Similarly, should I not be here, David will remove the collar. Once it is removed, you are not to speak. Also, when you come in, you are never to speak before it is put on. Only slave Marc speaks in this house, and then only when instructed or permitted to do so. Marc of the bank stays outside.'

'Again, I nodded.

I liked this demarcation.

Normally, I don't like commuting, but the few minutes I'd been told it took to reach the light rail system from The Professor's house, together with the ride to downtown San José, would give me time to adjust mentally from one role to the other at the start and end of each work day.

I felt good. By putting on the collar and locking the chain into place, The Professor was also accepting that he would be responsible for much, most, of me for those coming weeks. I looked up into his eyes and kissed his thigh. He must have liked the gesture, because he smiled and rubbed my head again.

'Stand.'

I did as I was told.

The Professor, for the first time, reached for my cock. It was throbbing.

'A first test, boy,' he said. 'Lose it. Lose the erection. As quickly as you can. Let's see how obedient you really can be.'

I was shocked. I'd never tried to do anything like that before.

I wondered how I'd do it. I knew about thinking of waterfalls and the sound of running streams if you wanted to make yourself piss, but never about losing an erection before.

The Professor was enjoying seeing me fight the blood supply.

Let me remind you, Marc,' he said quietly, but very firmly indeed, 'that that cock is now mine. By being here, you have given control of it to me until you leave. You will not touch it again without permission. You will certainly not ejaculate from it. If I say I want the cock attached to Marc's body to be hard, it will be hard. If I say I want the cock attached to Marc's body to be soft, it will be soft.'

If I hadn't been concentrating so hard on trying to will the erection away, I might, for the second time in a day, have shot my load there and then. I started to close my eyes, to increase my concentration.

'Let me show you what I mean, Marc,' he went on. 'David, get hard.'

I watched as his trapped cock seemed to get even bigger. I looked at David's face. His eyes seemed to be focusing on a non- existent horizon. His growing bulge made my challenge even more difficult. I was relieved when I heard The Professor say 'enough'.

I don't know how long it took, but I did it, or most of it.

When my cock was again sagging downwards, rather than pointing towards the ceiling, The Professor handed me a transparent cockring.

'Get everything through that,' he instructed.

I could feel my cock trying to get hard again as I pulled one ball through followed by the other. I nearly crushed my tumescent cock pushing it through the hole last of all. I gasped with disappointment as it seemed to be lengthening again.

'Get him ready, David.'

I didn't have long to wonder what this was for, as David picked up the pieces of white plastic and the cock cage from The Professor's desk. I had to fight my cock again as David's hands went to work. I wished I could enjoy the stimulation, but I also appreciated the effect that denying me the benefits of his ministrations was having. I spread my legs to try to help him as he fixed the cage into place.

I watched as he handed The Professor a small padlock. I knew now what was coming.

'I think this should fit OK, boy,' The Professor said, as he threaded the hasp of the padlock through the white plastic anchoring post. 'If it's too uncomfortable, there's a bigger version. David will check with you.'

I nodded.

'It's not the best design for cleanliness, but David will show you what to do. He will also remove it every few days to make sure that you are properly clean, but you are not, I repeat not, to touch that cock without permission, is that clear?'

I looked down at my dick, now trapped inside its polycarbonate prison. I'd fantasized about chastity control. I'd ever experienced self-control and self- denial, but never for more than a few days at a time. I remembered David's letter. He had mentioned chastity then. He'd also said that it would be unlikely, highly unlikely, I think were the words, that I'd be allowed an orgasm, or an ejaculation, during the weeks that I'd be staying with The Professor. This was coming true, becoming real, I realized. The Professor brought my attention back to the moment.

'Is there anything you have to say, Marc?' he asked.

I thought quickly and hard.

'Yes, Sir,' I said. 'There is.'

'So, speak boy.'

I licked my lips and swallowed.

'Sir, Professor, Sir, I offer you this cock, the caged cock attached to this body, Sir, for you to control, Sir, and to use, Sir, and for your pleasure, whatever that should be, Sir. And thank you, Sir.'

Tears were welling up in my eyes as I formed the words. I'd thought about offering myself as a slave before, but never offering a part of me, especially my cock, in such a particular way. I became aware that this ritual was almost a liturgy, my words an offertory prayer. Supplication, I realized, would soon follow.

I was surprised when The Professor leaned forward and again kissed me, first on the forehead and then on the lips. I felt his hand grasp my balls, and a finger running along the top of the clear plastic surrounding my cock, his cock. I could see as he looked across at David. He looked up and his head moved downwards just a little. It was a gesture of appreciation. From the corner of my eye, I could see David nod too.

'That, Marc,' said The Professor, 'was very beautiful, very beautiful indeed. I thank you very much for your generous offering. Yes, Marc, I shall obtain pleasure from knowing that you have willingly deprived yourself of the excitement of penile stimulation as a mark of your submission to me. I may well use that cock for my pleasure too, young man. Whether you accept that use as pain or pleasure, agony or ecstasy, will only be discovered when, perhaps if, I decide to use it. I thank you nevertheless, Marc. Yes. I thank you too.'

Tears really did flow as The Professor stroked the side of my face.

So, so many stories of 'leather' and 'leather sex', of sado-masochism and 'hard play' were of violence, not the true love and mutual respect that were the foundations of the most fulfilling, satisfying and longest lasting power-relationships.

I think I'd surprised The Professor. I wasn't quite sure why, but I felt that I'd knocked him off course a little, away from the ritual he had planned out for that first evening.

I was aware of David, standing to one side, watching this rite being played out. I looked at this Adonis. I couldn't think of a better expression than 'drop-dead gorgeous' to describe the hard thighs inside the white dance tights and the obscene bulge of his amble cock and balls, offset by the contrast of the black leather jacket and boots.

The Master noticed my gaze too, I think.

'David,' he said as he walked to his desk, 'handcuffs, a gag and a whiskey for me.'

David was light on his feet, even in the heavy boots. I stood where I was, trying not to move a muscle. I looked down. My cock was half-hard, as if it had a mind of its own and didn't know what to do with itself, inside the plastic cage.

I watched as The Professor pulled a plain wooden chair, like a dining chair, from a place beside his desk into the center of the room. He moved back to the armchair and sat down.

'Move the chair, Marc,' he said, 'so it's pointing towards the desk.'

Without acknowledging why, I did as I was told.

David knelt again on one knee at the door waiting for

permission to enter. When he received the necessary nod of approval, he walked to the armchair and, kneeling, offered The Professor the cuffs and the ball gag. As soon as they were taken, he kissed The Professor's feet and fetched the tumbler of whiskey.

This time as he knelt, The Professor indicated that he should put down the glass on the small occasional table beside the chair.

'Open your mouth.'

I caught the instant of surprise in David's eyes as he realized the gag was for him. I watched as The Professor buckled it into place.

'Go and sit on that chair,' he added.

David did as he was told.

'Sit as far forward as you can. Spread your legs.'

I watched as David obeyed.

He sat so he was supported by the top half of his butt. His hole and the butt plug were both forward of the edge.

'Hands behind.'

Again, David obeyed.

The Professor got up slowly, looking at the almost obscene beauty of David's openness. Halfway towards David, he stopped and went to his desk. The Professor had to open a few drawers before he found what he was looking for; another pair of nipple clamps.

He didn't bother moving David's tanktop. He quickly and firmly put a clamp onto each nipple. David smiled as The Professor pulled on the chain between them. He kissed David on the mouth too and then snapped the handcuffs into place so they held David's arms in place behind the chair.

'Kneel,' he said turning to me.

I was on my knees in the few seconds that it took The Professor to walk back to his chair and sit down.

He reached for the whiskey and took a sip. He let the amber liquor run round his mouth before he licked his lips and swallowed. He was savoring the moment. I think both David and I were wondering what would happen next.

'Marc, crawl to David's boots. Then put your mouth to good use. Show him how much you admire his body, worship his muscle, respect every moment he has spent running or in the gym. Start at his toes. You can use your hands too.'

I nodded. I must have done something right to get a reward like this, especially so soon.

'David, get hard.'

I watched as the outline of the man's formidable cock got bigger inside the layers of nylon and spandex. The control he had of his body amazed me. His obedience did too. I watched as David let his head back and his breathing deepened.

'You are not,' The Professor added, addressing David, 'even to think about cumming.'

The Professor sat back.

'Go,' he said to me.

I did.

I crawled round until I was kneeling in front of David's boots. I put my weight on my forearms as I brought my mouth to the toe. I started licking.

I licked the soles. I rubbed David's great thighs through the nylon of the tights. The sensation was new to me but delicate and delicious as if the thin material was adding a layer of skin, heightening the subtlety and grace of the contact. Those who believed intensity was directly linked to the strength and energy put behind a flogger or whip were wrong. The stimulation of the nerve endings by the most gentle of strokes and touches could be far, far more sublime and powerful. I intended to show David, and The Professor, what I could do and where I could take him.

I don't know how long The Professor let me do this. I do know that when he stopped me, David's pouch was saturated with my saliva, the cock inside was twitching, his head was back, his eyes were closed and his breathing exceedingly deep. I'd forgotten about the cock attached to my body altogether, locked away as it was.

I looked up when The Professor tapped me on the shoulder. He held his other hand in front of my mouth. The ejaculate was fresh in his palm. I knew instinctively what to do. I licked up the cum, relishing the slightly salty flavor.

That was then I saw The Professor's cock for the first time, standing proudly from his fly. I was reminded of another famous Mapplethorpe photograph, of the man in the polyester suit, only The Professor wasn't black and his suit was probably an expensive worsted.

He let me lick the last drip from his cockhead. I felt truly honored.

I watched as he put his cock away and zipped up his fly. I knelt forward and kissed the subsiding bulge.

He reached for my hand. I followed shuffling on my knees as he returned to the armchair.

He lifted the whiskey tumbler and held it to my mouth. I took a sip. The Professor leant forward and kissed me while the liquor was still damp on my lips.

'That Marc, was beautiful. I think you have talent, potential,' he said. 'I think this will be a good time.'

I bowed my head, acknowledging his generous words.

I think we both looked at David at the same moment. He was still sitting on the edge of the chair. However, his eyes were closed as he relished the bite of the clamps on his nipples.

My eyes met The Professor's. I was a little uneasy, sharing the smile with him, but he tapped my shoulder approvingly.

'Relax, David,' said The Professor. Within seconds, the man's erection was collapsing.

'It's been a long day for you Marc,' added The Professor. 'I think it's time you slept. David will take you through everything else in the morning. That's why we're starting at a weekend.'

I stayed motionless as The Professor moved across the room to fix another whiskey. Then, he unlocked David's hands. He put his feet against David's boots so that released icon could stand.

The moment was approaching I thought, as The Professor sat down again, David standing to one side looking at me.

'I believe,' The Professor said, 'you have something to tell me, Marc.'

I had talked to you Russ about a contract, Marc said to me, and you said The Professor didn't like them. You told me that he established more formal arrangements for longer-serving boys and men such as David, but I remember you saying that I should do something. I also remember you telling The Professor, in an e-mail, on the phone, I can't recall the detail now, that he should let me speak that first evening.

I could feel David's eyes on me, continued Marc. I glanced up at him first, looking at the dampness running from his waist to between his legs, almost as if he'd pissed himself. I think he smiled. I looked to The Professor. He knew I was getting emotional. He reached for my hands and held them. I swallowed hard.

'Sir, Professor, Sir,' I said, looking into his eyes, 'I offer you my soul and body, Sir, for your use and your pleasure, Sir. I offer you my obedience as an expression of my admiration and respect, Sir. I offer you my all as a sign of my affection too, Sir.'

I let my head fall, on to his knees. My tears were rolling on to his suit trousers. I felt his hand on my head. I felt David move. He knelt behind me. I could feel his bulge pressing against the plug inside me. I felt him leaning against my back, holding me as he reached for The Professor's hands. I felt their mouths meet over my head as they kissed.

# Nuts in May

My time with The Professor was everything I'd hoped it would be, expected it to be, and more,' said Marc.

The conversation had been intimate, revelatory, emotional, but had remained within social conventions. I was surprised when Marc unzipped the fly of the shorts he was wearing.

'It's still in place,' he said, indicating the chastity cage. 'I haven't touched my cock since that first night with The Professor.'

I was impressed. Marc noticed. I wasn't sure why, but I felt he'd grown as a person.

That afternoon was still relatively young. Although it was the first full day of the retreat event and the sound of play echoed around the site, others were still enjoying meeting old friends, catching up, making the most of the close, bonding time that came from being shut off from the world outside. For some, just being in or beside the pool in the sunshine that Friday afternoon was the restful change they needed from high-speed corporate responsibilities.

'Do you have to be anywhere?' I asked, conscious that Marc was there as a slave.

'I've done what I have to do for the moment,' he said. 'As long as I'm able to get everything ready for this evening, I'll be okay.'

'You can talk then?' I asked, seeking further clarification.

'In a moment,' Marc responded. 'If I may?'

He was asking permission to leave. I was about to say that he didn't have to do that for me, but quickly thought better of it. 'Of course,' I said, wondering what he was going to do.

I watched as he walked away. His back was in good shape, I noticed, and his butt looked really pert in the shorts. The chain around his ankle glinted in the bright sunlight. Yes, I thought, he's a hot man.

I was still dreaming of play in a gym when he returned, carrying two cups and a large bottle of water.

'Thank you,' I said as Marc knelt down on the concrete beside me.

He smiled.

'So,' I prompted. 'Go on.'

I smiled as Marc bent forward and kissed the Speedos I was wearing. I could have been naked. Nudity was permitted once the site was sealed. I preferred the aesthetic of a bulge and the constraint of the fabric.

'That's one of the few things I miss,' he said, noticing my expression. 'But I do get to appreciate nice underwear on other men.'

I smiled. I understood his predicament.

He stood up again and took off the baggier shorts he was wearing, folding them and putting them neatly away from the wet edge of the pool.

'I'm to be naked as much as possible,' he said, and, turning and bending to show me, 'plugged too.'

I could see others looking at him, from the pool and from the poolside deck. Some eyes were envious, some dominantly appreciative.

'Lie,' I said, 'don't kneel. Get some sun.'

Marc did has he was told. He laid a towel down on the concrete, then lowered himself onto it, face down. The end of the metal plug in his ass was clearly visible. I watched as he pushed the plastic cock cage down, his balls squashed back behind it.

'So, tell me more,' I said.

'The Professor kept his word,' said Marc. 'Life was very much as that first letter, you remember, said it would be. I let him continue his account in his own words.

I think David felt I was invading his territory at first, Marc said, but I reminded him that my assignment to the bank's offices there only lasted a month. After that, we became closer.

He was strict. He paddled me several times that first week, for not being careful enough with what I was doing or by being too slow. He never hit my butt though. That, he said, was for The Professor and The Professor only. He used my thighs. Within hours they were red, by the following morning, they were black and blue.

The Professor was working, so David took me through the house showing me where everything was kept. I had to concentrate hard to try to remember. We cleaned, we dusted, we scrubbed the kitchen and bathroom floors on our hands and knees. I learned how to make sure the grouting between tiles was scrubbed with a toothbrush. The Professor worries about the environment, so he prefers to see his boys and slaves use hard work rather than chemicals to keep his house spotless.

I polished brass as never before; the front door knob could dazzle, Russ, though I say it myself, but it didn't feel arduous. I felt good as I stood on the porch, wearing only the cock cage and some sandals. I wasn't worried about anyone coming onto the property and seeing me like that.

The most frustrating aspect of it was the smell of baking bread that wafted through the house as I worked. The Professor isn't a total food snob, Russ, but he reckons that if he's going to have boys, men, slaves working for him, then they may as well prepare meals which are fresh.

There's a vegetable garden on the property too. Sometimes he'll go himself to a farmer's market on a weekend. Sometimes he'll send a boy. Sometimes he'll go with a boy. If any of his boys work in The City, he'll expect them to go to the Farmers' Market near the Civic Center, to buy fresh food there.

It's good food too. It's not cheap, but there's no waste. David was baking that morning while I cleaned. I wanted to go to the kitchen, to offer to help, but I'd already learned that I had my orders. Every so often, David would come and check on me. He'd flirt with me too. I liked that. He looked so hot in a tight pair of square-cut shorts, his bulge obscenely appearing before he did, his brown work boots, the chain around his ankle resting over socks, and the heavy chain and lock around his neck emphasizing his shoulders and delts.

He'd lift my balls, gently squeeze them, or put one of my nipples between this thumb and forefinger, and start to dig the nails in. If I squirmed or slowed down in my work, he'd slap my already bruised thighs.

'Control, Marc,' he'd tell me, 'it's all about control.'

I'd have to concentrate; it was difficult. I wanted to stop, to appreciate the sensation, to go with it, to try to take more from him, for him, but he was making me separate it from the attention I was paying to the cleaning cloth in my hand.

I asked him about it when he finally allowed me a break.

'It's about discipline,' he'd said. 'A master may want you to endure pain, to enjoy it or to ignore it. He could get

186

pleasure from all or any of those responses, and you have to be able to do what he wants.'

I understood then.

'The more intense the stimulation you can take when you have to ignore it, the more you can take when a master wants you to enjoy it,' David added.

'You have to become accustomed to both very, very intense sensations which don't last more than a few seconds, or deeper, almost throbbing ones which may last hours. You need to learn how your body works separately. However much you may think you can deal with a steady pressure on your balls for several hours, and your brain learns to put the nerve signals coming from them into the background, the flesh is still being affected. It will be more sensitive, so when the stimulation changes, the response in the brain may go off the end of the scale. You have to remember that The Professor's colleagues have included some of the greatest neurologists in the world. They appreciate the chance to observe situations which they may not always be allowed to reproduce in a laboratory.'

David could see he was scaring me.

'It's always done under the most careful supervision,' he said, slightly more compassionately and understandingly, as he reached for my sac and pulled it again as he sent me back to work.

I had lost track of time when David called me for lunch. I was to carry a tray for The Professor out on to the deck at the back of the house. The repast, he called it, was simple. There were pieces of freshly- baked baguette, some camembert cheese and a plate of tomato, sliced with some fresh basil from the herb bed and some finely-chopped scallions. Beside this was a dish of fresh fruit and glasses of iced water and freshly-squeezed orange juice.

187

As I made my way towards The Professor, I didn't notice David following me with the two dog bowls. The Professor was reading. The day's San José *Mercury News* was beside *The Financial Times*, providing both the local and a global perspective. Both David and I were, I had also learned that day, expected to have read both papers well enough to discuss events and the commentators' analyses by early evening.

I waited a few paces away from The Professor. He finished whatever he was reading before indicating that I could approach. I knelt down to put the tray on a table beside him.

He smiled.

'How are you doing Marc?' he asked as I waited on my knees. He couldn't help but see the bruising on my thighs. 'I see David has been taking care of you too.'

I blushed.

'Yes, Sir, he has,' I said.

'You're eating with me today,' he added. 'David has your lunch.'

I looked round.

The military stud was standing a few paces away.

I wasn't sure how to react when I finally noticed the stainless steel bowls.

I think a grin must have crossed my face because The Professor was quick to speak.

'It's not funny, Marc, it's not a laughing matter.' I was chastened. 'It may seem like fun, but it's serious fun. There's a purpose to it.'

'Yes, Sir,' I said, nodding and watching as The Professor indicated where David should put the bowls.

I could see their contents for the first time. I'd never had a salad served like this before, I thought, as I looked at the mixture of leaves, beans, boiled egg and hard cheese.

'Cuffs, I think, David, for you both,' said The Professor as he too looked at the bowls and the food.

David seemed to be back before he had left to obey the instruction. He waited for The Professor's permission to approach then knelt to present the two pairs of Hyatts.

The Professor smiled and nodded as David offered him his wrists. The first pair was snapped into place. The Professor said nothing, but his eyes and his expression ordered me to follow David's example. I held out my hands, watching intrigued as the second pair clicked closed.

'You can balance yourselves,' said The Professor, 'but that's all. Now, let's eat.'

David and I shuffled on our knees towards the bowls. He nodded towards the one which he'd prepared for me. I bent forward. I wondered if he'd put any dressing on the salad. For a second, I had this ridiculous image of myself, kneeling there stark naked in the Saturday sunshine, eating salad from a dog bowl, with mayonnaise all over my nose.

I quickly realized that I needn't have worried.

Perhaps it was the circumstances, but I can remember that lunch so clearly. David had beautifully mixed the colors and textures of the food. It was a joy to lean forward, balancing myself on my knuckles to pick up each piece. I could see

The Professor smiling again as he watched us. He was savoring the cheese and the home-baked loaf, leaning back in his chair as he watched us on our haunches, munching and appreciating each mouthful.

The bowl started to move as it emptied.

The Professor was laughing now as I tried to follow it around on the deck.

David was having the same problem.

'Help each other,' The Professor instructed.

David knew what to do. He positioned himself so his

189

cuffed hands were holding my bowl. I gratefully licked out the final pieces. I held his for him. It wasn't until I looked up that I noticed the tomato pip on his nose. I tried to catch The Professor's eye. We weren't supposed to speak until we'd been spoken to. When he did see me, he spoke.

'Use your mouth,' he said.

So, I did. I carefully, gently moved into a position where I could lick David's face. I delicately removed the pip, then carefully licked the corners of his mouth and the slight gullies that ran to his chin. I licked under it too, clearing the traces of juice that had come from the tomatoes, apples and orange.

David returned the favor. As he finished, he kissed me gently on the lips. To outsiders the sight of two grown men licking each each others' faces so delicately and sensuously may have appeared at least curious, Russ. For us, those few moments were beautifully intense. I had to hold back the tears. I had found a heaven, a totem and an angel.

As the tears welled, I wanted to lean forward and kiss this majestic man even more. I restrained myself, letting my eyes feast upon his impressive physical grace. I tried to put myself in The Professor's position, to get his perspective. I thought again that we must have looked crazy but beautiful, glorious in our bondage and our nakedness, our butts raised as we balanced ourselves on our forearms. I'd never been into doggy play, but I wanted to nuzzle David, to sniff him, to lick him, to show my affection, my respect, my lust purely physically, through grunts, perhaps but not words. Words somehow would have lessened the emotion.

'Stop,' said The Professor suddenly.

We did.

'Lie together.'

David crept round me, then stretched his feet out, turning

on his side. He curled himself around me and then lifted his arms around my head, so I was trapped by his cuffed hands. I edged my butt into his groin.

I could feel his cock stirring inside the tight shorts. I felt his warmth against me. I bent my head to one side and kissed his bicep, then rubbed my face against his skin. I could just feel the hair starting to grow.

I'd never thought of myself as physically imposing. David was, is. He's a big man. He has military bearing. His face and his demeanor exude confidence. But here he was, lying almost naked on a deck with his arms around me, under the gaze of this other man. I'd never known anything like it.

'Relax, Marc,' said The Professor. 'Don't think about it; go with it. Let yourself into the moment.'

His ability to read my thoughts was scary.

'You'll get used to it,' he added.

I closed my eyes, shutting out the power of vision and letting my other senses take over. I could hear birds singing in the hedge at the far side of the garden. I could smell. I tried to breathe slowly and deeply, letting the scents pass through my nose without rushing. I concentrated. Flowers, I wasn't sure which. Grass. And David. There was some perspiration, pheromones. I could feel my skin tingle against his touch, the flesh of his chest and stomach pressing against my back, his thighs against my thighs, his knees against my knees.

I could see a delicious yellowy pink against the back of my eyelids. I could feel the warmth of the sun against my skin. My feet and toes felt so amazingly free. I ran my tongue around my mouth, savoring the aftertaste of the cheese, the apple, the tomato and the soupcon of saliva from the corner of David's mouth. Could I, I wondered, still relish the droplet of sweat that had been on his chin? I felt myself

191

drifting. My hands were in cuffs. A great stud of a man was circling my body but, as I opened my mouth, and pulled in the warm air, I felt freer than I had ever been. I wanted to reach for the sky. I grinned as I gently tested the restraints at my wrists. I wanted this moment to last forever.

I was brought to earth by The Professor's gentle laughter.

Again, he noticed that I'd reacted.

'Tell him, David,' he said.

I heard this gentle voice in my ear, a timbre to David that I hadn't met before.

'It's the irony,' David said. 'The Professor gets boys into positions he appreciates so much that he doesn't want us to move. It usually happens just when he wants something else, so he either has to go and get it himself or spoil the vision. It's what happened last night too.'

I understood. I kept my eyes closed as The Professor got up and went into the house.

I'm not sure how long we were there, but occasionally we'd be disturbed by The Professor saying something like 'sixteen across, seven letters, starting with a C, meaning business'.

It was David who moved first. He slowly took his hands away from my neck.

I think he had been given The Professor's go-ahead when he nudged me to kneel.

I don't know how David did it, but he managed to pick up The Professor's lunch tray even though he was cuffed. I managed to pick up and carry the dog bowls by wrapping my hands around them.

Stacking the dishwasher took David a few moments, but he succeeded. He wiped the tray and put it away. I was amazed by how much he could while still wearing the handcuffs.

'You'll learn,' he said, as he saw me looking on in amazement.

I must have still been in a daze when he led me back to our room. I was hard within the cock cage as David guided me onto the douche in the bathroom. As soon as he was confident that I was clean, he pulled off his shorts and squatted onto the nozzle himself. The tension in his thighs and glutes as he did so was awe-inspiring.

I closed my eyes as he pushed the plug into me a few moments later. I opened them to watch as he plugged himself. I started squeezing my sphincter as David pulled what looked like a thong from the laundry basket and stepped into it, however the fuller front was unlike any conventional posing pouch that I had seen before. I watched intently as he pulled it into place, then adjusted his cock and balls and made sure the thong back was over the end of the plug.

'We're swimming today, Marc,' he said.

His tone of voice seemed so matter of fact.

I put my finger to my lips. That was the sign that Marc had taught me to use if I wanted permission to speak.

After overcoming my morning desire to be sociable and chatty, I had actually started to enjoy being silent in the company of others. It was another aspect of my condition which was being challenged, I thought.

David nodded.

'Yes?' he said.

'Please, David,' I asked, 'what's that that you're wearing?'

He looked down at his impressive bulge before answering me.

'You don't know?'

'No,' I said. 'I don't. I wouldn't ask otherwise. I just know it looks sensational on you. And you look sensational in it.'

David smiled before replying.

'Thank you, Marc; I appreciate that,' he said. 'It's what's called a dance belt. I was using it properly last night, under dance tights.'

It was my turn to smile. I'd wondered for years how male dancers kept everything in place so well. I'd loved the image as long as I could remember, probably from the first time that I'd been taken to the ballet as a child. I remembered wondering what the dancers wore. Their butts seemed bare beneath the tights, while there were never the tell-tale side straps of a jock.

'Perhaps you can try one sometime,' said David, breaking my train of thought.

'The Professor likes them because he thinks they're so much more constraining than a normal jock. He thinks jocks let cocks and balls move around too much. He likes cups though, that's why you were instructed to bring cup jocks with you. They keep slave cocks out of his way,' he explained.

'I like them too,' I said.

After we had made our way back outside, we waited on the deck for The Professor to unlock us.

When that happened, he put his hand under my sac and slowly pulled it after telling me to put my hands behind my back. He then took one ball in each hand and slowly, ever so slowly, pulled. He rubbed the skin with his thumbs as he did so. The sensation was so delicate and distracting that it took me a while to appreciate that the pulling had become excruciating. It wasn't until my head went back and I grimaced that he released me.

When he turned his attention to David I appreciated why he liked the dance belt so much. With a cockring, David's balls were pushed prominently forward, making an inviting target.

Using the back of his hand, The Professor starting hitting David's balls. The military stud was grasping his hands tightly behind his back, trying not to flinch or scream as the intensity increased. I could see a bulge in The Professor's jeans as he started to count down. For an instant, there was relief in David's eyes. He knew the end wasn't too far away. The last ten hits were hard. The Professor used a lot of his strength in the upwards movement. David was doing toe raises as the final blows hit home. I saw the explosion of agony in David's eyes as the last made its impact. He looked as if he was screaming, but not a sound passed his lips. Inside the pouch, his impressive cock was twitching. The fabric around the tip was wet with pre-cum.

'He can shoot like that,' said The Professor, 'if I tell him to.'

David's chest was heaving. He closed his eyes as the pain slowly decreased. I wasn't sure whether he was enduring it or enjoying it.

'Marc.'

I looked up. I knew better than to speak. I let my eyes say 'yes, Sir'.

'Kiss them better. And clean him up.'

The Professor's instruction was firm.

I knelt down and, as gently as I could, I kissed David's balls. I could hear him inhale sharply as further stimulation rekindled the soreness. I used the tip of my tongue as delicately as I could to lick them, and then to tease the nerves in his cock through the nylon fabric as I guided my mouth to its head. I could taste the pre-cum. I tried to be quiet as I gently sucked it through the material. I could feel the cock growing. I wished I had permission to release it from its prison, to dive onto it and force the head down my throat. Instead, I sucked and licked delicately. The Professor chuckled and David started to groan softly. I guessed I was doing something right.

'Enough,' said the Professor. Swim.'

So, swim we did.

Having a metal plug in my ass as I did those lengths made that exercise period a whole new experience. The plug wasn't so heavy that I couldn't float, but I felt different in the water. Although it wasn't cold, I felt my sac shrink against the plastic cock cage too.

As David did a couple of lengths on his back, I could see the dance belt constraining his genitals as they shrank in the relatively coldness of the water.

David kept me going for about thirty minutes. If we weren't going to run at a weekend, we were going to swim. We had to exercise everyday, The Professor stressed. After each morning's workout, I was put to work in the yard. I checked the vegetable plot for weeds. I made sure there was compost around some seedlings. I mowed the lawn. David said I'd be spared doing it with scissors unless I really did something to upset The Professor. I did have to go round the edges with some sort of shears, on my hands and knees. The Professor stayed with his books, on the deck, watching while David made sure everything was tidy at the front.

The only breaks I got came when it was necessary to add more sun screen. That was hot. I got to rub the cream into David, all over and I appreciate the touch as he rubbed it into me. He also made sure that The Professor's head, neck and arms were also regularly protected.

I also found myself providing the artistic entertainment before dinner. I'd noticed the St. Andrew's crosses and other bondage equipment on The Professor's deck and I knew that, sooner or later, I'd probably be experiencing them. I hadn't expected it to be so soon.

I'd also probably not been thinking too carefully when The Professor called across the grass as I was working to ask whether I liked gin-and-tonics before dinner.

I think The Professor had gone to shower when David took me on to the deck. He bound me to one of the crosses, facing outwards, and checked that the plug was still firmly in my hole. He then strapped a leather parachute-like stretcher around my sac. The tension felt good, until a black plastic bucket was hooked on to it. I was still smiling as David inserted a gag between my teeth. I didn't realize until it was in place that the end was a teat, like on a baby's bottle, and a tube ran out of the other side. I was still examining it with my tongue when David went back into the house.

I didn't have long to think about what I was getting to drink. David came back carrying what looked like an enema bag. It was plastic and looked to be full of clear liquid and had a tube hanging from it. David didn't have to reach far to hang the bag from a peg above me on the cross. I was getting scared as David fixed the tube to the gag. I thought it would have been going into my ass. He smiled and kissed me on the cheek as he undid a fixing. Suddenly, my mouth was full of liquid.

'You know what to do?' asked David as I tried to swallow.

I shook my head, hoping that no drips were coming out of the sides of my mouth.

'It's your pre-dinner drink, Marc. The Professor said you liked gin-and-tonic.'

I was even more scared now. More than two quarts of mixed liquor would make more drunk than I liked being. The prospect was so daunting that David could see it in my eyes.

'Don't worry,' he reassured me, 'there's only a little gin, the liquid is mainly tonic water, with a little lime.'

I nodded, appreciating the sharp taste and the bubbles and

realizing very quickly that the building up of gas from the carbonated mixer may cause bloating.

'All you have to do is drink it all then piss it out,' said David. 'Once the bag is empty and the bucket is full, you can come in to dinner. One of The Professor's colleagues is visiting. I'll monitor you. I expect The Professor and his friend will both come to see you too.'

David kissed me again and squeezed my hand.

He must have seen the growing fear in my eyes. I hope my sac could take the weight and that I would not embarrass The Professor with a poor performance. This was only my second evening with him and I was being tortured in public. I know one other person isn't in public, but I was being exhibited, shown off. I felt as if it was too soon, but I was in no position to complain.

David went to get on with preparing and serving dinner, leaving me to come to terms with my predicament. Many guys I've played with have said that bondage is easier once you accept it, once you relax into it. I tried to do that now. All I could do as far as being displayed was concerned was to accept my predicament. I had no choice. I took some deep breaths between sucking on the teat. I felt myself calm down a little. Indeed, I had not swallowed very much tonic water before I realized that being put in this situation was really quite a compliment. I slowly understood that The Professor would not have done this if he hadn't had confidence in me. His reputation was on the line too. His colleague wouldn't be very impressed if the new material was a wimp. That belief in me was a boost. I found it hard to piss at first. I just wanted the tap open, a bit like having a catheter in place, where you have no control whatsoever about the flow. That sensation can be disconcerting initially, but it can be quite mind-blowing too.

I remember that I had my eyes closed and my head bowed when The Professor and his guest came out on to the deck. I had been trying to control the piss that had started to flow, hoping that it all dripped into the bucket rather than splashed onto the deck. I'd already worked out who was likely to be cleaning the wood – with his tongue – if that happened.

I looked up to see The Professor immaculate in black leather. The pants fitted him perfectly. The boots, with a mirror finish that I was sure had taken hours of David's time, were knee-high. The shirt, with a small pin on the flap of the left breast-pocket, was tailored perfectly. His hair was smart and he smelled clean. My instinct was to kneel and, as delicately as I could, kiss those beautiful boots. My predicament, instead, kept me firmly in my place.

The Professor's companion was equally smartly dressed. He was slightly taller than The Professor, his hair more gray, and slightly longer, but still very neatly cut. Although I was still drinking, my attention had moved from my bladder to this elegant man. I was trying to guage his age, possibly late forties or early fifties, when they approached.

'Edgar, this is Marc. He's come to me for a month, for training. He was recommended by a good friend, a protégé, as he is searching for a master. He arrived yesterday.'

I felt strangely honored. I'd never experienced being an object before, but at that moment, I didn't feel entirely human. I was confused. I felt like a man, a proud man, but at that moment I had no liberty. I had self-esteem, but I was being introduced to this man as if I was a prize horse, or a prized artwork.

I was even more confused when The Professor spoke directly to me.

'Marc,' he said, 'this is Edgar Vaughan-Brookes, he's dean

199

of the school of anthropology, I'm sure you'll enjoy talking with him later.'

I tried to nod, but found more liquid than I wanted at the back of my throat. I spluttered, hoping that I wasn't spitting tonic water all over The Professor and his friend. I was relieved when The Professor smiled.

'He's learning,' he said, explaining me away in two words.

I'd sucked as much of the tonic from the bag as I could when David appeared to tell The Professor and his guest that dinner was served. I suddenly noticed the tension in my ballsac only as The Professor and the Dean turned to go inside.

I didn't know whether the liquid in the bucket had hit a critical weight or whether, free from other distractions, the sensation was all that my brain had to process. I wondered how long it would take for the rest of the tonic to drain through me.

I was left, bound to the cross on the deck, as The Professor and the Dean sat down to dinner. I could see part of the dining room and I watched as David glided around them, the ever-attentive butler, filling their glasses and serving the meal. Trying to focus on his near-nakedness and watch what he was doing helped me deal with the weight pulling on my balls. I could feel the tension on the cords, tugging up, into my body. Looking at the heavy chain around David's neck, the lighter chain between clamps on his nipples and the bulge in the tight, striped, spandex shorts that he was wearing engaged some of my mind.

I had again closed my eyes, trying to focus on other sensations when David spoke to me. I hadn't heard him approach.

'Not long now,' he said, stroking my hair. 'They've nearly finished.'

I watched as he walked back across the deck to put out coffee cups and an ashtray on the table.

The Professor and the Dean both had cigars and brandy goblets in their hands when they came out of the house.

I had no idea how long I'd been tied against the cross. I tried to work it out. Dusk was falling now, and dinner certainly didn't look as it if had been hurried. Allowing for the time it had take to strap me to the cross and the relaxed aperitifs that The Professor and the Dean had enjoyed, I must have been there for nearly three hours I thought. Realizing that I had been there so long was not helpful. I don't know whether I was imagining the discomfort, but I could feel tension in my thighs, my wrists held high and a lack of feeling in my fingers, and in my upper arms. Suddenly my entire body was screaming for release. I wanted to move my calves and feet, to shift the way my weight – and the weight of the bucket of piss – were being supported. I wanted blood to return to my arms.

I was breathing more quickly as The Professor approached me. The Dean was a few paces behind him. I looked them both up and down. I thought that I could make out the bulge in the Dean's leathers growing, but it wasn't easy to see the black leather in the dimming light. My eyebrows hit my hairline and my mouth flew open as The Professor lightly stroked the chain between the clamps on my nipples.

I'd reached a state of almost super-sensitivity. I started trembling as he very, very lightly traced a finger tip along my naked thighs, running from my knee to the taut skin at the back of the parachute around my balls. I so wanted to scream. Keeping back the sound was just the latest battle my brain was having to fight.

'Such beauty,' said The Professor as he leaned forward and kissed me on the cheek. 'You're doing well, Marc,' he added.

'I'm pleased you didn't disturb our dinner. That wouldn't have been good.'

That thought hadn't even crossed my mind. Perhaps I was already more obedient, subservient and accepting than I'd grasped.

'Sir, thank you, Professor,' I thought to myself, reveling in his closeness and wishing I had permission to speak. I could smell his leather and his body, mixed with the aromas of the brandy and the cigar. At that moment, I wanted my body to melt into his. I wanted to rest my head against the leather of his shirt, to wrap my arms around him and to let tears run from my eyes as I sought solace in sleep. I knew too that that was unlikely.

The Professor read me. He lifted an arm, so I could inhale the odor coming from his armpit. The pheromones and the pure masculinity provided me with relief from my discomfort. As he turned, I looked into his eyes. He smiled, probably seeing – and enjoying – the pleading, the submission. He kissed me again.

'Such beauty, Dean, don't you think?' he said, turning to his guest.

'Certainly,' replied the Dean, 'I couldn't have wished for a more delightful aesthetic to accompany such a delicious dinner, Professor. You should be proud of your men.'

My attention was grabbed by the Dean's choice of words. We were slaves, I thought, boys, but not 'men'.

The Professor looked up too.

The Dean noticed.

'I don't like today's terminology, Professor,' he said. 'Yes, I understand the benefits of continually reminding our subservients of the difference, but I like a male who is mature, strong, masculine. A great general has his "men". Armies, proper armies, should not use boys to fight. Yes, I know that boys can make man's inhumanity to man look restrained, but I like "men" around me.

'Much as I love the great statues of this world, the beauty of the Enlightenment in Europe, I – like you, I think, Professor – really appreciate the living beauty of the adult male. I believe in the humanity of those who serve and obey me.'

I could remember the Dean's words very precisely.

'Yes, I love obedience,' he said. 'I find punishment for disobedience sexually exciting, but then I find that beating a man as a reward is exciting too. I also want initiative, Professor. You do too. You may want David to ask for your permission when he needs to piss, but you don't want to have to micro-manage him as he cleans the dinner table.

'I want strength, virility, I don't want immaturity. I want someone who allows himself to come into my service, my household to be an adult, who has come to know himself, his own needs, how he can have reached true insight into his own psyche and understand how he can achieve fulfillment through subjugation, satisfaction through subservience and submission. That's how, he can be appreciated, respected, even loved – as a man.'

Despite the tension on my balls and having my mouth full, I was smiling. I thought the Dean was talking about me, as if he too was reading my innermost thoughts. There was a light frown on his face when he looked at me.

'May I?' he asked The Professor, as he came nearer.

'Of course,' came the reply.

'You are a lucky man, Marc,' said the Dean, as he brought the lighted end of his cigar closer and closer to my left nipple. I could feel myself pulling back as the heat increased. The Dean smiled again, but looked at me challengingly. I obeyed. I pushed my chest forward.

'Good man,' he said, as he moved the cigar slowly

backwards and forwards. The sensation as he took the burning end tantalizingly close to the newly-shaved skin of my armpits was one I had never experienced before, intense but not painful.

The Dean was still the focus of my attention when I felt hands around my ballsac. I tore my eyes away from the Dean's to look down. David was kneeling, releasing the bucket. My gaze returned to the Dean, I was pushing myself forward. I wanted nothing more than to kiss him too. I knew just how large the emotions of lust and desire were written across my face.

From the corner of my eye, I saw The Professor nod as David undid first one wrist, then the second. The two leather-clad men came and stood at each side of me.

'Yes, Marc, you may,' said The Professor. David was there to help as I was allowed to let my arms slowly descend.

I didn't know which way to look. I was panting, drooling, tripping on their desire, their sadism and the sensory overload as neurotransmitters in my brain went wild. I could feel myself falling limp. David moved away a fraction as they held me, or rather they let me hold them. I had one hand on The Professor's shoulder and the other on the Dean's. I was almost oblivious to anything as they slowly led me down a few steps and on to a strip of gravel between the deck and the lawn.

I was still flying, floating, my mind somewhere between earth and heaven as they left me standing. I didn't even care about the sharper stones under my bare feet. My eyes were closed, my shoulders were forward, my arms hanging almost lifeless when the liquid hit me.

I raised my head and opened my eyes long enough to see David putting down the bucket that had been hanging from my balls. He had a tumbler in his hand. He dipped it into the bucket to fill. The Professor nodded, allowing David to raise it to my lips.

The liquid was cool, but not really cold. I opened my mouth and let some drips run in. I ran my tongue around my lips. I wasn't sure what to expect, but the piss was relatively tasteless. I smiled, exhausted, as I realized why David had had me drink so much water that afternoon. I drank deeply, seeing both The Professor and the Dean smile as I did.

'Clean him up then bring him back.' The Professor's instructions to David were clear.

I saw The Professor put his arm around the Dean's shoulders as he led him back onto the deck while David led me to the French windows and our barrack room.

I fell to my knees as David led me into the shower. I leaned forward and kissed his boots and then the pouch of his shorts.

He slapped me, on the face, but not hard.

'You shouldn't have done that,' he said.

'I know, David, but ....' My voice trailed off as the hot water hit me. It felt so good. I started to moan as the warmth brought new life to my tired muscles. I began to feel clean as the piss was washed from my head and my skin. I think David indulged me by putting his hands under my arms to help me stand.

I moaned again, deeply, as he washed my ass, rubbing a cloth around the end of the plug. I had forgotten it was there. He pushed it again, with each movement, the smile grew across my face, the stimulation like turning up a fader-controled light.

I spent the rest of that evening beside The Professor, kneeling, my head resting on his thigh, his hand rubbing my head. My eyes were closed most of the time. The rug that David had put out for me on the deck felt so warm, comforting. I tried not to think what others would think of us, of The Professor and the Dean in full leather, of David in shorts, his boots and heavy neck chain, of me, splendidly naked and servile. I looked at the light darkness behind my closed eyelids and let my brain drain of every thought except the emotion of sublime happiness. I may even have slept.

# California whirls

I don't think I had a moment to myself during those first four weeks in California, Marc went on.

The morning alarm would go off at about fifteen minutes before six. David kept to the word of his letter. We'd be out at six, running for half-an-hour. We'd have put out tanktops, skimpy shorts and running shoes before going to bed. I'd put my work clothes out too. I was allowed to remove the plug before sleeping each night.

When we got back, I'd have to hurry to shower, shave – my face of course, and my hole, balls and as much of the area between my legs as the cock cage allowed – as well as making sure everywhere else was smooth too. Sometimes David would come into the bathroom and run his hands over my body to check.

David would have prepared my breakfast; some oat cereal and a protein drink. He would have made another drink and prepared some lunch for me, usually a salad, and put out some fruit. The backpack I took to work would contain all this, a tanktop, some spandex shorts, training shoes, a jockstrap and a plug. Oh, yes, and my journal.

Unless there was a particular meeting, I didn't have to wear a coat to work. I would wear chinos, with a jockstrap as underwear, and a shirt and tie.

I'd leave the house about seven and be at the light rail stop by about ten past seven. Sometimes, I would pick up a newspaper and read that on the ride downtown. More often though, the thirty five-minute ride gave me the time to make the psychological transformation from slave to bank official.

I'd make use of the gym a block away at lunchtime. I'd shower again, put on a clean jock but also plug myself for the afternoon. I'd usually eat lunch sitting in the sun before heading back into the office. Some days I'd have to go to other bank premises in the area. I'd try to arrange those meetings for the afternoons. The staff usually felt less busy then than in the mornings, so it was easier to talk to them and get the information about procedures and policies that I needed. No one worried whether I hired a car or used public transportation. I preferred buses and trains, getting cabs from the stations when I needed to. I could think more than if I'd been stuck on the freeway, or trying to find my way around some parts of the East Bay that I didn't really know.

Evenings were rarely the same from one day to another. The Profession taught classes a couple of days a week and David's research post meant that there were times when he had to be on the campus too, although he could work several hours most days from home. He'd stayed in the military reserve too, so there were those duties he had to fulfill.

When he was away, I stepped up, taking over his responsibilities at home. Sure, I was tired and I don't think I'd slept better at any time in my life, but I was on a buzz. I had to plan, think ahead. If I was going to working a particular day and wouldn't be back by the time The Professor had got home wanting a meal, I'd have to get as much done for him in advance as I could. I knew he would have preferred to have had someone around full-time, but David's career was important to him.

The Professor likes to entertain too. There would be guests

to dinner at least once a week, probably twice. Weekday guests would be his faculty colleagues. These would be more conventional. David would be allowed to sit at table, talking with his co-workers too. I'd have to wait table. I'd be dressed, usually in a polo shirt and black or gray 501s, but with my butt still plugged.

Word had gotten around that The Professor had domestic staff, a perk of not having to finance a family some said, so my presence was always accepted. Some, I'm sure, wondered just how personal the service was, but they were always far, far too polite to say anything.

Sometimes the guests would be political, from party committees or even, a couple of times, State legislators. I think the Governor had stopped by a few times too.

If we weren't entertaining, then David and I would be working, managing the household. The Professor would dine then retire to his study. He'd read, write, make calls, check e-mails. Occasionally, he'd watch TV, but not often. Sometimes he'd listen to music, but more often than not he'd have the radio on. He'd listen to NPR. It would be on his bedroom in the mornings and his study in the evenings. I'm sure he'd be listening to *Morning Edition* in the car going to the campus each morning and *All Things Considered* as he came home in the afternoons.

KQED became part of my life too. If there was a rare, quiet evening, he'd lock me or David into the cage in the basement, despite the threat in his original letter to you that this would happen every night. The lights would be out, we'd be cuffed or bound in some other way, but the radio would always be on in the background. There was nothing to do but relax physically, but there was always something to think about.

Fridays and Saturdays were different. Those were the days

when men from The Professor's network would visit. They were men of means, men who had done well for themselves. A few had pretentions, but most were unassuming, taking their success in their stride, but knowing what they wanted, and making sure they got it.

Some lived in The Bay Area. I was introduced to two academics from Berkeley, very senior executives from corporations based in The City, a Senator from a southern state, and others visiting on business were invited, usually alone, but sometimes in twos and threes.

Most came with their secretaries or personal assistants, highly-educated men in their thirties or forties. They would be dressed in suits when they arrived, but be naked within seconds. Most would have chains around their necks, their bodies shaved from head to toe. Many were in cock cages, some had brands, tattoos or other marks of ownership. The house would be busy then.

Some would fly to San José especially. Some even had either personal jets or the use of corporate aircraft, which explained why the men with them could be permanently locked or shackled into chains or other metal restraints; security checks for private aviation were far less exacting than those facing passengers at commercial airport terminals.

Dinner would be very civilized. David would cook well, but not too richly. Service was attentive without being too fussy. The Professor appreciated good wine. Indeed, he had taken to driving south to explore some of California's lesser-known vineyards and estates around St. Luis Obispo. He didn't, he said, want to deal with some of the industrial producers of Napa Valley or Sonoma. His guests appreciated that. They also preferred quality to quality.

The men with them varied greatly too. Some would be 'put away' for the duration of the visits. They would be taken straight to the basement where they'd be douched, plugged, cathetered and strapped into body bags. They'd be fed through a tube and not move for thirty-six or sometimes even seventy-two hours. Without solid food, nothing reached their bowels that needed to be expelled. The catheters drained away the protein and roughage liquid that they had been fed. Some other men would be caged or beaten severely.

I remember one man in particular. He was supremely muscled, a competitive bodybuilder, I later discovered, as well as having several degrees and a doctorate in a particularly obscure, but very valuable, aspect of corporate law. Every hair on his body had been removed by electrolysis. He was almost scarily silent. He would bow, slightly turning his head, acknowledging instructions with his body whenever he received an order, but I never heard him utter a word. I didn't notice for a while, but he never seemed to open his mouth either.

The first time I saw him, he had been brought to celebrate an anniversary and a birthday. I learned from David that tis Master had discovered him working in a bar in Cologne about ten years earlier. He had been fit then, but not as built as he'd become.

When they had arrived on the Friday evening, the muscled guy had been taken into the basement by David. The Professor had spent the previous evening briefing David carefully and in detail to make sure that that every one of that Master's wishes could, and would, be accommodated. I was allowed to serve the drinks and dinner that night, I remember.

The Professor was quite relaxed, wearing a leather shirt with jeans. The Master, a small Asian man, had changed from a very expensive suit into exquisitely cut cream leathers. His black boots shone like a mirror.

I knew that David was busy outside as I served them. Although they drank champagne, a vintage which I guessed must have cost several hundred dollars a bottle, both men also drank large quantities of water. The Professor also made me drink water too. I kept bringing in jugs, filled with ice and slices of fresh lemon and lime. They drank it by the pint. I thought I knew why. The Professor kept a glass for me on the table beside him. Each time I approach, I had to stand, one hand behind my back. I was not permitted to move until the glass was empty. I could feel my bladder filling, but I knew better than even to suggest to The Professor in any way that I might deign to seek permission to piss. That liquid was clearly being produced and stored for a purpose.

I had been told to wear tight leather shorts that evening, and black boots. David was dressed the same way, except that, when he came open to the doors onto the deck, I noticed that he was now wearing gauntlets that reached up his lower arms and an upper body harness that emphasized further his impressive pectoral muscles and nipples.

I followed The Professor and The Master outside, bringing a tray with the champagne and yet more water.

While I had been serving dinner, David had been working hard.

Dieter – The Master had used the bodybuilder's name while talking to The Professor – was suspended upside down in one of the frames.

His feet were in boots attached to a pulley. I could see something black sticking out of his hole. He had his back to us. Beside the frame, in a bucket of ice, were another bottle of fizzy white wine, a large jug and a large container of lube.

I had put down the tray and was standing to one side when The Professor spoke.

'Marc,' he said, 'go and piss in the bucket.'

The instruction confirmed that I had abdicated control of my bladder as well as any ejaculations. I looked around and, for the first time, noticed the large black container beside Dieter's head.

I nodded, acknowledging the order.

Pissing was difficult with the cock cage still in place. I pulled down the leather shorts and squatted over the bucket. I hoped The Professor and The Master would enjoy watching. I looked at Dieter as I waited for the first drips.

His hole was being kept open by a speculum, with a big black dildo resting inside it. Alligator clamps had been attached to his nipples, with a heavy chain pulling down on them. His balls were in a leather stretcher, a cord running from a D-ring to another ring in middle of the suspension bar. I followed the line of the cord; it ran down his front, under the chain between his nipples to the heavy padlock chained around his neck. His sac was carrying that weight. Along his tumescent cock, David had placed dozens of small metal clips. I couldn't even begin to count how many. I just knew that the sharp edges on the sensitive skin must have been excruciating. Through the glans of the cock was the biggest gauge Prince Albert piercing that I had ever seen, the steel shining against the sizeable mushroom head. It was I then that I noticed the head was entirely black.

David was standing beside me by then.

'It's tattooed,' he whispered, following my eyes. 'It's done every month, so it's always healing and sore.'

I swallowed hard.

'It looks good though, doesn't it?' whispered David. I couldn't remember hearing jealousy in his voice before.

Although I hadn't pissed for at least a couple of hours and I must have obediently swallowed several pints of water, it

212

took a few minutes for my bladder to empty. When I'd finished, David took my place.

He was locked in chastity too. When he'd finished, I licked the last drips from the outside of the Goethals device that encased both his cock and balls.

The Professor was next. I could see his cock getting harder as he pissed. I was envious as David knelt to lick the end clean.

We all watched as The Master moved towards Dieter. He positioned the bucket immediately below the muscled man's head.

'David.'

The Professor spoke as The Master got into a position in front of Dieter.

I watched as The Master opened his fly and pulled out a cock that was, in relation to his tight, terrier-like frame, disproportionately large. That cock too, I saw, was pierced and had the head tattooed.

I could see that, despite his predicament, Dieter was watching The Master intently as walked round the frame to face him. The Master brought his cock towards the bound man's lips. Dieter moved to kiss the head. As he did, The Master's piss started flowing.

Dieter tried to take as much into his mouth as he could, as if he wanted none to be wasted. His efforts were in vain. Dieter closed his eyes as the piss ran down his face and dripped into the bucket.

At The Professor's instruction, David started to lower the man's head into the bucket of urine. Dieter took a deep breath as his nose went under the liquid.

The Master had finished pissing by then. I watched as he walked to the bucket and lifted out the wine bottle. He opened the cork carefully, before pulling the dildo out of Dieter's hole. Dieter spluttered in the piss as The Master ran his finger round inside the open sphincter. Then, he leaned forward and blew into it. The Professor had put his arms around David and I and pushed us closer so that we could see what was happening.

I watched, my jaw dropping, as The Master proceeded to pour the entire bottle into Dieter's open ass. As soon as it was empty, he motioned for David to raise Dieter out of the bucket of piss. The big man gasped for breath as his nose reached the air. His chest was heaving, moving the weights and the clamps and adding to his torment.

David noticed the fear in my eyes.

'Don't worry,' he reassured me, 'it's low alcohol only about three per cent. The Master doesn't want him too drunk.'

Once Dieter was clear of the bucket, The Master pulled it forward out of the way, indicating that the muscled man should again be let down. The Master nodded for David to stop when Dieter was resting with his shoulders on the ground.

The Master then used the jug to pour piss from the bucket into Dieter's ass. The bucket was nearly empty when The Master picked it up, lifted it between the open legs and poured the last of the piss down the big man's body.

I jumped to The Professor's touch as The Master took off his shirt. Although not much more than five feet tall, The Master was wiry and well-defined, free from more than a few ounces of body fat. My mouth dropped open in appreciation. I took the shirt and placed it over the back of one of the chairs on the deck.

At The Master's indication, David poured a substantial amount of lube through the speculum. Satisfied that enough had been used, The Master nodded. David loosened the speculum and took it from Dieter's hole.

The Master too was using the lube, using his left hand to make sure that his entire right forearm was well-coated.

When he was ready, The Master looked down to Dieter's face. The big man's eyes were closed.

The Master placed his fist against Dieter's hole. There was no attempt to stretch the fingers forward, to tuck the thumb into the palm to make entry easier. The clenched fist rested for a second against the closed sphincter. I watched, amazed, as The Master touched the hole once, then twice. The third time, he punched. Some lube splashed back past The Master's muscled wrist.

My eyes and my mouth flew open as The Master's forearm disappeared. In seconds, the hole was nearly at his elbow.

David added more lube as The Master's hand came in and out like a piston. Sometimes he'd bring his wrist out as far as the hole before plunging back in. Sometimes, he'd bring the entire hand out, before ramming the clenched fist back against the gaping, greedy hole. I stood, struck dumb, as Dieter's hole withstood this onslaught. I noticed The Professor too. He smiled and raised his eyebrows, as if asking me if I'd like to be in that position. I shook my head. Dieter's tolerance was beyond anything I'd seen before.

I was caught equally unawares as the roar began. I think it must have started deep in Dieter's guts, forcing its way downward through his diaphragm and into his huge bodybuilder's lungs.

Suddenly the piss was flowing too. He'd lost control. The Master plunged his arm into Dieter's hole even deeper, taking it past the elbow, then stopping as violently as he'd been punching. Dieter's entire body was clenching against the arm inside him. His mouth was open as he tried to catch and swallow his own piss, at the same time releasing his immense, lion-like bellow. This was an orgasm of a dimension that I'd never even imagined, let alone seen.

The Professor pushed me to my knees. I'd been

215

concentrating on Dieter so much that I'd not noticed The Master's impressive erection. With his arm deep inside Dieter, The Master was starting to shudder while The Professor guided me into position directly in front of The Master. I opened my mouth. I was again surprised, this time by the power as The Master's cum hit the back of my throat.

'Don't swallow,' said the Professor. The Master moved forward so I could lick the last drops from the Prince Albert and his piss slit.

'Now,' said The Professor, 'go and put that where it belongs, in Dieter's mouth.'

I edged around the muscled body and bent forward. I could smell the piss and the sweat on Dieter's skin. He kept his eyes closed as he opened his mouth. I opened mine and let The Master's cum fall onto his tongue. When he closed his mouth again, I bent further and kissed him gently on the lips. Despite the physicality of the fisting, the punch-fucking, Dieter looked quietly delirious.

The Professor detailed me to help The Master clean up. I went with him to the guest room, picking up his shirt on the way.

David took care of Dieter.

The Master summoned me when he was in the shower. He too was a man of few words. I knelt as his eyes instructed and opened my mouth in front of his huge cock. His thighs, I saw, were as muscled as Dieter's; the two men represented a powerful, impressive duo.

I had to swallow hard and fast as his piss came. The warm water from the shower ran down my back as I drank. When he'd finished, again I kissed the metal of the PA and the cockhead.

The Master put his hands under my arms, guiding me upwards. He kissed me and whispered 'good man' into my ear as he made sure my body was clean from any extra piss. He stood silent again as I dried him down. He spread his legs letting me make sure no dampness was left between the back of his sac and his hole. I kissed his feet when I'd finished.

In his room, I noticed a photograph had been put onto the nightstand – of Dieter in a bodybuilding competition. The big man looked truly mighty, the bright yellow posing brief contrasting well with his tan. The bulge was impressive too; his cock up and balls forward.

The brief from the picture was on The Master's bed, clean and laid out ready for him.

He stepped into it before pulling on a pair of jeans and a sweatshirt. He noticed me looking on.

'Dieter only ever wears what I have already worn,' he said.

Dieter was kneeling on a mat on the deck when we arrived back downstairs. The Professor was sitting in front of him, nonchalantly playing with the bodybuilder's cock and balls with his foot. The stretcher and the clips on his cock were still in place as were the clamps on his nipples.

The Professor stopped when The Master sat down beside him.

Dieter moved to face The Master. The Master kissed Dieter then let the big man take his tongue into his mouth before starting to remove the metal clamps from the cock. I could see the determination as Dieter concentrated, making sure that the agony did not distract him from his Master's tongue.

The Professor had David and I kneeling beside him to watch. We were allowed to rub The Professor's tights as he rubbed our heads.

We saw Dieter released from the long ball stretcher and the alligator clamps on his nipples. We saw The Master open his fly and let Dieter kiss the yellow posing brief. We

217

watched as The Master stood. Dieter followed on his knees as The Professor's guest retired to bed.

* * *

David had more work to do with Dieter the following day. Once again, the big man was hung from the frame, this time upright and facing forward. He was wearing the yellow brief that The Master had worn the night before. I noticed too that David had bound Dieter against a wire frame.

Both men had spent time in the basement gym while I'd prepared and served breakfast for The Professor and The Master.

I suppose Dieter had been in bondage against the frame for at least an hour when The Master went out to him. He smiled and looked deeply into the bodybuilder's eyes as he kissed the muscled man, cupped and squeezed his balls, played with his sore nipples.

The Master looked good too. He had changed into tight black leather pants, boots and an upper body harness. The Professor and I watched from the deck as The Master read from some papers. Dieter would nod every so often. I thought I could see the words 'Yes, Master' form on his lips at times. The Master would then let him kiss the paper and his hand before moving on to the next section.

When The Master finally put the papers down, he stood in front of Dieter. He let the big man kiss him on the lips, then raised each arm so that each pit could be licked and kissed too.

The emotion, the connection between The Master and Dieter was so powerful that, even sitting silently, thirty feet away, my presence, The Professor's presence, together felt intrusive.

I wanted to leave, to let them have these moments to themselves, but I waited. The Professor had sensed my anxiety.

'They wanted witnesses, Marc,' he said, quietly into my ear, so The Master would not be disturbed. 'That's why they're here.'

I wasn't sure that I understood.

It was only then that The Master signaled to David. I hadn't been watching him until that moment. He too was, if anything, even more impressive than usual as he walked towards The Master. He too was wearing a harness and boots, but – most dramatically – he was holding a brand in one hand and a blow torch in the other.

I gasped as I saw the end of the brand glowing. The metal was on the cusp of changing from red to white hot. The Professor held on to my shoulder.

'Perhaps one day, Marc,' he said, noticing that I was simultaneously fearful yet intrigued.

Dieter's eyes nearly left their sockets as The Master brought the brand down against the flesh above his right nipple. A moment later, the smell of the burning flesh reached my nostrils.

Even then, Dieter's use hadn't finished. The fresh mark was covered with a dressing, but he was left bound while The Professor and The Master had lunch.

At some time, David turned him round, so that his back was towards the house. David had also given him some water to drink too, I think, and made sure he was still ready for what was to be the climax of the weekend.

Again, The Professor had David and me beside him on the deck as The Master went to work ...

I was sure I could see the muscles in Dieter's face and neck grew tense as he heard the first crack of the single-tail.

The Master looked impressive again, his upper body starting to sweat as he put in some practice strokes.

'Dieter was thirty-five last week,' explained The Professor, and he has been with The Master ten years this year. That's why they are renewing their vows and their commitment.'

Suddenly the passion of the rituals was clear. I could feel tears again welling up in my eyes. The power, yet the delicate intimacy between the two men had been a wonder to behold.

'Dieter has signed a contract committing himself to The Master for fifty more years,' said The Professor, 'undertaking to be The Master's slave until at least his seventy-fifth birthday.'

I swallowed. I'd never really thought about slavery that far into old age.

'So, he will receive seventy five strokes in recognition of each of those years, another fifty to represent the service to come and a final ten to mark the years which have passed,' added The Professor.

The whipping when it came was beyond words.

The Master was so attentive. He had used a flogger as a warm up, stimulating Dieter's nervous system so that the bound man was getting high on the endorphins. Only then, did he started with the long single-tail.

We could hear as The Master gave Dieter his final instructions.

'You will call out each that you consider a hit,' he said.

My mouth could not have been open further as I watched Dieter remain silent as the first strokes crossed his back and shoulders. Even then, he seemed only to acknowledge about one stroke in three. The Master was having to work hard.

Unsurprisingly, the big man was soon sweating.

The Professor sent me out to him with a towel, to wipe

Dieter's arms and back and his hands while David took The Master a glass of iced water.

It must have taken the best part of an hour before Dieter finally said: 'Seventy five, Master, Sir; thank You, Sir.'

More than two hours had passed when he said: 'Fifty, Sir; thank You, Sir.'

The Master came and spoke quietly to The Professor before starting the final ten.

David and I were led from the deck to a position where we could see Dieter's face and body. We watched as The Master went up to the big man and suddenly, violently, tore the yellow briefs from his body.

He threw the torn material to me. I caught it and held it to my face. The Master smiled.

We watched as The Master whispered to Dieter. I know I was impressed as the big man's cock grew to an erection.

'Ten, Sir; thank You, Sir.'

Dieter's voice was still strong as the whip again hit his shoulders.

'Nine, Sir; thank You, Sir.

'Eight, Sir; thank You, Sir.

'Seven, Sir; thank You, Sir.'

I thought I saw Dieter's cock subside a little as, eyes closed, he absorbed the pain.

'Six, Sir; thank You, Sir.

'Five, Sir; thank You, Sir.

'Four, Sir; thank You, Sir.'

The big man's voice was quieter now. His back was raw.

I knew he had counted nearly one hundred and fifty strokes. In fact, there had been many, many more. I knew too, at that moment, that he wasn't insulting The Master's skill by seeming to reject the strokes, but showing that he could take more, that he would give even more of his body, his being, to The Master's pleasure. Again, I was choking on the emotion.

'Three, Sir; thank You, Sir.

'Two, Sir; thank You, Sir.'

The final blows were coming so hard and fast that Dieter could hardly catch his breath to utter the acknowledgements.

'One, Sir; thank You, Sir.'

The relief was such that Dieter's voice almost disappeared. I was so captivated by his endurance that I wasn't watching The Master.

Then, suddenly, I noticed as he approached Dieter. He had thrown the whip to one side and torn open his leather pants. The Master's huge erection was pointing skywards.

The penetration was raw and brutal. Dieter's eyes opened again as The Master's cock forced its way passed his sphincter. His back must have been in agony as The Master pushed himself against the raw flesh, almost raping the muscled beast.

The Professor pushed me forward, placing me in front of Dieter, his hands forcing me gently but firmly to my knees. From the previous night's experience, I thought I knew what was to happen.

'Dieter, shoot.'

The Master's order was clear.

The big man was concentrating hard. His thighs tightened, his breathing became quicker.

'Five.'

This time, it was The Master who was counting down.

'Four. Three, Two, and, and, and ... one.'

With exemplary control and obedience, the cum left Dieter's cock as The Master spoke.

'Don't swallow,' I could hear The Professor remind me.

I caught it all.

I could not see The Master behind Dieter, but I could hear him panting against the big man's savaged back.

As Dieter's breathing subsided, The Professor guided my mouth upwards. I licked the last drops of semen from Dieter's awesome, black cockhead and then stood. I kept my mouth open, Dieter's cum on my tongue as The Professor lifted me to my feet and steered me towards The Master.

The Master's cock was still deep within Dieter as we kissed and I pushed his slave's cum into his mouth. I felt him swallow some.

He pulled his mouth away from mine and, pressing his mouth against the big man's back, let the remaining white liquid run into the wounds. The Master pushed me back down onto my knees then, moving my mouth until it was right beside Dieter's buttocks.

I moved slightly to lick The Master's cock as he pulled it from the hole. Instead, I felt my head pressed between Dieter's ass cheeks.

'Suck.'

I did as I was told.

I was surprised to find myself tasting latex as well as cum. Dieter had been lubed and his hole prepared before the beating.

'Don't swallow.'

I didn't need telling again.

When The Master thought I'd got as much of his cum as I could, he pulled me to my feet. He kissed me again, sucking some of the white liquid back from me. I was about to become more passionate again, when he pushed me away, moving my body towards Dieter.

I tried not to disturb the dressing over the brand as I put my face towards his. He opened his mouth and sucked the semen from mine.

He held it, refusing to swallow.

I moved away as The Master pulled the latex from Dieter's ravaged hole. I could just a small amount of cum inside it. We watched as The Master rolled up the condom, forcing the liquid out, spreading it with the other, across the beaten back and shoulders.

\* \* \*

I was surprised how relaxed Dieter looked at breakfast the following morning considering his exertions and battering the previous day.

It was my last few full weekend with The Professor and I'd taken five days vacation from the bank. Not having to rush to get to work felt wonderful. My only duty, David had said, apart from helping out around the house, was to drive The Master and Dieter to the airport.

I was surprised to see my own bags on the porch of The Professor's house when I drove back.

I'd almost run up the stairs and into The Professor's study when David had grabbed me.

'Remember, Marc,' he said. 'You want to be a slave, to be controlled and owned. The Professor has a gift for you.'

I stopped suddenly.

'Kneel.'

David's instruction was clear.

'Look at the floor.'

I waited as David went to our room. He came back with a leash that he attached to my collar.

'Stand.'

Despite my time with them, I was as nervous as hell as David led me towards The Professor's study.

There, while The Professor looked on, he indicated that I

should strip. I did so, as quickly as I could without losing my balance.

A plug and handcuffs had, I noticed from the corner of my eye, been laid out on one of the coffee tables.

The Professor looked on nonchalantly as I was plugged and cuffed.

David stood to one side. We both waited quietly. I took deep breaths as I knelt. I knew something was about to happen but not what.

Despite having my head bowed, I could just see as The Professor took a sip from a glass on the desk before standing. He walked slowly towards me. I hadn't noticed the blindfold on the table until he picked it up.

'I will see you when I see you,' The Professor said, as he pulled a blindfold into place around my eyes.

I could feel his hands on my shoulders and the gentle caress of his breath as he bent forward and kissed me on the forehead.

I raised my head and kissed his fly.

'This,' he whispered, leaning forward to my ear, 'is another beginning.'

I had no idea what he meant. I knew my time with him was due to end the following Sunday. I had the ticket for my flight back to you, Russ. My immediate thought was that, for the next few days, David might be using me or that I'd be experiencing a really long time in bondage

I crawled along the corridor from The Professor's study, obediently following David on the leash. Fingers, I think they were his, had pushed my cuffed hands to the floor when I had felt the first tug. I trusted him enough by then not to worry about being in the blindfold.

Only when we were at the front door did David let me stand. I was scared but didn't say anything as he led me across the gravel to the truck.

'Don't worry, Marc,' said David quietly as he helped me get into the back of the vehicle. I appreciated the support as I tried to maintain by balance. 'The Professor promised Russ he'd look after you. He won't break his word.'

I was still worried as I felt David fixing the restraints on my wrists and ankles to the corners of the truck bed. A moment later, I could sense the cover for the back of the truck being pulled into place.

I didn't quite know what to think during the drive. I had no idea how long it lasted. I felt the bumps and some movement but they seemed incidental against the scenarios rushing through my mind. Perhaps The Professor was just testing me. Perhaps David was just driving me around like this before taking me back?

Despite my predicament and the bumpy ride, I tried to relax.

Just as I'd had to strip in the cab of the truck when I arrived, here I was spread-eagled in the back, the only concession to comfort being a small cushion behind my head.

I was starting to control my emotions enough to calm down a little when, suddenly, I became aware of sound and how the background noise of the engine had changed. The truck was backing up but the echo suggested it was indoors, or in a garage. Then, just as suddenly as the sound had changed, silence fell.

I had to wait for a few moments in the stillness before I heard voices. I could, I thought, recognize David's but not the other one.

I tried to concentrate. First, I heard a door opening end then the sound of the cover being undone. Air, a drier air, hit my naked skin. I tried to raise my head as my wrists and ankles were released.

A moment later, I was being lifted.

I recognized David's aroma and nuzzled into his shoulder. I kissed material, but I knew it was him. For an instant, the embrace tightened reassuringly.

A moment later, I was kneeling on a mat. I was still blindfold as he kissed me on the lips. He put his arm around me and hugged me.

I understood why when I heard the truck engine start again.

I could feel tears in my eyes as I heard him walk away. I was aware, just, of voices, a door opening, and then an engine coming to life.

Listening intently, I could hear the crush of the gravel. I knew that the truck was pulling away, David at the wheel.

I felt very alone. My rational mind was fighting hard against the irrational, trying to reassure me that neither The Professor nor David would have put me in danger. I tried not to shiver, despite what I could feel was warm air around my nakedness.

I wondered where I was. I could smell fresh air, unlike the mustiness that still hung around the basement at The Professor's house. I wondered if he and David were playing mind games, before I remember that, although a vehicle could be backed up close to the door, it was too small to get the truck inside.

I tried to concentrate. I sat back on my haunches. If I spread my knees a little, I could touch the floor, even though my hands were cuffed. It was wood, polished wood.

I tried to make my slight movements as inconspicuous as possible. I tried to relax too, opening my legs a little to let the cage around my genitals move. I clenched my sphincter around the plug in my butt. I kept my mouth closed as I tried to inhale as deeply through my nose as I could.

My focus on myself was broken when I heard the relatively distance sound of a garage door closing.

I thought I would not have much longer to wait.

I tried to distract my mind by counting slowly. When I reached six hundred, I realized that I probably was not a priority for my captor, or captors, whoever he was, or they were. I felt tears welling up. I kept them in check by trying to remember as much as I could, in detail, about my time with the Professor – and David.

I have no idea how long I was kneeling there. Indeed, I was so deep into these particular reveries that I had a shock when I suddenly became of a figure near me. I could smell leather and perspiration. I felt hands on my shoulders, and a face near mine. I was kissed on the lips, then on the side of my face.

I licked my lips – trying to recover whatever evidence I could of this unseen figure. The sweat tasted fresh, with a hint of salt.

Feet, booted feet, pushed my knees together. The cage was crushed under me, as if that mattered. I could feel leather pants pushing against my chest and face.

My view was limited when the blindfold was removed. I kept my eyes closed for a few moments, aware of light through my eyelids. I tried to open them as slowly as I could. Even before I could blink and focus properly, I knew I was looking at an erect cock, sticking out from black leather pants. I moved my head forward to kiss the mighty, circumcised glans.

Before my lips could move the few inches, a hand reached under my chin and directed my gaze upwards,

I was still trying to identify the chin as the first words were uttered.

'Welcome, Marc.'

I squinted, trying to make out the features of the face. I recognized the voice first; it was the Dean.

I could see him smiling as he took his hand away from my chin. At that moment, I bent forward and kissed the head of his cock.

# Epilogue

My transfer within the bank couldn't have come through more quickly, Marc told me.

Although he didn't know it at the time, and only discovered later, the Bay Area management team had been so impressed with Marc's work that they were already trying to find ways of keeping him in San José.

When he went in – during his vacation week – to ask for the move, they were delighted, he told me.

'Having done without me for a month, Russ, the office near your home weren't too worried,' he explained. 'You've kept an eye on my property, Russ, while I was away and we've spoken briefly on the phone, but now you know it all.

'Mister Dean – I call him that – allowed me to tease The Professor the next time we saw him. He, or rather David, is arranging a collaring ceremony for us. I hope you'll come out for that. I don't think I'm going to be branded, but I suspect Mister Dean and The Professor have already talked about tattoos and other marks. I won't know until the day, but I trust them. Apart from which, I've already signed a document giving my consent.'

\* \* \*

I saw Marc every day during the retreat but we never talked like that again. He was busy being the Dean's man, taking care of everything. I'd kissed him that night, on the

229

lips, then put my hand on his shoulder. I didn't say anything. I didn't need to. I knew that the Marc whom I had rescued had found what he was looking for. I knew that he loved the Dean too. The affection was mutual. I was happy for him.

I left him, kneeling, waiting for the Dean as I walked back towards my room. I stopped under some trees and wept, mourning the friend I'd half lost and celebrating the joy that Marc had found.

I slept fitfully. It wasn't until dawn had broken that my mind found the answer it had been seeking. Marc wasn't a so-called born slave. In finding the Dean, he was a slave who had been re-born. He had found joy, a new life, a new Master and he'd found his renaissance.

I slept then, happy for us all.

THE END

# ABOUT THE AUTHOR

Chris Charlton is nearly 60 and has been interested in power relationships and SM for more nearly 40 years. He is a professional writer and journalist, covering health, including HIV, and the media. He takes his play and relationships seriously, being a long-standing member of one of the leading SM clubs in the US. He read psychology at university in England.

Taking inspiration from leading writers such as John Preston, Race Bannon, Joseph Bean, 'Fledermaus' and Guy Baldwin, Chris Charlton looks for the beautiful, the positive and the inspirational in the honesty that allows people to appreciate the power dynamics of dominance and willing submission.

Chris's interests include many aspects of physical SM, the exploration of the body and its responses. He is also intrigued by the ways in which finding and being open about the power dynamics between people can keep the most intimate relationships alive and exciting.

*Renaissance* is the second in a series of stories exploring domestic power relationships and the minds of those attracted to them. Look for the other titles – Revelation and Retirement – online.

You can write to Chris at chrschlrtn@gmail.com